First Love and Forever

FIRST LOVE AND FOREVER

A Novel

Anita Stansfield

Covenant Communications, Inc.

Covenant Communications, Inc.
American Fork, Utah

Printed in the United States of America
First Printing: September 1994
02 01 00 99 98   12 11 10 9 8

Library of Congress Cataloging-in-Publication Data
Stansfield, Anita, 1961-
    First love and forever : a novel / Anita Stansfield.
        p.   cm.
    ISBN 1-55503-714-3 : $9.95
    1. Man-woman relationships—United States—Fiction. 2. Mormon
women—United States—Fiction. 3. Widows—United States—Fiction.
I. Title.
PS3569.T33354F57   1994
813' .54--dc20   94-21535
                                                         CIP

This book is dedicated to my Father in Heaven. It is He who gave me this gift and an endless string of miracles to make it possible to give it to you, the reader.

And to the memory of Ellen Strate Cox.
Thank you for believing. You are a true friend—forever.

CHAPTER ONE

Orem, Utah

"THANK YOU, LORD." Emily breathed more easily as she heard the car pull into the driveway. A moment later Ryan came through the door, and despite the protest of her conscience, Emily pretended indifference. Would she ever learn to keep from worrying when he didn't call?

Without so much as a glance in her direction, he hung up his coat and began leafing through the mail, pausing to look through a sale booklet for a local department store that advertised things they couldn't possibly afford.

A familiar infuriation rose in Emily when she glanced at the clock. He'd been home for twelve minutes and hadn't acknowledged her. But she knew her anger was a secondary emotion. It was one of many concepts she had learned in college psychology that helped her cope. *You're not angry, Emily,* she told herself. *You're hurt and frustrated and disgusted. And anger won't remedy any of it.* This she had learned from a hard-won experience that had nothing to do with college.

"Where have you been?" she finally asked, her voice purposely toneless to disguise the anger.

"Got hung up at work," he replied, not moving his eyes from the brochure.

"You missed Allison's program," she said, hoping for some

kind of remorse in his reaction.

"I know." Still he didn't look up. "It couldn't be helped."

Emily wanted to scream. She wanted to tell him she was tired of being both parents while his work absorbed him. She was tired of feeling like a piece of the furniture, or a lap dog to be patted on the head at his convenience. A thousand biting words rushed through her mind, but she bit them back, not from self-discipline, but rather an unwillingness to begin a typical, fruitless argument that always ran the same circles and came to the same stale end. All her years of prayerfully and prudently attempting to deal with this relationship seemed in that moment to have gotten her nowhere.

An uncontrolled depression mounted inside her.

"I need to get out." She impulsively pulled her coat from the closet. Ryan looked up.

"Where you going?" he asked, his eyes reflecting mild panic. For a moment Emily thought he might be concerned about her welfare, or perhaps even her feelings. "What if the baby wakes up?" He glanced helplessly toward the hallway.

"You know how to fix a bottle," she countered, proud of herself for disguising the disappointment in her voice. "I'll see you later."

"Where you going?" he repeated.

"I don't know." She put her arms into the coat sleeves and buttoned the gray wool together. "I don't care. I haven't been out of this house without children for a month. My biggest outing is a trip to the grocery store." She felt tears collecting in her eyes. "I've got to get out. That's all." Emily picked up her purse and dug into the abyss for the keys.

"No kiss good-bye?" He grinned, but his teasing only made her more angry.

"You didn't give me a kiss hello."

Knowing what his reaction would be to her tears, she took hold of the doorknob. He looked slightly distraught by her odd behavior, but she knew he wouldn't ask her to stay and talk. How she longed to just talk to him! If they could only talk to each other, she knew it would make such a difference. But how many times had she tried, only to be rebuffed?

"Be careful," he said mechanically, already distracted by the unopened mail. Emily pulled the door shut behind her, resisting the urge to vie for his attention with a house-shaking slam.

Knowing Ryan's car would be warm from his drive across town, she slid into it and fumbled for the right key to turn in the ignition. An irritating cacophony assaulted her ears. She hit the eject button on the tape player and dug into her purse for a more inviting cassette. Even their taste in music didn't mesh.

Once on the road, Emily felt the anger finally melt into tears. The hurt and frustration trickled down her face while the lights of State Street businesses flickered past. With practiced efficiency she wiped the tears and pushed the feelings away, concentrating instead on a destination. Her mind quickly filed through the possibilities, which were few, and she decided the safest place to go was the mall. It would still be open for a while yet, and it seemed forever since she'd been there. A twinge of guilt reminded her she'd forgotten to tell Ryan that his dinner was in the fridge, ready to be heated in the microwave. But she figured hunger would move him to investigate.

Emily pulled the car into a stall near the north entrance of Mervyn's. She opened the door and glanced into the rearview mirror to make certain the tears hadn't left any traces. But it wasn't until she had walked past other shoppers for five minutes that her embarrassment set in.

Emily had never been prone to follow fashion. Her ability to choose inexpensive, classic pieces of clothing had saved her these past years. She still used some of the clothes she wore in college, and never felt terribly out of place. But she couldn't recall the last time she'd worn anything new. This reality struck with impact as she noticed the chicly-dressed shoppers and rows of new fashions in the stores. *No wonder I've avoided this place,* she thought.

A self-conscious hand gingerly straightened ash-blonde hair, pulled back from her face in natural waves that hung past her shoulders. She tried not to think how it hadn't been brushed since early this morning, and what little makeup she'd started with had likely faded. Her clothes had seen a day of diapers and bottles, cooking and cleaning. At least the coat helped. Though it too was a remnant of college, it hung long and loose on her five-foot, three-inch frame. Emily pulled it tighter around her and walked on, avoiding the clothing stores.

Pausing to browse through the latest in music, she found little she even recognized. She admired some hair bows, lingering over a flagrant red one, but she couldn't justify the $2.99. The endless rows of chocolates in Kara's windows were a temptation. She found enough change in her wallet for an orange truffle, which she savored carefully with a feeling of extravagance. Where had she read that chocolate produced the same endorphins as love?

The indulgence lifted her spirits, and she instinctively decided that perhaps buying something for herself might be just the thing to perk her up. But knowing that whatever she spent would come out of her carefully-guarded grocery budget, Emily sat on a bench to watch the bubbling water fountain while she contemplated a prospective purchase. Certain she couldn't possibly afford any item of clothing in this mall, she pondered the red hair bow. No, it didn't seem right.

By way of habit, she sought silently for some advice. *Please,* her mind prayed as naturally as any conversation with her closest friend, *help me find something to make me feel better. I know it's silly, but . . .*

Emily was surprised at how quickly the answer came. A book.

That's it! Emily headed to one of the mall's two bookstores. The thought of something to read excited her. She envisioned finding a novel that would give her a chance to escape—just a little. But she reminded herself to choose carefully. She needed to be uplifted, too, and she counted on the same divine guidance to help her seek out the perfect book.

Looking over the romances, nothing felt right. She

concluded that reading romantic fantasies would not help her situation at all. After a brief look over the other fiction available, Emily headed further down the mall and around the corner, walking briskly to get to the other bookstore before it closed. Just inside the entrance, a large display caught her eye. Pausing to look closer, Emily felt a rush of adrenalin before she consciously realized what she was looking at. Across the top of a cardboard stand, filled with a number of identical hardbound books, the silhouetted picture of a man and a horse stirred a warm memory. Emily picked up a copy, knowing she couldn't possibly afford a hardbound, but investigating nonetheless. Not until the book was in her hands did the author's name jump out at her like a slap in the face. She had been seeking something to lift her, but just reading the name *J. Michael Hamilton* sent all emotions to rest in the pit of her stomach. Like a rock thrown into still water, it sent ripples of memories—and perhaps regret—to every part of her.

After a long, frozen moment staring at that name, Emily willed herself to open the cover and read on the inside of the dust jacket: *J. Michael Hamilton, born in Queensland, Australia . . .* She scanned further down to continue: *Beyond his lifetime experience with the breeding and racing of horses, he received degrees from Brigham Young University in humanities, English literature, and . . .*

Emily knew all of that. Frantically, her eyes searched for some evidence in his biography to give her a degree of peace. But it mentioned nothing personal. Whether or not Michael was married still remained a mystery.

Emily closed the book determinedly and set it back with the others. She stared at it helplessly for several moments, then picked it up again and carried it to the checkout counter, writing a check for $15.95 plus tax that would cut into her family's meals for the coming week. But she didn't think about that, nor did she think of what Ryan's reaction might be when he came across the amount in figuring the checkbook. In that moment, she could only think of Jess Michael Hamilton.

"I'm sorry?" Emily heard herself say to the sales girl. "Were you talking to me?"

"I was telling you about the autograph signing. We just had it verified, so there isn't a sign out yet. But the author of that book is going to be here. I thought you might be interested. It's always fun to meet the authors."

Emily's reaction was a blank gape until she found the will to close her mouth. Her voice became lost somewhere down in that pit in her stomach, and she felt grateful when the girl asked, "Would you like me to find out for certain the time?"

Emily nodded helplessly. She was left alone for only a moment until the clerk returned to announce, "It's this coming Thursday, from noon until closing. I'd suggest coming early. The book seems to be a big seller around here."

"Thank you," Emily murmured, watching her put the book and receipt into a plastic bag.

Emily returned to the car, where she sat for long minutes filled with numb apprehension. She hadn't been to the mall since long before Alexa had been born, and she hadn't purchased a novel off the stands for years. Reading fiction was rare for her, and when she did it was usually borrowed from the library or loaned by a friend. And here she sat, in the mall parking lot, dome light on, staring helplessly at the book in her hands as if it had fallen there by some miraculous means. *"Verity,"* she spoke the title aloud, then added with hesitance, "a contemporary novel by J. Michael Hamilton, author of the bestselling title, *Crazy's Day.*"

Emily sighed. "Oh, Michael," she uttered and tossed the book into the passenger seat. She nearly put the car in reverse, but lacked the motivation to do anything more than turn off the dome light and press her forehead to the steering wheel, sighing heavily.

The last time she saw Michael Hamilton, he had been standing on the porch outside his apartment, his hands deep in the pockets of his jeans, his eyes brimming with an emotional plea that Emily could never forget. The memory of that moment as she had driven away was as clear as her memory of the day she had first heard his voice.

Michael Hamilton was an easy man to notice as he filtered in and out of the Book of Mormon class where he sat directly behind her, silently absorbing the knowledge as if he thrived on it. Emily heard him described as "the non-member who got straight A's in the class, even though he only took it because religion classes were a requirement at BYU."

Emily was almost as intrigued by that characterization as she was by his appearance. It wasn't just his slightly waved brown hair that looked neatly styled and wind-blown at the same time, or his hazel eyes that changed hues according to his mood. It wasn't the six foot, one inch of him that dressed in a studied simplicity which seemed to astutely express his manner. It wasn't even the little courtesies he showed her as they passed through doors near each other and exchanged silent greetings. What made Emily take notice of Michael Hamilton was something she couldn't pinpoint. But when she finally heard him speak, that first time he chose to make a comment in class, all of Jess Michael Hamilton fell neatly into place. If not for the accent, she might not have realized that she had been in the same class with him for weeks and never heard his voice.

"Mr. Hamilton," the professor pointed him out, looking past Emily to the seat behind her.

"Thank you," was all he said before Emily had to turn and make certain they were referring to the same Mr. Hamilton. Sure enough. And as he continued with his comment, the evidence deepened. Michael Hamilton was not American.

"I have found," he said in a deep, warm tone, "that in studying what you are referring to as the Psalm of Nephi, the segment, despite its added poignancy, still carries through a style that is typical of Nephi's writing. I believe the man to be a gifted writer."

"Very well put," the professor replied and continued with the discussion. But Emily's mind stayed with that comment. Michael's accented insight to one of her favorite passages was stirring.

When class ended, she couldn't resist the urge to turn and

speak to him as he gathered his books. "That's quite a brogue you've got, Mr. Hamilton." She meant it as a compliment and felt relieved to see his eyes catch a sparkle of humor.

"It is not a brogue," he stated as if he were telling her the reason the sky was blue. "What I speak is perfect Australian prose."

Emily smiled. "Your perfect Australian prose has some excellent insight, Mr. Hamilton," she complimented him further. "I have similar feelings about Nephi."

"Then we have something in common." He came to his feet and she did the same. "And my name is Michael. You are . . ." He leaned toward her, a question in his eyes.

"Emily Ladd," she stated and held out her hand.

"It's a pleasure, Miss Emily Ladd." He blended her two names together as if they were one note of an Australian folk song. Then for the first time in her life, Emily's hand was kissed rather than shaken. His eyes were full of humor as he squeezed subtly and let it go, saying with an upward twitch of his lips, "But you'd best mind your manners about my prose, Miss Ladd, or I might drag you to Australia and see how *you* feel being the foreigner."

"Ah," she laughed, feeling a little unsteady as he followed her to the door and held it open for her. "A rogue with a brogue."

Michael Hamilton laughed. Emily nearly expected him to deny being a rogue the way he had denied speaking a brogue, but he proudly said, "I'm told that my grandfather was a rogue. I dare say I've got a little of him in me."

A week later, Michael Hamilton sat across a table from Emily at J.B.'s, with two very big sundaes between them. Michael was animated in a histrionic tale of his grandfather. The story seemed so outlandish that Emily doubted its truth, but Michael assured her it had been recorded in family journals. Michael William Hamilton had kidnaped Emma Byrnehouse-Davies for ransom and taken her and her sister into the outback. He not only got the ransom, but a few weeks later ended up working for Emma's father, with Emma as his wife to boot.

"You have a very colorful past," Emily admitted.

"Michael and Emma are just one of many stories in my family's history," he said proudly, lifting an eyebrow with subtle mischief. "Sounds a little like Michael and Emily, doesn't it." It wasn't a question, and as time went on, Emily realized that he clearly meant it to be an implication.

After seven months of bowling, ice cream cones, football games with matching blue sweatshirts, picnics in the park, studying, long talks, cooking gourmet for Emily and her five roommates every Tuesday evening, and a firm declaration of "I love you, Emily Ladd," it became evident that if Michael Hamilton was a rogue, the term could only be admirable.

Emily tried hard to find something wrong with him. She had been raised to be practical and would not fall into a relationship blindly. She picked Michael apart in search of imperfections, and once she told him that he didn't clean the sink after he used her kitchen for his cooking escapades. She never found it dirty again. He bit one thumbnail when nervous, and he walked too fast on his way to the cafeteria for lunch. But Emily found that if she took his hand, he slowed to match her pace without being asked.

Michael Hamilton had only one real flaw, and even that was almost excusable by its incompleteness. At the top of Emily's mental list of husband requirements, there stood a big, bold: *Member of the Church*. Michael Hamilton attended church with Emily, continued to get perfect grades in LDS religion classes, attended firesides and General Conference, and even shared regular scripture study with Emily.

Michael had come to BYU at the suggestion of some LDS missionaries who had approached him in Australia. He hadn't been interested in baptism, but a reputable college with high standards was something he'd been in the market for. One of his dreams had been to attend college in the states. The other was to be a writer.

But becoming a member of the Church simply didn't seem

to occur to Michael. And that was fine. Emily wanted for nothing in their relationship. He was a perfect gentleman, attempting nothing more than a gentleman's kiss through all their months of being together. He made Emily happy, and their general talk of marriage gradually became more focused in a way that made his one flaw seem insignificant.

That summer, Michael conscientiously traveled to Emily's home in Idaho to request permission of Mr. and Mrs. Ladd to escort Emily to Australia to meet his family. He phoned with reverse charges to his home and introduced Mrs. Ladd to his mother. The two mothers found much in common and talked for nearly an hour, after which permission was given. Once Emily's visa was finalized, she embarked on the most wonderful month of her life.

It wasn't until they drove into the Hamilton family's *station,* as he called it, that the full spectrum of Michael's life came into view for Emily. She looked over at him in surprise, and he answered with wide-eyed innocence. But the evidence clearly indicated that Jess Michael Hamilton was a wealthy man. He was so frugal and conservative that Emily had never suspected money was a part of his life. As Michael's mother welcomed her with open arms, Emily became acquainted with the reality of the Byrnehouse-Davies Home for Boys and Racing Facilities. She found that the Hamiltons were backed by fourth-generation wealth in amounts beyond Emily's comprehension.

But they didn't act wealthy. They were conservative, good-hearted people who could get lost in the crowd of struggling farmers Emily had grown up with. Emily fit right in. Michael taught her to ride and they shared many hours on horseback. They also found a new common interest as they pored over family journals and records, illuminating a family history that intrigued and fascinated Emily more than any of her aunt's genealogical efforts ever had.

Emily returned from Australia certain that Michael Hamilton was on the verge of proposing. She loved him and was prepared to accept. The evidence ran deep that he was a good man, and she felt certain he would be a good husband. He had repeatedly made it clear that he would support her in everything she did, and she felt totally alive and fulfilled when she was with him. He encouraged her in her activities and interests, making her feel certain that she could accomplish anything.

Yes, it had all been fine . . . until Emily returned to Idaho following her Australian adventure to catch up on some time with her family. Michael stayed on campus, dedicating himself to a thesis.

Emily's parents started the wheels of conscience spinning with an innocent statement. "Michael is a nice young man, Emily, and we understand how you care for him. But could you really live without the blessings of the priesthood and the temple in your home? Is that really what you want?"

The following day Ryan Hall stopped by, fresh from his mission, anxious to see if anything still remained of the no-commitment relationship they had shared prior to his leaving. Emily accepted an invitation from Ryan to attend a church dance, her purpose being to help him with the social transition following a mission. She was honest concerning her relationship with Michael Hamilton, and though he seemed disappointed, he said nothing.

Ryan continued to seek out Emily's company, and she gradually began to feel torn. Confusion became as commonplace as breathing. Each day Michael called her, and she knew her life should be spent with him. Then she would see Ryan and wonder if she had fallen in love with the wrong man.

Ryan Hall was handsome, a little taller and more muscular than Michael. He had been a star football player on their high school team, and he and Emily had dated on and off until his mission. He came from a good, active family, and the success of his mission radiated from him.

The night before Emily returned to Provo, Ryan Hall proposed to her. Instead of being ecstatic, Emily was afraid. She felt totally confused. From her youth, she had been taught to marry within the Church. Her parents expected it. Though the emotions were somehow different from what she felt for Michael, she couldn't deny that she loved Ryan. She begged him for time to think, to search her feelings.

The instant Michael saw Emily, it was evident that something was wrong. Four weeks in Idaho had left shadows beneath her eyes. "What happened?" he demanded immediately. Emily was tempted to skirt the issue or wait until a more appropriate time. But she knew there was little point. "An old friend of mine returned from his mission. I . . . spent some time with him."

"Is he a rogue?" Michael smiled, but the severity in his eyes clearly indicated he could see through her attempt to make this sound trivial.

"Actually no," she said too seriously. "He's a very nice man, and . . ." Again Emily was tempted to soften the impact, to avoid it, but she drew back her shoulders and looked away from his inquisitive gaze. "He asked me to marry him."

Michael laughed. "I hope you told him no."

Tears brimmed in Emily's eyes as she turned to face him. "I told him I had to think about it."

Michael sat down. His expression became so somber that Emily wanted to take the words back. He gave a humorless chuckle. "I can't believe it," he uttered. "After what we have shared, in a few weeks you would . . ." He stood and turned away, unable to finish the sentence. He ran his fingers through his hair, then turned to her. "Am I mistaken, Emily? Was it wrong for me to assume that you and I were going to be married?"

"It was never official," she said.

"Well, I'm making it official," he said with determination. "So call the man and tell him you're already engaged."

"I can't," she said, her voice barely audible.

"Why not?" he nearly pleaded.

Emily swallowed hard. "I have to make a decision first."

Michael attempted to catch his breath. "I can't believe this." He threw his hands in the air, then pushed them through his rumpled hair. "What you're trying to tell me, then," he said more calmly, "is that it's between him and me."

"I suppose that's it," she had to admit.

Michael shook his head. "I don't understand, Emily. How could you become so . . . close, in just a few weeks?"

"I've known him for years, Michael."

"I see." He nodded skeptically. "So, what has he got that I haven't got?"

Not until he put it that way, did Emily ever ponder the thought that perhaps if Michael joined the Church . . .

"Michael," she said carefully, "is there a reason why you . . ." She faltered before she could say it. His goodness made it seem trite to put such a condition on their relationship.

"Why I what?" he demanded in a tone that made it clear he would not give up until he had a straight answer.

Emily looked down and mumbled, "Ryan wants to marry me in the temple, and my parents believe that—"

"Ah." His voice filled with enlightenment, edged only slightly with bitterness. "So that's what it comes down to. Emily's parents want her to marry a Mormon." He paused and asked pointedly, "But what does Emily want?"

"I want what is best for me, for my future," she insisted. "I have to consider the prospect of raising a family and facing the trials of life. I have to do what the Lord wants me to do, because without his support, I cannot function."

"Emily," he spoke softly, "I think the Lord knows I would make you happy. He should know, as you do, that I have always, and forever would be, completely supportive of your beliefs."

"Yes," she replied, "but it's not the same." She drew a deep breath and added, "Why do you hesitate to become a member, Michael?" With everything they had discussed, all they knew about each other, the subject had simply never come up in quite this way.

Michael sighed and put his hands in his pockets. He looked at Emily with an intensity in his eyes she would never forget. "I believe in God, Emily, and I believe that much of the doctrine of your church is true. It makes perfect, logical sense, and I enjoy being a part of it. But I will not do it just to do it. Maybe I lack the conviction or dedication. I don't know. I do know my life has been good, and I see no reason to change it."

"And what if I said that I want a temple marriage?"

"I'd say it would be unfair for you not to accept me and my beliefs, just as I accept you and yours. Besides, even if I were baptized tomorrow, we couldn't go to the temple for a year. I don't think it would be wise to wait that long to marry."

"No, but we could work toward it together and—"

"That's not the point, Emily. I am not going to join the Church just so you can marry a Mormon. Marry me for me, or don't marry me at all. I was raised to respect a woman. You've told me yourself you could not ask for more in a relationship than what we have here. There could be worse things to live with, Emily."

Confusion fell over her like a dark cloud. She turned away and groaned in frustration. Attempting to be rational, she said firmly, "I need time. I need to fast and pray about this."

"Why don't you do that," he said almost spitefully, but with an edge of confidence in his voice. Looking back, Emily believed that Michael felt certain he was the right man for her.

"You must respect my choice, Michael," she said.

A week later she made the decision to marry Ryan, feeling the confusion fall away and a calm peace settle over her. Recalling that peace had gotten her through many difficult days; and by staying close to the Spirit for much-needed guidance and comfort, Emily came to realize that what the Lord wanted for her was not necessarily the easiest marriage, but the one that would help her grow.

And grow she had. But there were moments when she felt the oppression of her circumstances would eventually stunt her growth permanently, even though there was a part of her that believed Ryan needed her, and that perhaps she had the strength or the patience to help him achieve his own potential. If only she could reach him!

Now, more than ten years after her decision had been made, Emily lived with an inactive husband who made virtually no effort to share anything emotional or spiritual with her. Their only common bond was three children, but he took no part in raising them beyond providing a living, and paying condescending attention to them when he had nothing better to do.

The emptiness Emily felt often came close to crossing the line of something beyond her capacity to bear. And now, in seeking something to give her hope and an uplift of spirit, she had been led to a tangible reminder of Michael Hamilton. After making the decision to marry Ryan, she'd forced all thoughts of Michael out of her mind. She had made her decision, and at the time the Spirit had told her it could only be right. There was no good in questioning that now. She knew it was right then. She had to believe it was still right.

A glance at the dashboard clock made Emily gasp. She should have been in bed by now and felt certain Ryan would be worried. Tabling her memories for the moment, she hurried home.

The house was dark and Ryan was sleeping. With a sigh Emily stuffed the book under the edge of the bed before she wearily climbed between the covers, only to stare for hours into the darkness above her. For the first time since she'd married Ryan Hall, Emily's thoughts were with Michael Hamilton.

CHAPTER TWO

EMILY AROSE EARLY to prepare a finer than normal breakfast, perhaps hoping it would appease the gnawing guilt she felt for entertaining thoughts of another man. But she couldn't help wondering about Michael. What was he doing? What kind of life had he found without her?

Knowing these feelings would bring no good to her marriage, Emily attempted to distract herself for the few minutes left before Ryan went to work.

"Ryan." She sat beside him at the table and reached for his hand. "I've been thinking that perhaps we should get away, spend some time together, and . . ."

"Really, Em, you know we can't afford motels." He took a bite of his eggs and turned a page of the *Sports Illustrated* at his side.

"We don't have to get a motel." She spoke with hope in her voice, briefly touching his dark hair. "You know Penny's mother has that cabin she's offered to let us use anytime, and it's only an hour's drive. I could make arrangements for the children this weekend, and . . ."

"Emily." He drew her name out to imply she should have remembered something that she hadn't. "I've got plans Saturday. The guys are all meeting at Lane's to watch the game."

Emily had heard nothing about it until now, but she pushed that issue aside. "Then next weekend," she persisted, hating the way her voice was beginning to sound desperate. "Our marriage is surely worth an investment of some time. It's been so long since we've done anything together."

"Maybe we can go to a movie or something." He stood, pressed a mechanical kiss to her cheek, and headed out to work.

Emily wanted to cry, but sounds from the other room summoned her. Numb with confusion, she went about her normal routine of dressing and feeding Alexa, seven months, and Amee, twenty-one months, intermittently checking on nine-year-old Allison to make certain she accomplished her assigned tasks and got ready for school.

Emily sorted laundry, scrubbed the bathroom, and did what she could to keep the babies entertained. By noon she finally got to the breakfast dishes. Standing by the sink to sort through pans, she felt tears burning her eyes. She blinked them back and continued her work, certain that she had somehow brought this confusion upon herself.

Nevertheless, when the babies went down for naps, Emily put the remaining work on hold. She took advantage of this quiet time by digging out the sack from beneath the bed. She looked at the book, thumbed through it, read the brief biography three times, but she couldn't bring herself to read. Instead, she carried it to the front room and knelt in front of her cedar chest.

Carefully she opened the chest and lifted out the blessing gown worn by each of her three daughters, then dried wedding flowers and a cake-top. There were scrapbooks, baby books, and books of genealogy. She pulled out two dresses from high school dances, then took a deep breath before lifting out the double layer of folded blue tissue paper that divided the contents of the chest. Lying in the center, between the folds of tissue, was one last item—until last night, the only possession she had that crossed the barrier between two worlds.

It was a copy of the novel *Crazy's Day*, autographed and sent to her three years earlier by way of her mother. Emily recalled the day it arrived as she lifted it gently and cradled it in her hands. This book, too, was unread. It had been stashed here the day she received it, with a subconscious hope that if she didn't read it, she wouldn't feel the ache. Emily opened it now, and tears filled her eyes as she read the familiar script: *To my first love, forever. J. Michael Hamilton.*

Emily set aside the book and carefully folded back the tissue. She'd not looked beneath it since the day she'd put it there, two weeks before she married Ryan. Now she laughed and cried as she pulled out the keepsakes—a dried rose; a ballet ticket stub; a shoe box filled with cards and letters; another filled with photographs and negatives. She found her airline tickets, passport and visa; a necklace he'd bought her in Australia, and a stuffed koala bear the size of her fist that he had declared should remind her of him because it was cuddly and Australian. And at the bottom Emily found a pair of classic black riding boots that Michael had bought her as a reward for learning to ride his prize stallion.

A light knock at the door startled Emily. She turned, fighting the urge to furtively shield the open chest.

Penny pushed the door open without waiting for an answer, as she often did when she knew Ryan wasn't home. "What *are* you doing?" her friend insisted.

"Just . . . reminiscing," Emily answered, hoping Penny wouldn't notice any evidence of tears.

Penny glanced from Emily to the objects scattered over the floor. Her eyes came to rest on the books. "Hey, isn't that the book you got from that old boyfriend of yours?" She picked up *Crazy's Day* and thumbed through it, plopping herself on the floor near Emily.

"Yes, it is," she answered. As Penny picked up the other book she added, "That's a new one. I bought it last night."

Penny grinned. "Just a minute. Just a minute." She put her hand to her forehead in a teasing gesture of shock. "You . . . you? . . . bought a book? Why, you frivolous child!"

"Oh, hush." Emily couldn't help smiling. Penny had a way of making the challenges in life seem easy.

"Is it any good?" Penny asked.

"I don't know. I haven't found a chance to read it."

"I mean this one." Penny indicated the book tucked away for years.

"I don't know," Emily repeated.

"You didn't read it?" Penny sounded appalled. "This dashing Australian you almost married writes a novel, sends you an autographed copy, and you didn't read it?"

"Sometimes I think you know too much about me, Penny."

"Someone's got to. So, why didn't you read it?"

"I don't know. Scared, maybe."

Penny paused to absorb the confession. What she knew of Emily's relationship with the Australian writer amounted to a ten-minute explanation because Penny had been present when the book arrived. Any effort to prod Emily further was always thwarted. She simply didn't discuss it. Putting the pieces together now, Penny had a pretty good idea why.

Penny knew Emily's situation and tried to support her. But all efforts on Emily's part to get Ryan to open up, to go to marriage counseling, and any number of other attempts to ease the problems in their relationship, always left Emily more discouraged than ever. Could it be possible that Emily actually regretted the decision that she claimed to have been so certain of?

"You're going to read this one, aren't you?" Penny asked directly. "I mean, you didn't spend $15.95 to put it in your cedar chest, did you?"

"I suppose I should read it." Emily took the newer book from Penny, and a warmth filtered through her confusion. "Maybe I'll read them both."

Penny opened the book in her hands. "Ooooh," she teased with a raised eyebrow, then read with drama, "To my first love, forever." Her tone softened. "How do you rate? Such a personal autograph from a famous writer."

"The books have sold well," Emily replied, "but I wouldn't exactly call him famous. If he's going to be at the University Mall Thursday, he can't be too famous."

Penny looked up in astonishment. Emily nearly regretted

letting that slip out. She had already decided not to go.

"He's going to be here?" Penny almost danced with excitement. "Oh, of course you'll go and have him autograph this one, too. I mean, you were close once, you said. Surely he'll remember you. It would be good for you to get out. I'll watch the kids, and—"

"Don't be ridiculous," Emily insisted. "I can't run off to meet an old boyfriend and—"

"It's just an autograph signing!" Penny protested. "What's the big deal? You give him the book. He signs it. You ask how the weather has been for the past few years, and that's it."

"I'm afraid it's not that easy." Emily abruptly began putting back her keepsakes of Michael Hamilton.

Penny frowned. "I think there is more to this guy than you've bothered to tell me."

"No, there is not. I told you he asked me to marry him, but I married Ryan instead."

"But things with Ryan aren't so good, and I can't believe that you don't wonder if . . ."

Emily's glare silenced Penny, and she knew she'd hit a nerve.

"Yes," Emily insisted, "I do wonder. I wonder what he's doing, what he looks like, and yes, I am scared. I'm scared to face him, because I don't want to know how great he is doing without me. I don't want to hear about his wife and children, and how wonderful his life is." Emily's voice broke. "I just don't want to know."

"You're not a good liar." Penny folded her arms. "You are the most honest person I have ever known, and I know as well as I know the sky is blue, that you *do* want to see him. Try to tell me you're not intrigued, or at least curious. If my old love, who just happened to be a famous writer, was going to be at the mall Thursday, I'd certainly go."

"That's because you have the confidence of a good marriage behind you, Penny. I'm not sure I can face up to the feelings that seeing him would bring out."

"Maybe that's just what you need."

Emily looked at her friend carefully as the challenge pierced deep.

"Think about it, Emily. You're in a rut. Your marriage is going nowhere fast. You don't get out. Your whole life is your children and your Relief Society lesson."

"What's wrong with that?"

"There's nothing wrong with that. But you're like a well, only willing to give water but never taking any back. I fear that you're going dry, Emily, and it worries me. Now, why don't you just make a point to go out Thursday? Maybe seeing him and hearing about his wife and kids will help you get over the fear and face it. Maybe it's not knowing that's getting to you."

Emily contemplated it. "You might have a point there." She put the tissue paper back in place and returned the remainder of the contents to the chest, leaving only the two books on the floor. "I think I need to pray about it."

"You always do," Penny said with a teasing respect, "and when the Lord lets you know that it's okay to do something for yourself, let me know and I'll tend the kids." Emily smiled gratefully at her friend as she headed toward the door, adding with a sly grin, "I'll be very angry with you if you pass this up, Emily. It's a once-in-a-lifetime shot."

Left alone with Michael's books, Emily felt the confusion again. Her commitment to Ryan was sometimes difficult to comprehend, but she didn't take it any less seriously for that, or any other reason. But Penny had made some good points, and Emily felt something inside of her spring to life as she pondered the prospect of seeing Michael again.

She nearly picked up a book to read, but instead she went to her room to pray, certain she needed that more. Once off her knees, Emily put both books beneath the bed. Then, with fresh motivation, she settled into her housework.

The following day spring kicked in with bright skies, but Emily still wasn't certain what to do. After Ryan went to bed without exchanging more than ten words with her, and those words concerned his own plans for Saturday, Emily got on her knees again and felt an excited peace about spending a day at the mall.

Emily dialed Penny's number the minute Ryan's car backed out of the driveway. "Did you say you were in the mood to babysit today?" Emily asked in a more cheerful tone than Penny had heard in weeks.

"I'll be right over." Penny hung up the phone before Emily could blink.

"Really, Penny," she said to her friend at the door minutes later, "the big event doesn't start until noon. And I think I'd rather not be one of the first to show up."

"Fine, but you've got to find something to wear." Penny went to Emily's closet without permission and began rummaging through it. "And you need to take a long bubble bath, and do your nails, and—"

"Penny!" Emily laughed and decided it felt good. "I'm just going to the mall."

"No, you are having a day out—for you. And that begins with a long bubble bath. Now hurry along. I'll take care of the babies. I've watched you do it enough. I know what they need."

Emily couldn't argue, but she did whisper a quick prayer of gratitude for Penny's friendship. It was the one thing that kept her treading water, especially these past few years since her mother had been gone. Penny's children were all in school now, and she spent her days either scouting out garage sales if she wasn't organizing one of her own, or helping neighbors in need. Emily was often at the top of Penny's list.

Emily sank into the steaming water and made up her mind to forget, just for today, about the difficulties in her life. Today she was going to enjoy herself.

Choosing something to wear wasn't easy, but the decision came down to a classic black skirt from college days. A pleated pink blouse that buttoned down the back was added because the color flattered Emily, and the neckline was good for the necklace she wanted to wear. The real trouble came with the shoes. Everything either looked worn, matronly, or too out of style. Emily sat on the edge of the bed in dismay. She wondered if praying for new shoes to appear would help, then decided to work on her hair and makeup and think about it. She did her face like she would for Sunday, with only a little more makeup than the bare minimum she wore every day. Pink combs held her hair back on the sides, rather than tied into a practical pony-tail.

Brushing her teeth, Emily remembered the boots. Eagerly she dug through the cedar chest while Penny kept the babies from helping. Emily laughed when she pulled them out, realizing she'd seen some much like them just the other day in a display window at the mall. Michael told her when he'd bought them that it was the same style of riding boot worn by both men and women for decades, maybe centuries. And now they were fashionable.

"Now," Penny instructed when she was ready to leave, book and receipt in hand, "shop, eat an orange truffle, relax, enjoy, and don't forget to get that book autographed. Don't worry about the time. Even if it gets late, I'll manage. I know how to feed husbands and put babies to bed."

"I won't be late," Emily insisted.

"You just have a good time, and don't decide right now when you're coming home. I'll see you later."

"Thank you, Penny. You're a gem."

"So you tell me. Now, get out of here."

Emily bubbled with excitement and eager anticipation until she arrived at the bookstore, realizing that Michael Hamilton was nearby. A small crowd of people hovered around the display where she had found the book earlier in the week. As they milled around and formed some semblance of a line, Emily caught a glimpse of him, seated on a high-backed stool, scribbling in a copy of his book.

It *was* him!

The crowd shifted and she lost sight of him before she hardly had a chance to absorb his reality; but her heart pounded, reminding her that she hadn't imagined it. It really was Michael

Hamilton. How familiar he looked—just when she had begun to believe that she didn't remember what he looked like.

Nervous beyond reason, Emily turned and fled. What was she doing here? She headed toward the nearest exit, but as her heart slowed so did her feet. She turned back and wandered idly through the mall, looking at everything but seeing nothing. She nearly got an orange truffle but felt certain she'd end up with chocolate smeared somewhere. She wondered if food would ease the gnawing nerves in her stomach, but decided it would only make them worse. There was little good in spending precious money on something she doubted she could bring herself to eat.

Emily sat on a bench, hugging the package tight. She looked toward the bookstore, took a deep breath and walked back, pretending to browse and attempting to ignore the pulsebeats in her ears. The line had lengthened. Was he so popular? Discreetly she moved closer for a better look. The nervousness settled into something warm. He hadn't changed, except for a deepening of the laugh-lines that crinkled at the corners of his eyes. He wore a tasteful pair of wire-rimmed glasses. He looked so handsome, so dignified. Just watching him was easy and seemed natural.

Moving subtly closer but turning her back, pretending to examine a picture book, she heard his voice as he exchanged trivialities with a fan. That rich Australian brogue! Emily wanted to laugh and cry at the same time. She was tempted to just turn around and speak to him. He was so close. But fear overtook her and she took a place in line, browsing through the book to pass the time. In her mind she rehearsed what she might say to him—*Michael, I don't know if you remember me . . .* Or maybe, *Michael Hamilton. Is that really you?*

Emily shook her head. This was ridiculous. Her nerve was leaving fast. Then she remembered the peace she'd felt in her decision and knew there was no harm in this. Perhaps, in a way, Penny had been right. Maybe the opportunity to see Michael again would help her face some of the difficulties in her life. If she could see and hear for herself that Michael Hamilton was happy and content without her, it would be easier to let go of any fear and enjoy the memories for what they were.

Emily's distracted thoughts ended abruptly with the realization that she was second in line. She heard him laugh and decided she wasn't ready. Discreetly she moved out of line to stand at the rear, adding another three bodies between herself and Michael Hamilton. Again she approached too quickly, and again she moved to the back of the line. But approaching once more, she turned to find no one behind her. With only one person between them, Emily glanced helplessly over her shoulder, certain that someone else must be hovering nearby to meet the esteemed Mr. Hamilton. But there was only her.

Emily took a deep breath as the person in front of her moved away. She waited where she stood, expecting him to look up, but instead he looked closely at his pen as if to investigate a malfunction, then he fumbled in his jacket pocket. Emily approached timidly as he withdrew a fresh pen and clicked it into place. Without looking up he took the book from her hands and said in a kind voice, edged with dramatic humor, "And to whom would you like this dedicated?"

Emily hesitated. All rehearsed phrases escaped her. With a shaky voice she whispered, "To my first love, forever."

The pen remained motionless, poised against the page. Emily held her breath, waiting for him to perceive it, wondering if he would. His head shot up. He pulled off his glasses and his eyes filled with warmth. Those smile lines deepened as his lips moved to silently form the word, "Emily!"

The world blurred around her. Ten and a half years dissipated as their eyes met. The past was like a dream. The future was non-existent. Emily could only feel now, and she was grateful for whatever means had made it possible for her to stand here at this moment.

"Hello, Michael," she finally said, proud of herself for the steady tone.

He smiled, then chuckled. "I don't believe it!" With no hesitance he engulfed Emily in an embrace of steel. She could do nothing but return it, squeezing her eyes shut to more fully absorb the reality. How familiar he felt. The very scent of him took her to another time. He finally drew back to look at her, and Emily could feel his eyes marveling as if she were a work of art in a museum. She had forgotten how it felt to be looked at that way. Self-conscious, she glanced away from his silent appraisal but quickly found her eyes drawn back to his.

"What are you doing here?" he asked breathily.

"I live here," she stated, as if it were obvious. "I have for nearly ten years."

He nodded slightly. "I . . . I didn't know . . ."

Emily laughed tensely. "I don't need to ask what you're doing here." He shook his head with a humble chuckle. "You made it, Michael. I knew you could do it."

For a long moment they were lost in silent embarrassment. It seemed there were no words to begin to bridge the gap created by the years. Recalling the last time they'd seen each other could only bring to mind the emotions that had seemed unbearable at the time, and perhaps still were.

Their eyes shifted mutually to a young couple now hovering near to acquire an autograph. Michael cleared his throat. Emily motioned toward the book on the table.

"Aren't you going to sign it?" she asked lightly.

"Ah, yes." He eased back onto the stool, replaced his glasses, and set his pen again to the blank page. He hesitated, then quickly wrote something and handed Emily the book.

"It's good to see you again, Michael," she said with sincerity. "It's been so long."

"Yes, it has." His eyes met hers and she sensed that his words implied deep meaning.

"Well," she said, glancing quickly over her shoulder to the others waiting in line, "I should be moving along and let you—"

"Emily." His voice bordered on panic. He stood and took hold of her arm. Turning to those waiting, he said with an easy smile, "I'll be with you in just a minute, if you will excuse me." He guided her away from the table, then turned to face her. For a moment he just looked at her while she waited expectantly for him to say something.

She wanted to ask what she had wondered all these years. There was no wedding band on his finger, and she didn't want to pry. He finally spoke. "Can I see you later? There's so much to catch up on. Maybe we could have dinner or . . ." He paused when her gaze dropped. "No," he answered himself, the disappointment evident in his voice, "I guess you can't do that."

Emily shook her head. "I really need to be going. I've got to get home and . . . cook dinner, and . . ." Her voice faltered when his eyes turned heavy with questions and frustration. Emily suddenly didn't want to be here, but he continued to hold her arm. "Like I said, it was good to see you again, and—"

"Wait!" He tightened his grip as she attempted to move away. "Please. Can't we at least talk? There is so much I want to ask you, to tell you. So much time to catch up on."

Emily felt herself becoming a spectacle and nodded in agreement, if only to escape the discomfort of this moment. He smiled and she realized what she had done. Frantically she tried to think how to handle this. She was a married woman! How could she possibly meet with him and feel all right about it? She knew the rules of such things. It simply wasn't acceptable or smart for them to be alone. She glanced around the crowded bookstore. The public. That's what they needed. If they were in public, she could talk to him and not break the rules.

She finally put a voice to her agreement. "All right," she said, "but I can't tonight. Will you still be here tomorrow, or—"

"Yes," he said quickly, the relief in his voice all too evident.

"Meet me here, tomorrow morning at ten."

He nodded eagerly. "I'll be here."

Emily met his eyes once more and hurried away. She paused at the store entrance and turned back, surprised to find him still watching her. She felt his eyes recognize the boots, but there was something in his expression that made her suddenly afraid. What had elated her a few minutes ago now filled her with a formless dread. Her life had once again crossed paths with

Michael Hamilton's. And somehow she knew that facing up to the years lying between them would not be easy.

CHAPTER THREE

ONCE BEYOND MICHAEL'S SIGHT, Emily ran. She didn't stop until she sat safely in her car. Laying her head back against the warm upholstery, she attempted to catch her breath while the late afternoon sun shone in her face. She closed her eyes to avoid it and instead was assaulted by a vividly clear image.

"Michael," she said aloud, as if it might convince her the encounter had been real. Recalling that she had promised to meet him tomorrow, Emily groaned and pressed her head to the steering wheel. "Oh, what have I done?" she asked herself, then groaned again.

She would simply not show up, she told herself, but immediately decided against it. Emily had been raised to be dependable and responsible, and she could never live with leaving Michael to wait and wonder. She had agreed to meet him, and she would just have to do it. But she reminded herself to stay clearly in touch with the rules. Emotions were too vulnerable, she hovered too close to the edge of unhappiness to allow herself to be set up for any kind of trouble. She needed the blessings of righteous living, and she would not jeopardize the presence of the Spirit in her life for any reason. They could talk as long as they stayed in public view. And that was all. She would not do anything tomorrow morning that she couldn't tell Ryan about tomorrow evening.

Reminding herself of the time, Emily drove toward home, stopping at the store to buy groceries for a quick meal. Getting back into the car with her bag, she looked down at the book lying in the seat. She hadn't even read what he'd written. Hesitantly, almost fearfully, she picked it up and opened the cover. Emily could nearly hear his voice adding life to the scribed words: *To my first love, and my last. You will forever be a part of me. Michael.*

Emily sighed—a soothing, poignant sigh, as if she had just watched the end of a romantic movie. She cherished the disarming evidence that she was still a woman worthy of such affection. And yes, she had to admit that although her decision stood strong, he would forever be a part of her, too.

Driving the brief distance from the store to her home, Emily wondered what she would do in the morning if Penny couldn't tend the babies. She'd never left them with anyone but Penny. Emily chuckled at the image of meeting Michael Hamilton, accompanied by a double stroller and a diaper bag.

Relieved that Ryan's car wasn't in the driveway, Emily walked in the door to find her babies playing among the typical scattered toys, with Penny's younger children sprawled among the mess.

"Is that you?" Penny emerged from the kitchen, towel drying the empty vegetable drawer from the fridge.

"You didn't clean my fridge!" Emily protested, setting down the groceries.

"I was bored."

"Then read a book or something. You don't have to clean my fridge."

"I like to clean other people's fridges," Penny admitted.

"Yes, I know," Emily said, opening the shining fridge to put away her purchases, "and other people's toilets, and dishes, and floors, too. I'm well aware of what you like to clean around here. If Ryan knew how much of this house is clean because of you regularly taking pity on me, he'd probably start giving you my grocery allowance."

"I won't tell him." Penny pushed past her to put the drawer away. "And one day you won't have babies that keep you from getting extra things done. I was there once." Penny leaned against the counter and folded her arms while Emily washed and cut lettuce. After a reasonable silence she nearly shrieked, "Well?"

"Well what?" Emily asked without looking up.

"Did you see him?"

Emily had to smile. "Yes, I saw him."

"Do I have to squeeze it out of you? Tell me!"

Emily set the knife aside and repeated only the necessary details of her encounter with Michael Hamilton, ending with the announcement, "So I guess I'm meeting him tomorrow at ten. Do you know where I can get a babysitter?"

"I think I can manage to fit it into my schedule." Penny grinned triumphantly. "You said he wasn't wearing a ring. Do you think he's married?"

"I don't know." Emily finally resumed her task. Glancing at the clock, she wondered what could be keeping Ryan. "But it doesn't matter. You should know that I—" A loud cry from the other room interrupted.

"I'll get her," Penny offered, returning a moment later with the baby on her hip. "You were saying?"

"I was saying that it doesn't matter whether he's married or not. I am. I don't like the way you're implying that there is still some great romance going on here. He's an old friend. He asked to see me so we could catch up. That's all. Nothing changes."

"I wouldn't be so closed-minded about it if I were you," Penny said in nearly the same tone that she added, "Hand me a cracker there for Alexa."

Emily dried a hand and passed the box of saltines. "I can't believe you said that, Penny. You know I love Ryan, and I would never—"

"Emily," Penny interrupted while she put the baby into the high chair and offered a cracker, "I think it's time I said something that I have wondered if you need to hear." Emily worked more vigorously, already knowing she wasn't going to like this. "And let me add first that I wouldn't be saying it if I didn't know well that you are the most reasonable, cautious person I have ever known. But really, Emily. I have watched you give everything you have to this marriage, and what have you got to show for it? It's not like you haven't given him every chance in the world. Maybe the decision to marry Ryan was right ten years ago. Maybe something else is right for you now."

Emily tersely set down a pan. "Penny, honestly there are moments when you sound like the devil's advocate."

"Sorry," Penny uttered, and Emily knew she meant it. But she also knew that Penny wouldn't have said what she had if she didn't feel a certain conviction about it.

"You know as well as I do the seriousness of wedding vows, Penny. Despite it all, I love Ryan, and I don't believe he intends to hurt me. He just—"

"Never mind." Penny held up a hand to stop her. "I don't want to hear this speech again. Quite frankly, I can't take it. It's your life, Emily. All I ask is that you keep an open mind. I'll see you in the morning. I'll be here early so you can get ready."

Penny headed out of the kitchen but Emily stopped her. "Penny, thank you—for everything. You are such a blessing to me."

"Even if I am the devil's advocate?" Penny managed a smile.

"I didn't really mean that."

"I know. I'm sorry if I . . . well, I'm just concerned. You say I'm such a blessing to you, but I wouldn't dare think what my life would be like without you. Do you realize how many years we have practically been living in each other's laps?"

"Yes, I know."

"And I just want you to be happy, Emily. If you're determined to stay with Ryan, I can only pray that he comes around one day."

"That would make two of us." Emily smiled. "Thanks again. I had a good day."

"And an even better one tomorrow, I hope." Penny waved and went to the front room to gather her children.

Emily could hear toys being picked up and hollered, "Don't

do that. I'll take care of it later."

"Aw, shut up and cook," Penny called back.

Three minutes after Penny left, Amee came running into the kitchen with a bucket full of blocks which she dumped in the middle of the floor. Emily sighed as Amee looked up at her proudly and said in perfect toddler, "Pay bocks."

Emily squatted down to hug her. "Mommy missed Amee today. Did you have a good time with Penny?"

"Pay bocks."

Emily hugged her again and left her to build with blocks, carefully dodging them while traversing the kitchen floor to set the table. Alexa began to protest and Emily put dinner on hold to spoon feed her. Then she cleaned up the highchair so she could put Amee in it.

"Allison? Are you here?" Emily called, realizing she'd not heard from her oldest daughter yet.

"I'm doing my homework," Allison called back.

"Good girl, but can I have a hug?"

A few minutes later Allison appeared to give her mother an eager embrace. Emily felt blessed. Her daughters were beautiful and healthy. A day didn't pass without her acknowledging that she had much to be grateful for.

"Did you have a good day at school?" Emily inquired, passing Alexa over to her big sister who made silly faces at the baby.

"It was okay."

"Any problems?"

"No."

"If there were, would you tell me?"

"Mom," Allison feigned disgust, making it evident that she would. But Emily always checked.

With the table barely set, Ryan came through the door, his attention turning first to Amee, who called "Daddy! Daddy!" eagerly from her highchair. He grinned and tousled the child's curls.

"How was school?" he asked Allison, who repeated the same answer then disappeared into her room after handing Alexa over to her father. He tickled the baby a minute, then set her down to look at the mail. Emily's peaceful observance of father and children was shattered by the same old reality. The mail was always greeted before the wife. The one time she had gently suggested that it should be the other way around, Ryan had laughed and told her she was being silly. Emily bet that Michael Hamilton wouldn't come home to his wife and . . . She stopped the thought as abruptly as she stopped cutting tomatoes. Squeezing her eyes shut to block out the image, she silently uttered a quick prayer to free her mind of such thoughts, knowing they could not possibly help her marriage.

Emily set the green salad on the table where Ryan waited to eat while he shuffled through the bills. She set his plate in front of him, called to Allison, and turned to cut a hot dog into bite-size pieces for Amee.

"What is this?" Ryan asked, obviously irritated.

"It's a hot dog, dear." She kept her tone light. He looked up at her dubiously. "You know, the great American food. It goes along with all those football and baseball games that you love to—"

"I know what it is," he said, "but . . ."

Emily glared at him and was relieved when her look stopped what she knew he wanted to say. "There's plenty to go with it to make a decent meal," she said. "I think we will survive one night of hot dogs."

Ryan said nothing more, but through the meal Emily sensed that he'd rather be eating anything else. She felt that familiar anger, but suppressed it with practiced agility. There had hardly been a day in ten and a half years of marriage when she hadn't put a good meal in front of him, but she couldn't have a day out without feeling guilty because she didn't have time to prepare any more. Her mind filed through a thousand justifiable retorts to his insinuating silence, but she held them back and instead chose to say, "You'll never believe who I ran into today."

"Who?" he asked absently.

"Well, Penny insisted that I get a day out, and I decided to go to the mall. There was an autograph signing at the book-store, and guess who the honored author was."

"I can't imagine." He showed a degree of interest.

"Michael Hamilton." Just saying the name sent a delicious tremor down her spine.

"Who?" Ryan repeated.

"You remember. My college sweetheart." His eyes showed no recognition. "The Australian," she added, and Ryan's expression showed a vague enlightenment. "He's a writer, you know. It seems his books are rather popular, and I . . ." Emily figured this was as good a time as any to discuss that extra check she'd written. "I bought one."

Emily hoped he might ask if he could read it, or maybe inquire about Michael Hamilton; perhaps even an indication that he might be intrigued—or maybe a bit jealous—at the thought of his wife running into her college sweetheart. But all he said was, "How are you going to pay for it?"

"I wrote a check," she said tonelessly.

"And where do you think that money comes from?"

"I know where it comes from." Emily willed herself to stay calm. "You work very hard to provide for us, and I appreciate it. I think I'm worth buying one book every five or six years."

"Maybe you should get a job and you could buy one more often." His tone almost teased, but Emily knew well that he clearly meant what he said.

"I have a job," she insisted. Allison looked up from her meal in dismay. "Caring for our home and children is more than a full-time job."

"If you can leave them with Penny to go to the mall, why can't you leave them with her to do something worthwhile?"

Emily put down her fork and closed her eyes, willing herself to not get caught up in this. His tone was turning all too serious, all too biting. They'd had this conversation a hundred times and it never changed. His idea of solving the financial strain was for her to get a job. Her idea was to faithfully do the best they could to live within their means as long as they had children at home who needed her. It was only money to her. To him, money was everything.

Amee began to scream when the baby crawled through the blocks. She spilled her milk attempting to get out of the high-chair to stop the invasion of her toys. Emily calmly handled the crisis, grateful for the distraction.

It was nearly ten before the girls were asleep, the dishes done, a load of laundry put into the dryer, and the toys picked up—again. Emily checked on the children, then got ready for bed and crawled between the covers. But instead of settling into her pillow as she normally did, Emily reached underneath the bed to retrieve her freshly-autographed copy of *Verity*.

She opened it, glanced over the inscription, then turned the page and began to read:

Verity was born in the early morning. Murphy chose the name and he had earned the right. If not for his skilled hands and patient manner, the foal would not have survived its harried trek into the world. For seven grueling hours, Murphy had . . .

Emily became distracted by a rare reality. Ryan was kissing her—on the lips. "Want to snuggle?" he asked with a teasing smile.

Emily knew what he was politely referring to, but with little thought she gave a rare response. "Actually, I think I'll just read a while and go to sleep."

Ryan scowled. "How much did you pay for that book?" he inquired tersely. "It's a hardbound. Couldn't you wait for it to come out in paperback?"

"If I had done that, I wouldn't have been able to get it auto-graphed."

Ryan took the book from her hands. Emily was briefly tempted to take it back before he could see what Michael had written, but she reminded herself that she had nothing to hide. Ryan's scowl deepened as he read the words scribbled there with Michael's signature. While he stared at it, Emily waited for a reaction. Much to her disappointment and relief, he only grunt-ed and tossed the book at her, then turned over to settle himself for the night.

"If you're going to read," he muttered, "why don't you do it in the other room? I can't sleep with the light on."

Emily stuffed the book under the bed and turned out the light, deciding that what she needed was sleep. Habit and an ever-present need urged her out of the bed and to her knees. She didn't know how long she silently poured her heart out in prayer, but when she crawled back into bed, Ryan was snoring softly.

The next day, Emily immediately recognized the signs of the "if anything can go wrong it will" morning. The first symptom was Ryan getting out of the shower to declare that he'd used all the hot water. He checked the water heater and found the pilot had gone out. It was relit and declared sound, but the only time Emily could possibly take a shower, she had no hot water to do it. The next problem came in a diaper soaked through, which meant changing the crib linens. Then Alexa ate a piece of Allison's homework, and Amee dumped her bowl of milk and Cheerios on the floor, insisting that she wanted Rice Krispies. How could a child less than two be so opinionated?

A fork fell in the garbage disposal while it ran. A glass dropped on the counter and shattered. The toaster wouldn't work, and the pair of jeans Emily had intended to wear suddenly had an unexplainable stain. After all of that, Allison's ride to school came late.

When Penny walked through the door at nine o'clock, Emily nearly fell apart, rambling off a forty-five second report of how long the day had been already. Penny quickly took over. She sent Emily to the shower, gave the babies each a cookie, checked the kitchen carefully to make certain the glass was all cleaned up, threw away the mangled fork, and started washing the breakfast dishes.

Emily glanced at the bedroom clock while she dressed and nearly panicked. If she was late, he might not think she was coming and . . . Frantically she wondered what to wear. In the interest of time she went with the same skirt and boots, but put them with a lightweight white sweater. Her hair was barely fluffed a little with a brush. She put on a bit of makeup, checked the contents of her purse, then went to the kitchen to find her world under control.

"Bless you, Penny," she muttered gratefully.

"Well, it's not every day you get to meet a dashing Australian," she teased. "But you'd better hurry, or he'll think you chickened out."

"Yes, I know." Emily fastened her Mickey Mouse watch around her wrist.

"And remember," said Penny, pointing a stern finger, "it's like I told you yesterday. I don't want you to even think about the time. If it takes all day to talk it through, fine. I can feed husbands and put babies to bed. I don't have any plans."

"Thank you, Penny." Emily embraced her and hurried out the door. She hit every red light on State Street, and came through an unexplained traffic slow-up near 400 south. She went through the rear entrance of the bookstore and walked quickly toward the front, unnerved that she couldn't see him. Mickey Mouse said five after ten. Telling herself not to panic, Emily gathered her wits and caught her breath while she pretended to browse. The cardboard display for Michael's books was empty, but sported a handwritten sign that read: "We'll have more Tuesday. Sign up on our waiting list."

Emily reflected briefly on what made the book so popular. She hadn't read it so she couldn't say for sure, but a quick guess would be that his values came through in the story and were appreciated by the people in this community. Whatever it was, Emily felt a warmth for his success. She had clear memories of Michael musing endlessly about stories that he could see in his head like movies. A driving desire had been with him from his early teens, to record his observances of the world. His success was a testimony to the kind of man he was—determined and positive.

Again Emily glanced at her watch. Ten past ten. She looked around tensely, searching for his face. Perhaps he wasn't coming.

What if she couldn't talk to him? Would he look for her? Could he find her even if he tried? Her parents were both dead now. He didn't know any of her relatives well enough to know where to contact them. She doubted if he even remembered her married name. And she knew she didn't have his Australian address. He'd lived only in Provo when they had dated. Perhaps she could write to his publisher and have something forwarded.

A studied perusal of her surroundings made her heart heavy. He wasn't coming. Perhaps it was better in the long run that he didn't show up and—

"Emily!" She heard his breathless voice and turned, heart pounding. He was breathing hard, but his eyes sparkled as he looked at her face. "I'm so glad you didn't leave. The car I rented wouldn't start and I had to get a cab, and . . ." He smiled. "Well, I made it."

"I was a little late myself," she admitted.

Emily watched his eyes travel down the length of her. Despite feeling self-conscious, she couldn't help doing the same. He wore casual gray slacks with pleats and big pockets in the front. Showing from beneath them were black boots, nearly identical to those she wore now. The glasses he'd worn yesterday were in the pocket of a blousy white shirt, tucked in. He looked as lean and fit as he had when they'd been in Australia, nearly eleven years ago.

"Your husband must be doing well," he stated when his eyes finally returned to hers.

Emily's brows furrowed together. "What makes you think so?"

"Because you look like a million bucks."

Emily smiled timidly from the sincerity in his eyes. "You don't look so bad yourself."

Michael glanced around tensely, then held out a hand. "Let's walk."

Emily shoved her hands into her pockets and moved beside him into the mall's wide corridor.

"Thank you for coming," he said, setting an easy pace. "I

suspect you don't feel totally comfortable with this, but I really do appreciate it."

"And why is that?"

"It's like I told you yesterday. There's so much to catch up on." He paused and looked down at her. "I've missed you."

Emily looked straight ahead and continued to walk. "Am I to assume there is no reason for you to feel uncomfortable, meeting me this way?"

"I'm not married, if that's what you mean."

Emily unintentionally cleared her throat. "There's no one in your life?" she had to ask, still not looking at him.

"No one worth mentioning." The words had a subtle bite.

"That's not my fault, Michael," she stated in response to his tone. She almost expected an argument. If she had said something like that to Ryan, she'd have gotten one.

"No," he agreed humbly, "it's not your fault. Let's just say that holing up with a word processor can be a little . . . unfulfilling at times."

Emily attempted to steer the conversation elsewhere. "Are you working on another, then?"

"Yeah," he said as if it were nothing. "This last one was part of a three-book contract. It keeps me busy because I'm not a very fast writer. I have to pull every word up from the tips of my toes."

"However you do it, it must be working," she complimented. "Your success is apparent."

"Did you like the book?" he asked intently.

"I'm afraid I haven't had a chance to read past the first paragraph. I've only had it a few days."

"I mean the other one. I sent you a copy of the first one. You did get it, didn't you?"

"Yes." She tried to conceal the embarrassment. "I got it. But I'm afraid I didn't read it."

He stopped walking and Emily was three steps ahead before she figured it out and turned back to face him. "Why not?" he asked.

"There was a lot going on at the time," she justified, "and

soon after that I got pregnant." She looked away.

Nothing more was said until some passing shoppers regard-ed them oddly as they had to walk around their stationary bod-ies. "Couldn't we go someplace a little more . . . quiet?" he asked tersely. Emily said nothing and he shook his head. "No, I guess we can't."

"I do prefer remaining . . . public," she said, hating this ten-sion between them. She had thought that after all these years, so much would have changed. But she felt as if it had been just last week that she'd told him she wasn't going to marry him, and he was still in a bad mood because of it.

"Are you implying you don't trust me?" he asked pointedly.

"It's not a matter of trust, Michael. It's a matter of princi-ple." Her voice softened. "There is no reason on earth why I shouldn't trust you."

Emily began to walk and Michael followed, wondering what he had done to deserve having Emily Ladd come back into his life when he'd finally begun to believe he could be happy with-out her. But he reminded himself that this little rendezvous was his own doing. He had practically begged her to meet him, and however difficult it might be, he wasn't going to let her leave until he got the answers to some questions that had haunted him for more than a decade.

CHAPTER FOUR

MICHAEL FOLLOWED EMILY SILENTLY to the sunken sitting area near a jewelry store where they had once dreamed together over wedding rings in the window. Emily sat on a bench and he sat beside her, leaning forward with his forearms against his thighs.

"I really wish you had read my book," he said. "There were things that only you could understand. In a way, I suppose I wrote it for you."

"I'm sorry," she said, and he knew she meant it. He looked over his shoulder to see her face. "I'll read it soon, I promise."

"Let me know what you think."

"I'll do that."

He looked ahead and pressed his fingers together in a fidgety manner. "So, how are your parents?"

"They're both dead," she answered, and he snapped his head back quickly to check her expression. He couldn't believe it. "Yes," she assured him, "soon after I was married my father got cancer. What treatment they could afford didn't make much difference. My mother died nearly three years ago of a heart attack, just a few weeks after you sent me that book."

"I'm so sorry, Emily." He sat straight and turned toward her. "I truly am. I didn't mean to imply that—"

"It's all right, Michael. I should have read it, and I apologize. I'm touched that you thought of me. The truth is . . ." She nearly said that she was afraid to read it, but she decided to tell him a different truth. "By the time I dealt with losing my mother, I found out I was pregnant, and from then on everything got more complicated by the day."

"Like how?" he asked in genuine curiosity.

"I'm sure you didn't meet me here to listen to the trivialities of my life."

"On the contrary, Emily, that is exactly why I'm here. I want to know." Emily marveled at the sincere interest in his eyes. "Tell me how it got more complicated by the day. No," he corrected, "tell me everything."

Emily fidgeted with the small purse in her lap while Michael watched her face. "Well," she chuckled tensely, "the pregnancy itself was a surprise. For years we had tried to have another baby, but—"

"Another?" he interrupted.

"Yes," she clarified. "Allison is nine." Michael nodded, feeling a little lost and helpless from the reality. "But I had some difficulties with the birth, and for years we . . . well, I began to wonder if she would be the only one."

Emily recalled the difficulty of facing up to being denied the opportunity for more children, and the fasting and prayer that had given her peace not long before she'd discovered her pregnancy. "As I said, I found out I was pregnant soon after Mother died. She came to stay with me when Allison was born, so I felt a little out of sorts, but we managed. Amee is twenty-one months now."

"I bet they're beautiful," he smiled.

Emily took the opportunity to produce her wallet and show him pictures. "This is Allison." She pointed to the copy of her most recent school picture.

"She looks like you." He put his glasses on and bent over it to look closely. Emily attempted to turn it to the next set, ignoring the wedding picture opposite Allison. But Michael took the wallet from her hand and looked at the picture with a blank, studied gaze. "You haven't changed," was all he said, shifting to her face as if to compare.

"You didn't make it to the wedding," she observed.

Michael's dry chuckle indicated she might as well have expected him to go to Mars. "No," his voice turned husky, "I didn't make it to the wedding. I was out of the country at the time." He turned the picture in his hand to look at the next.

"That's Amee," Emily declared proudly, grateful to move on. "And yes, she's as mischievous as she looks."

"She really is adorable," he grinned, then pointed to the baby picture beside it. "And who is this?"

"That's Alexa."

Michael looked up in question. "That was my great-grandmother's name."

"Yes, I know. I hope you don't mind. Alexa will be seven months old tomorrow."

"She's yours too?"

"Funny, isn't it?" Emily laughed. "I couldn't get pregnant for years, and then I had two babies fourteen months apart."

"They must keep you busy," he said distantly. "It certainly keeps you in shape." He glanced quickly to her waistline.

Emily ignored the compliment. "Actually, I believe I am barely sane. I don't get much time for reading." He looked up from the pictures and she smiled as if to say "touché"

"Three daughters." He handed back the wallet. "I'd say that's quite an accomplishment for ten and a half years. It's worth a whole lot more than two and a half novels."

"Accomplishment is relative. Sometimes I'd like to think I'm capable of more than changing diapers."

"There's a lot more to parenting than that," he said with due respect.

"I suppose there is," Emily admitted, "though at times it's difficult to see the results."

Michael chuckled. "It reminds me of some of the stories in those family journals I showed you. My grandmother had twins and another daughter soon after."

"I don't think I could survive twins," Emily laughed. She was enjoying this. Raising children was something she rarely discussed with Ryan.

"You practically had twins."

"I have wondered which would be more difficult. One of the hardest times for me was being pregnant while I still had a baby waking up nights, and then carrying a toddler around while I could barely walk myself. But I think the worst was recovering from childbirth with a fourteen-month-old who thinks this infant is no different than her Raggedy Ann Doll."

Michael was filled with compassion for something that had obviously been difficult. The light way she laughed it off didn't fool him. He wished he had been there to help her, the way he wished it was him in that wedding picture. He wished he had been there to see these beautiful girls be born, and grow, and . . . Michael stopped himself. He was only inflicting useless self-torture. He wondered, as he often did, why he hadn't dealt with this ten years ago. Emily was obviously happy, and nothing he wished would ever change the circumstances.

"You must have help at least part of the time," he said to reassure himself.

"Oh, I have Penny," she said brightly. "She's my neighbor. She's the most wonderful thing in my life. I'd be lost without her."

"And your husband, of course," Michael stated, not really expecting any reaction. He was quick to notice her faltering expression, though she covered it smoothly. A subtle unease started to creep up the back of his neck, but he couldn't find words to define it.

"Oh," Emily said flippantly, "his work keeps him busy much of the time."

While Michael attempted to read between the words, he impulsively confessed, "I envy your life, Emily. A man my age should have two or three kids by now."

Emily gave a slight chuckle and leaned her head back against the brick wall. "At times I could envy yours. All that peace and quiet and time to yourself."

"But one day those babies will be grown and you'll have

something to show for what you're doing. All I will have is more peace and quiet."

"Is there a reason you haven't married, Michael?" She felt she had to ask, despite the nagging fear involved with what the answers might be.

There were a thousand things Michael wanted to say, but the only thing he could tell her without making a scene was simply, "Just haven't found the right girl, I suppose."

"Have you looked?"

"Yes," he insisted, "I have."

"I was just asking."

"And I told you."

Emily looked away, certain that their terseness was a symptom of many unvented emotions that she had no desire to face or even think about. She changed the subject.

"What have you been doing these years besides writing?"

Michael sighed and stretched out his legs, crossing them at the ankles. "I've traveled quite a bit. I spent nearly a year in Europe, and I've been getting more involved with the horses, though I stick more to breeding and training and leave the racing to the gamblers. One of our horses did very well last year at Melbourne. You would have enjoyed it." He wondered if she remembered how they had discussed putting the Melbourne Cup on their honeymoon agenda.

"Yes, I would have." Emily smiled at him. "Tell me about it."

Emily relaxed again as Michael talked freely of horse races, and the people and animals he worked with. She asked him about Europe, wishing he would never stop. She thoroughly enjoyed just listening to him, watching him, and completely ignoring the urge to regret not being able to share all of this with him.

Michael stopped talking when Emily's stomach growled. He laughed and she looked down in embarrassment. "You didn't eat breakfast, did you?" he asked. "How many times have I told you that you've got to eat a good breakfast? Come on." He took her arm and urged her to her feet. "Let's get something to eat." He gave her a teasing smile. "I didn't eat breakfast, either."

Emily glanced at her watch. "I don't believe it." Emily showed it to him and said in a voice like she would to her children, "Mickey Mouse says it's twenty past one."

Michael chuckled and paused to imitate Mickey's arms poised to the correct time. "I think Mickey Mouse has dislocated shoulders," he concluded.

"I can't believe how the time has flown." She glanced at her watch again, fearing it deceived her.

Michael sounded panicked. "You're not in a hurry, are you?"

"No," she replied, and he gave an audible sigh. "Penny has the children. She told me to enjoy myself and not to worry about the time."

"I think I like this Penny." He smiled. "Do they still have a J.B.'s in this place?"

"I don't think so." She smiled in return. "But I'm sure we can find someplace to eat."

Michael barely touched a hand to her back to guide her into the restaurant, but Emily felt the warmth linger long after they were seated and facing each other. She watched Michael smile kindly at the hostess who handed them each a menu. He put on his glasses to read it, but Emily left her menu on the table. Michael glanced over his and smiled. Again Emily felt as if the years separating them had never existed. The entire ritual seemed so natural.

"Still no individuality," he teased.

"I simply trust your judgment when it comes to food."

"Then I assume you'll have whatever I have."

"It always worked before."

"Yes," he replied with deeper meaning in his eyes, "it always worked before."

Emily ignored the implication. Michael went back to studying the menu and finally ordered.

"Now it's your turn." Michael leaned toward Emily. "What have you been doing all these years besides having babies?" He removed his glasses and returned them to his shirt pocket.

"Nothing exciting, I can assure you."

"Tell me anyway."

"I've lived in the same house for nearly ten years. It's on a street with a hundred other houses that look exactly the same. I spend a lot of time with Penny. She's lived there longer than I have. I keep in touch with my sisters through letters. I've stayed active in the Church, of course."

"Of course."

"How about you?" She couldn't resist asking.

"I haven't been to church since the last time I went with you." Emily sighed and began playing with her napkin. "And I must confess that I've missed it."

"Then you should start going again. Maybe you'd meet a nice girl and—"

"The only girls I'd find at church would not want to marry a man like me."

Emily's lips tightened in response to the edge in his voice. A quick retort came to mind, but instead she paused to analyze his comment briefly. "Why don't you just come out and say it, Michael?"

"Say what?" He feigned innocence so perfectly that it was obvious he knew what she meant. She explained anyway.

"I get the feeling there is something you'd like to say to me, and this might be your last chance to say it. So maybe you'd better just get it over with. I can take it. The past ten years have toughened me up good."

Michael jumped quickly to the defensive. "I've been the one alone all these years, Emily. Don't talk to me about being toughened."

Emily thought of too many examples she could give him to illustrate how difficult these years had been for her, but the last thing she wanted was for him to know the reality of her marriage. She tried to turn it to empathy and said with a gentle voice, "Why don't you tell me about it?" He said nothing. "That is what you want to talk to me about, isn't it?" Emily knew she was guessing, but it was a good place to start. "I know you wanted to say a lot the last time we talked. Why don't you get it out now, and let's get on with our lives."

Michael knew she was right. Despite the pain he felt in facing it, Emily made it evident that she still knew him, perhaps better than he knew himself. It was time he did learn to live with it.

"Emily," he said gently, "there is nothing I can say that will make any difference now. It's been too long. Whatever I haven't dealt with is my problem. But you're right. There is something I want to say—something I have wondered about a great deal."

Michael shifted in his seat and crossed his legs beneath the table. He realized as he hesitated that the question wasn't easy to ask, but deep inside he knew it would make a difference. Perhaps if he knew for certain that Emily had made the right choice, that she was happy, he could get past his wallowing and resign himself to finding somebody else. Not that he hadn't tried, but maybe what held him back was the wondering.

"Emily," he said again, "I simply want to know that you're happy."

Emily shot back a reply so quickly that it startled him. "What makes you think I'm not happy?"

"I didn't say I thought you weren't happy. I simply asked if you were. You are, aren't you? I mean, you've got a beautiful family, and you . . ." Michael stopped cold when she turned her head to the side with a jerk, and the muscles in her face tightened. He might have believed she had turned to stone if not for the subtle quivering of her bottom lip just before she bit it. A foreboding chill ran through him.

"Emily." He drew her name out huskily and leaned further over the table. "You are one of the most honest people I have ever known. I don't think you are even capable of lying. Look at me and tell me if you're happy."

Emily squeezed her eyes shut. She wanted to die. Why hadn't she realized, before she ever agreed to see him, that he would want to know, and he would demand the truth? But even worse, much of the pain she had suffered was choosing this moment to rush up and hit her between the eyes, where an unbearable pounding made it difficult to keep her head upright. Why here? Why now? What was she doing here in the first place?

The food arrived at their table, and for a moment Emily was relieved by the distraction. But as soon as the waitress left, Michael pushed it all aside to clear a path between them. He stretched his arm across the table.

"Emily," he insisted with a hoarse whisper, "look at me!"

She glanced around helplessly, as if something might rescue her from this. If nothing else, she was relieved to note there was no one sitting close by.

"Emily!" he repeated, and she snapped her head forward defiantly. "I want the truth, and I want it now."

Emily used great self-discipline to swallow the knot in her throat. She pressed her fingers against that pounding between her eyes and willed herself to speak. Experience told her he wouldn't let it drop. She recalled other times when he had sat facing her for hours, until whatever might have bothered her was straightened out.

"Emily," he urged with an insistent whisper.

"I . . . I don't know . . . where to start. Ryan is a good man, Michael. He works hard to provide a living for us, and I don't believe he intends to . . . hurt me, but . . ." Michael stiffened visibly and she hesitated before going on. "I . . . I don't . . . well . . ." She leaned her elbows on the table and pressed her forehead into her palms. "I don't know what's wrong. I've tried so hard to figure it out. I think the biggest problem is, well . . ." Emily hesitated, but she knew it was something he'd ask. She might as well tell him before he had a chance. "Ryan stopped going to church nearly seven years ago." The tears finally welled up. Emily squeezed her eyes shut and they trickled out. "He hasn't been to the temple since Allison was born."

In one concise movement, Michael leaned back and folded his arms. "So that's temple marriage."

Emily wiped at the tears with her napkin. "That's not fair, Michael. There are countless people who—"

"You are not countless people, Emily." He put his hands on the edge of the table and leaned toward her. "You are the woman who refused to marry me, so you could marry someone who would take you to the temple and bring the benefits of the priesthood into your home."

"You're upset," she whimpered.

"Upset?" He chuckled humorlessly, then clenched his teeth as if it might keep him from shouting. "I'm not upset, Emily. I am *furious*. I don't think I have ever been so furious in my entire life."

The pain between Emily's eyes intensified, and the knot in her throat tightened until it threatened to explode. She clamped a hand tightly over her mouth in a feeble attempt to hold it back, but an occasional whimper escaped as he continued his quiet, impassioned speech.

"You were the best thing that ever happened to me, Emily. And your leaving me was the worst. Every day for ten and a half years I have coped with not having you, and I've done it by telling myself that the important thing was your happiness. I tried to forget you. I tried to distract myself. I took every opportunity I could muster to get to know other women, to find someone who could make me forget you." His hands clenched into fists and his voice lowered further. "But I had to compare every woman to you, and they always came up lacking. And now you sit there and tell me that all of the anguish and the hurt and the emptiness was for *nothing!*" He slammed a fist on the table and the dishes rattled. Emily winced and another whimper escaped the hand still pressed to her mouth as if it held back a storm that had been brewing for too many years.

Michael watched her through narrowed eyes, and the anger subsided into something far more difficult to deal with. The pain emanating from her became a dagger twisting in his already aching heart. Looking back, he wondered what he might have done differently. But the past was behind them. It couldn't be changed. He had to think of now. And right now, Emily was hurting. In a feeble attempt to offer comfort, he stretched his hand toward her.

Emily shrank back and folded her hands in her lap. "No, Michael," she sobbed from her throat. "You mustn't touch me." His hurt deepened along with the question in his eyes. "I fear if you touch me I'll never be able to let go." Michael curled his outstretched hand into a fist and withdrew it.

Emily stood. "I'll be back in a few minutes," she said, turning to walk toward the restrooms. Michael groaned and hit the table again.

The waitress approached and asked if everything was all right with the meal. "Fine," Michael told her, "but we could use some more napkins."

Emily was grateful to find the ladies' room unoccupied. She went into a stall and leaned her head against the door to sob. When some of the pressure in her head had been released, she willed herself to gain control and blew her nose. The mirror revealed that there was no disguising what she had been doing, and she regretted leaving her purse at the table. A splash of cool water helped a little. Blotting her face with a paper towel, she took a deep breath and mustered enough courage to return to the table. She had no idea what to expect from Michael now, but she reminded herself that their time together was brief. He would be gone soon, and they would probably never see each other again. He knew the truth and he was going to have to learn to live with it, the way she had learned to live with it. Or had she?

With an attempt at normalcy, Emily sat down and began to eat without looking at him. "Eat, Michael," she said when he just stared at her. "Your mother wouldn't be pleased if she knew you weren't eating properly." Still he didn't move. "How is your mother, by the way?"

"She's fine," he answered sharply. "I talk to her every Sunday. She misses you, too." Emily couldn't help looking at him then. "She was very upset about what happened. Every once in a while she mentions you and wonders how you're doing."

"Don't tell her," Emily insisted and took another bite. "It's good. You really should eat."

"I'm not hungry, Emily. And I don't lie to my mother." Emily continued to eat. "Why are you suppressing it, Emily? Do you ever tell him how you feel, or do you pretend everything is all right the way you're trying to pretend right now?"

Emily put down her fork. Suddenly the food didn't taste so good. She didn't know where the extra napkins came from, but she was quick to grab some when the tears threatened again.

"Yes," she answered, "I have told him how I feel. There is nothing more I can do that I have not already done with diligence."

"Maybe you should try some counseling."

"That's a good idea, Michael," she said with sarcasm, "but I thought of it six years ago. He refuses."

"You said he didn't intend to hurt you. I want you to define 'hurt.'"

"You're really determined to make this day miserable, aren't you?" She sniffled and dabbed at her eyes.

"I am trying to get you to face reality here, Emily. I don't believe you've changed so much that I can't figure out what's happening. My guess is that you're living with a whole lot of patience and long-suffering. You're pushing the pain inside because you don't want to, or don't know how to, deal with it. In the meantime, you're not doing yourself—or him—any favors by letting it simmer until it explodes. Remember, I took psychology too. And I didn't create best-selling characters by reading the funny papers. Now, I repeat, *define 'hurt.'* I want to know exactly what we are dealing with here."

"What *we* are dealing with?" She stifled a sob. "This is not your problem, Michael. I am the one who made the decision. I am the one who has to live with it."

Michael reached across the table and grabbed her wrist, whether she wanted to be touched or not. "Don't you dare tell me that *you* are the one who has to live with it. I have had to live with it, and I will continue to live with it. I was one-third of that decision, Emily, but I was the one left on the outside. You know, three's a crowd. I was the crowd. Your dear Ryan is obviously not doing anything to solve these problems, but I certainly am not going to walk away from you today without doing something about it. Now talk, Emily. Define 'hurt.'"

"He doesn't beat me, if that's what you mean. Sometimes I wish he would. If I had bruises, it would be easy to define the problem. I wouldn't have to lie awake at night and wonder why I feel the way I do if I could look at my husband and simply say that he beats me, he abuses me, he drinks, he's unfaithful. But he's done nothing tangibly wrong. He works hard for us. So why am I so miserable?"

"That's what I'm waiting to hear. You said he hurts you. I want to know how."

"And I would love to tell you if I knew."

"You must know something. I think you're avoiding it."

Emily groaned and pulled her arm from his grasp. "You're a hard man to face, Michael Hamilton."

"Yes, but at least I'm facing it. I'm not cowering behind who knows what while my wife suffers in silence."

"And what makes you so certain that if you and I were married now, our life together would be so blissful?"

The fury returned to his eyes. "I am not a perfect man, Emily. I'll be the first to admit I have faults. But I can tell you one thing for certain. I would *not ever* allow my wife to hurt for any reason, intentionally or otherwise. If someone who loved me told me I had a problem, I'd do something about it."

"You can't judge Ryan. You don't have any idea what makes him do what he does."

"No, I don't. But I know that whatever he is doing is hurting you. If nothing else, that gives me some rights. I deserve to at least know what's going on here. You owe me that much, because whether you like it or not, I am a part of this. Now define 'hurt.'"

"I don't know." She hung her head. "I just feel so . . ." The pressure returned, and Emily clamped a hand over her mouth. Michael waited patiently until she lifted her head and managed to say, "I feel like a part of the house; the same as the pantry or the couch. My opinion is not valued. My feelings are invalid. My intelligence is disregarded. My efforts in the home and with the children are treated as unimportant trivialities. But do you know what the worst of it is, Michael?"

He shook his head. His eyes filled with empathy.

"The worst of it is the subtlety." She pressed her palms over the table and leaned forward. "It's all so undefinable that I can't question it without being told that I expect too much, that it's my imagination. All I ever wanted, Michael, was to do the right thing. All I ever tried to do was be the best possible wife and mother I could be. I am a sound, intelligent woman, but in my home I often feel worthless. Why? I just don't understand . . . why."

Emily put her face into her hands and cried, doing her best to remain quiet. Michael watched her, feeling as helpless as if he were bound and gagged. He wanted more than anything to just take her in his arms and soothe the hurt away. But she was as out of reach to him as the moon.

The waitress approached timidly and addressed Michael while Emily tried to discreetly dry her face. "I don't suppose you want dessert." She nodded toward the barely-touched meal.

"No," he said kindly, "I think this will be plenty. Thank you."

"Is there anything else I can do?" she asked, sliding the check across the table.

Michael picked it up to look at it. He pulled a twenty out of his pocket, which he straightened and handed to her along with the check. "Nothing except paying that for me. Keep the change."

Michael took Emily by the arm and urged her into the mall corridor, where she leaned against the wall to compose herself.

"Are you going to be all right?" he asked, unable to resist helping her wipe away some of the tears. He almost regretted it as touching her face ignited once-familiar sensations in him. He couldn't deny that he loved her every bit as much now as he had the day she had told him good-bye.

Emily nodded feebly in answer to his question, and he decided there was one more thing he had to know before she had a chance to escape. He leaned a hand against the wall and looked at her closely.

"Emily," he said, "you told me the day you left that you had fasted and prayed, and you knew that marrying Ryan was the right thing to do. I'm sorry, Emily, but I don't understand how—"

"Oh, that's easy," she said firmly. Michael had expected her to stammer or rationalize, or maybe start to cry again. But instead she said, with the same firm conviction showing in her eyes that had always been there, "I came to realize long ago that I did marry the right man."

Michael resisted the urge to gape in disbelief.

"I have no doubt that what I felt then was right. There was a reason for it, Michael. The right marriage is not necessarily the one that would make us the happiest, but perhaps the one that would help us grow, to achieve our potential. My marriage is my refiner's fire, Michael. And when I get down on my knees, I know beyond any doubt that my Heavenly Father loves me very much. He must have a great deal of faith in me to give me such trials. He must have something wondrous in store for me to find me worthy of such refinement. The rewards may not come in this life, but if I strive to do His will, they will come. Of that I have no doubt."

Emily was surprised by the moisture glistening in Michael's eyes, but not as surprised as he. The only way he could define what he felt at that moment was to say that he knew beyond any doubt that what she had said was true.

Emily Ladd had taught him a lot of things about life and love, but what he had just learned from her was the true essence of faith. Her faith in God, in His willingness to bless her and be mindful of her, was unlike anything Michael had ever learned in any religion class. Despite the torment of what he had discovered in the last hour, he was deeply grateful for whatever force had made it possible for him to be with her now, absorbing the glow that radiated from her spirit. That was it, he decided. Beside Emily, all other women lacked that glow, that faith, that spiritual wisdom.

Yes, what she had said was true. Her Heavenly Father loved her very much. And so did he.

CHAPTER FIVE

"BEFORE YOU GO, EMILY," Michael said, "I want your address." She looked up, nearly panicked. "I want to keep in touch with you, and don't try to tell me there is any harm in exchanging letters with an old friend." Michael knew he was helpless to change her marriage, but perhaps he could give support from a distance.

Emily nodded helplessly and fumbled in her purse for a pen. She couldn't find one and realized she was trembling, so she just tore a deposit slip out of her checkbook. Michael glanced at the printed information and folded it in half before he stuffed it in his pocket.

"Thanks," he said quietly.

"Do you have to go?" she asked, trying not to sound disappointed.

"No, but I thought you—"

"I don't want to go home." She barely managed a steady voice. "Not yet. I can't. Penny will keep everything under control. I . . . I . . . just want to . . . I don't know!" She bit her trembling lip.

"How about a little browsing and carousing?" He smiled and the pain briefly dissipated.

"Only rogues carouse," she insisted lightly.

"Then we'd best settle for browsing." Michael put his hands in his pockets and walked beside her.

"Speaking of rogues," she said, "I must say I'm relieved that you haven't lost that brogue."

"I never had a brogue," he retorted, pretending to be insulted, "but my family claims that my perfect Australian prose has been tainted with some Americanism."

"Sounds perfectly Australian to me."

For hours they wandered in and out of various stores, looking over everything from shoes and clothing to sporting equipment and books. They made up for what they hadn't eaten of their lunch by indulging in cookies and frozen yogurt at one end of the mall and double chocolate muffins at the other. They even had an orange truffle, which Michael declared to be pure nectar. When Emily smeared chocolate on her lip, Michael gently wiped it away with his thumb. She briefly wondered what might happen if she ran into someone she knew, but forgot all about it when he told her a joke that made her laugh harder than she had in months. Maybe years.

Emily's mind was irretrievably lost in the present. For these few precious hours, she had nothing to worry about except basking in the presence of a man who truly made her feel alive again. In one day, Michael had displayed more adoration, dedication, and feeling toward her than she had seen from her husband in a decade.

While Michael observed Emily, he started piecing bits of evidence together. There was a sallow weariness in her eyes that became more apparent as she let her guard down. The years and childbirth had changed her physical appearance very little; but still, she was different. He couldn't pinpoint it exactly, but he sensed an intangible lack of the vibrancy that had once been so prominent.

Michael watched Emily admire things that caught her eye with a hesitant awe, as if they were somehow forbidden to her. The evidence of financial strain deepened as he took notice of what she wore. He knew well where the boots came from, but he doubted she had worn them to impress him. That wasn't like her. And the skirt he recognized not only as the one she'd worn yesterday, but he had little doubt that it was the same skirt she'd worn to see the "Nutcracker" with him in Salt Lake City well over a decade ago. His memories of that night were vivid, and there was something about the way she looked in that skirt that he couldn't forget.

So why was she wearing clothes from college and walking through the mall like an urchin in a toy factory? The answer was simple. She was struggling financially. That in itself might not have disturbed him. He knew how she felt about money, and he believed she could be happy to have her basic needs met; she'd said twice that Ryan worked hard to provide for them. But Michael suspected, as he observed her, that money was not only absent, it was an issue in her marriage. Impulsively, he decided to test his theory.

"Why don't you buy it?" he said, noticing the way she fingered the navy-colored sweater hanging on a sale rack.

"Oh, I couldn't," she said without too much regret.

Michael looked at the tag. "It's only fifteen dollars. It would look good on you."

"That's almost as much as I spent on a book earlier this week." She smiled with genuine affection. "I'd rather have the book. I'm going to go home and start reading it tonight."

"Read *Crazy's Day* first," he said, then went back to his purpose. "Is it necessary to choose between a book or a sweater?"

"Michael," Emily replied, beginning to feel irritated, "I know this might be difficult for you to understand, but I can't afford either one."

Michael sighed. She wasn't skirting the issue. But he didn't like her explanation.

"Emily, I have known a lot of people who are poor and happy, and I have also known many who are rich and miserable. The point being, it's the happy that matters, not the money. I know you can live without the sweater, and you probably could have lived without the book. But facts be faced, this world runs with money, Emily, and not having enough of it can be very stressful. Do you have enough?"

Emily wondered if she felt angry because of his presumption, or because he implied something that she had to admit was difficult to deal with. She knew well that Ryan didn't make a great deal of money, but she could have been content being poor if she felt the poverty was shared equally. The truth was that she suspected there was more money available than she was led to believe. Money was just another thing that she and Ryan avoided discussing, because they only argued in endless circles about it.

"I have enough for my needs," she stated emphatically.

"And once in a while every woman needs a new sweater." He took it off the rack to check the size. It looked good to him, so he carried it to the counter and produced a fifty-dollar bill.

"What are you doing?" Emily whispered behind him.

He didn't turn around. "I'm buying a sweater for Ryan Hall's housekeeper."

Emily ignored the gibe. "And what makes you think I'll accept it?"

"What's the matter?" he whispered. "Are you afraid your husband will find out that some strange man bought his wife a gift? Maybe a little competition would ruffle his feathers."

"Don't count on it. I doubt he'll even notice."

"Good. I shall have to buy you books and sweaters more often."

Emily made an infuriated noise and walked away. She pretended to examine some earrings until Michael stood beside her and put the handles of the shopping bag into her hand.

"There," he said triumphantly. Then he made certain she was looking at him as he added, "Now, do you need anything else? Can I help you out?"

Emily was angry and made no effort to cushion her response, feeling it was an important point to make. "Michael, you cannot solve my problems with your fourth-generation wealth."

"I was not attempting to, or even implying that I could. I just asked if I could help."

"And I told you I have enough to meet my needs."

"Which do not include books and sweaters."

"Why are you making such an issue out of this?"

"Because it *is* an issue, and you know it."

Emily turned her back to him, feeling like her mind was being read. "What makes you so certain of all my issues?"

"Because I know you, and unlike your dearly beloved, I can look at you and see what you're feeling."

"I shouldn't find that surprising." She turned back to face him. "But I want you to remember something, Michael. Don't think for one minute that you can go back to your hundreds of acres in Australia and believe you know what it's like to struggle from day to day. You've never lived without money. You couldn't possibly know what it's like."

"You're right, Emily. I have been very blessed that way. But I have lived without you."

Their eyes met momentarily and exchanged a thousand unspoken emotions. Fear and anger flew like sparks that threatened to burn until tears pooled in Emily's eyes and she turned away. He could have the last word on that one; she didn't even want to touch it.

They walked and browsed further, until Michael insisted they eat a decent meal. The food was enjoyed in silence, while Emily began to think of her children. Michael noticed the distress in her expression. "What's wrong?" he asked.

"Oh," she smiled, "I was just thinking about the girls. I don't believe I've ever been away from them for so many hours."

Michael wondered if that meant she'd had so little recreation in the past ten years, but he only asked, "Do you need to get back?" The dread of separation engulfed him as Emily glanced at her watch. "What does Mickey say?"

"He says that my children will survive this day without me. I need this. Do you know how long it has been since I've gone out to dinner? Wait. Don't ask me, because I can't remember." She sighed. "I don't want to talk about that." Her expression brightened. "Why don't you tell me some of those stories about your ancestors? I love the one about Michael Hamilton the rogue."

"What?" he laughed. "The kidnapping story?" Emily nodded eagerly, and he repeated his grandfather's story aloud for the first time in years. He found he enjoyed it until his mind became distracted. Something formless about the story combined with his own words of earlier, and a thought began to germinate, much like a new idea for a novel. When he finished the oration, Michael tried to recall exactly what he'd said to Emily over the sweater that suddenly now seemed significant. When it came to him, the idea fell into place instantaneously and he looked at Emily as if he'd never seen her before. Her eyes narrowed in question, but he couldn't answer for the echo of those words pounding through his head: *Maybe a little competition would ruffle his feathers.*

"Is something wrong?" Emily asked.

"No," he said, biting his thumbnail.

Emily knew the habit was a sign of nerves, and she questioned him further. "You're nervous. What's wrong?"

"I'm fine," he insisted and continued to chew at his thumbnail. He saw her gaze deepen, and for a moment he became lost in her eyes. He glanced down, feeling somehow guilty for looking at her that way. But his eyes were quickly drawn back to her as she coyly fidgeted with her napkin. "You're beautiful, Emily," he whispered with intensity, "and the years have only made you more so."

Emily looked up, silently questioning his motives. But all she saw was pure sincerity. "Are you certain you're all right?" she asked, trying to ignore the delicious tremor caused by his compliment.

"Yes, I'm certain," he smiled, realizing he needed a moment alone. "I'll be right back."

His brief jaunt to the men's room was enough time to decide that what he really wanted had nothing to do with the classic strategy of getting Ryan Hall's attention with manipulated jealousy. What Michael wanted was much more than that, and no blossoming idea for fiction had ever filled him with such eager delight. It was too bad he didn't live in a time when kidnapping a woman and three children could be a feasible course of action.

"Finished?" he asked without sitting back down.

Emily hovered in the corridor while he paid for their meal. If she didn't know he was wealthy, she could feel guilty for all the money he'd spent on her today.

She sensed a certain purpose to his step as she walked beside him to the center court. He sat on a bench and patted it, motioning for her to join him.

"There's something I want to talk to you about before you go home, Emily." The severity of his tone put her on edge. "All I ask is that you hear me out." He glanced away briefly, then drew back his shoulders and lifted his chin in a courageous gesture. "Emily, I want you to marry me."

Emily laughed, but only for the moment it took her to realize he wasn't joking. "Michael," she chuckled breathily, "you know I can't just—"

"And why not?" he interrupted. "Okay, so it was right to marry him. I can see that maybe what you and I have gone through in these years was necessary for us to become whatever we are supposed to become. Maybe your children were supposed to be born where they were, and to whom they were, for a reason. I can accept that. But what might have been right before may not necessarily be right now. What I see here is a no-win situation for you. How much more can you give before you snap?" He lowered his voice and put his face so close to hers that she could feel the warmth of his breath. "Leave him, Emily. I'll take you and the girls to Australia. We'll make a fresh start. I'll accept it all. I'll make you happy."

Emily opened her mouth to speak, but he could see the protest in her eyes and stopped it before it could start. "I don't want you to say anything now. I want you to go home and fast and pray like you never have before. And yes, I will respect your decision. But I am not leaving here without knowing that I gave you an option. I have a hard time believing the Lord only brought us together again so we could open old wounds."

Michael took a deep breath to continue. "I'm flying to Denver tomorrow. I have another nine or ten days of promotionals to cover, and then I'm going home. I'll come back here first, and with any luck I'll be taking you with me, as soon as we can get visas for you and the girls."

Emily put a hand over her pounding heart, finding it difficult to absorb this new turn of events. Suddenly weak, she leaned back with a breathless sigh, staring at nothing with furrowed brows while Michael waited patiently for a reaction. She couldn't believe it. In her wildest imaginings, she could not have fathomed something like this happening to her. She thought of her life, its oppression and discouragement, and the thought of leaving it all behind kindled something deep inside. Her mind began itemizing all that would have to be done and considered, but she stopped herself. How could she just turn her back on Ryan and leave everything she had worked so hard for? She was bound to him by sacred temple covenants. Could she void them so easily? But then, hadn't his attitude done that long ago?

As Emily realized what she was considering, her eyes turned to Michael. To see him now, to try to comprehend what he was offering, made her breath catch in her throat. "Michael," was all she could manage to say, but he seemed to understand. A faint smile touched his lips, and his eyes sparkled.

"You think about it," he whispered, "and we'll talk when I come back."

Emily nodded feebly. "Michael, I . . ." A twinge of fear pushed tears into her eyes. "I . . . love him."

Michael looked away and pressed his lips together.

"Despite it all, he is dear to me. You have to know that."

Michael looked at her searchingly.

"But I will think about it."

Michael felt hope. At least she wasn't completely disregarding his offer. Watching her now, familiar sensations came to life that reminded him of another time. He wanted to kiss her, but knew it was forbidden. He would be a fool to try and cross lines that would only bring them pain. Instead, he meekly took her hand and fingered her wedding rings idly.

Emily looked down at her hand in his, then back to his eyes. She could almost feel him longing to take the ring off and throw it away. There had been moments when the anger had made her want to do the same. Yet there was so much at stake here, so many lives that would be affected. But he wasn't asking her to make an impulsive decision. He had told her to fast and pray. He respected her need for that, and Emily knew she could do nothing so significant to her life unless she had the Lord's support. Without it she would be lost.

But in that moment Emily hoped the Lord would understand how she felt about Michael Hamilton. All the feelings she had pushed away these many years, fearing they would add to her discontentment, came back to her openly and she had to admit it. She wanted him, wanted to be his. She knew they could make each other happy, and he would be a good father figure to her children.

When she began to wish that he would kiss her, Emily cleared her throat and turned quickly away. She took her hand from his, pretending to look for something in her purse. Her lip gloss seemed like an appropriate thing to be searching for, and she pulled it out to apply a dab with her fingertip.

"It's getting late." She glanced at her watch. "The mall will be closing soon. I suppose I should go home and . . . face it." She chuckled tensely. "Ryan will wonder what's become of me."

"Are you going to tell him?" Michael asked softly.

"What?" She glanced down at her fidgety hands. "That I spent the day with my college sweetheart?"

"And that he asked you to run away with him?"

Emily knew that telling Ryan would only add stress to the situation, not allowing her the space to ponder and feel the Spirit. "No," she answered firmly, "I'm not; at least not until I make a decision."

Michael smiled. "Thank you, Emily, for meeting me today, and for considering my offer. You have rejuvenated me."

Emily's heart began to pound. "I would guess it's more the

other way around."

Their eyes met with an intensity that held the moment in suspension. She smiled, and Michael saw a hint of the vibrant Emily he'd fallen in love with.

"Come on." He stood. "I'll walk you to your car—unless you don't want me to, of course."

"That would be fine," she replied distantly, feeling somehow numb and disoriented.

"Don't forget your sweater." He picked up the bag she'd left on the bench.

"No," she smiled, "I wouldn't want to forget that."

They walked in silence toward the bookstore. Searching for anything that might ease the tension before they parted, Michael asked casually, "I don't suppose you've done much painting lately, taking care of those babies and all."

Emily laughed softly. "No, I don't get much time for such things these days."

"Have you kept up with it at all?" he asked, recalling his fascination for her talent with oils. She'd always kept an easel set up in the front room of her apartment. "You did so well in those art classes, and I'd hate to see you waste such a gift."

"I painted some when Allison started school. It helped me through the time when I was longing for another baby and thought I couldn't have one. I did well enough, but it was difficult to afford the oils, and . . ." Emily caught herself, deciding she had talked enough about such things. The difficulties of her life were beginning to sound like a broken record.

"And what?" Michael asked before she could change the subject.

"Well, I . . . put it away when I started looking for a job."

He covered his surprise as she continued.

"With Allison in school, I couldn't justify staying at home, but I got pregnant and ended up staying home anyway." Michael sensed the relief in her voice.

"I've often wondered if I might be able to supplement our income with some freelance artwork," Emily mused. "I've seriously considered looking into it. Perhaps one day when I have a little more time . . ."

"That would be great," Michael encouraged. "I'm sure you could do anything you set your mind to. Have you continued with any art classes or—"

Emily laughed tensely. "The only such classes available to me are for painting ceramics and little wooden things to clutter your home with."

Tired of talking about herself, Emily turned her mind to the present. "You said you took a cab this morning. How are you getting back?"

"The same way. I'm quite accustomed to such things."

Emily felt disoriented by the dark when Michael pushed open the door and they stepped into the brisk air. "I can give you a ride," she said, suddenly not caring about propriety in these final moments of her day with him. If she was a woman considering leaving her husband, giving Michael a ride seemed incidental.

"It's all right, Emily. I can get a cab. There's no reason for you to feel you have to—"

"Don't worry about it, Michael." She turned the key in the lock and opened the car door. "I think I can trust you for ten minutes in a moving car." She gave him an almost teasing smile.

"It's not a matter of trust," he replied, his lips twitching upward. "It's a matter of principle."

"Get in," she insisted and handed him the keys to open the other door. "Considering what you and I are contemplating, I'm not sure if . . ."

Emily couldn't finish. The words felt foreign and strange. This just wasn't like her. Had the years of suffering left her so vulnerable?

She sat in the bucket seat and fastened the seat-belt while Michael got in and put the key in the ignition for her. "Where are you staying?" she asked absently, putting the car in reverse.

"The Park."

She smiled. "Of course."

"I was surprised to see how downtown Provo has changed," he commented.

"Yes. I suppose you couldn't miss the new high-rise."

"It looks a little strange next to the Tabernacle. But I'm glad they left the lawn." He looked at her. "And the trees."

Emily glanced toward him and her insides fluttered to recall the afternoons they had spent on the Tabernacle lawn, sprawled on a blanket, studying and discussing their views of the world.

Uncomfortable with the tension and her own romantic urges, Emily pushed a cassette into the player and turned it on, concentrating on the music rather than the starvation for affection she was beginning to feel.

A quick glance at Michael told her it wasn't working. If anything, the poignancy of the music only intensified the reality of the moment. To distract herself she attempted concentrating on the lyrics.

Life in your new world turning round and round
Making some sense where there's no sense at all
No promises, but if you should fall . . .

"That's Icehouse," Michael said jubilantly.

"Yes," she smiled. "You're familiar with them?"

"Emily!" he laughed. "They're Australian."

"I know, but I guess I never thought of it that way."

"I saw them play in Sydney a few years back."

"Really?" Emily was excited to find someone who shared her musical interests again. "I'll bet it was wonderful."

"It was," he agreed. "I took my nephew."

The conversation fell into another lull and their ears tuned back to the song.

I could give you more than just the shape of things
Break every word, we'll get it all again . . .
But as . . .

A formless fear rose in Emily with the relation of those words to the reality of this moment, and she abruptly turned the stereo off. She wished she hadn't when Michael looked at her and finished the phrase: ". . . but as love lies bleeding in your hand, heaven sends you no promises."

"That's not funny," Emily insisted.

"I was not intending it to be, nor was I implying anything. I think it's a beautiful song."

"That song makes me cry," she admitted.

"Why?"

"You tell me why," she snapped, "since you know it so well."

"Because it's about disillusionment?" he guessed.

"I suppose that covers it. Could we talk about something else? Have we discussed anything today besides my disillusionment?"

"Actually, yes, we have. But if you want to talk about something else, fine. How about this?" Michael lowered his voice to a near whisper and repeated lines from another Icehouse song. "So if I'm dreaming, don't wake me tonight. If this . . ."

Emily joined him. "If this is all wrong, I don't want it right."

Hearing the words come back to her in a silent echo, Emily cleared her throat and gripped the steering wheel more tightly as she turned the car into the hotel drive.

"But you do want it right," Michael said, and she wondered if he could read her mind. A brief silence enveloped the confined space around them, amplifying their mutual ache.

"Think about it, Emily," he whispered, a huskiness turning his voice dry. "It may be right."

"I can't live with it if it's not," she replied. "We could not be happy living with the heartache of regret, Michael. The ravages of divorce would always be with us."

"I know," he said softly and took her hand.

"If I don't have verification from the Lord that it's right, I could never live with it."

"I understand, Emily. Really, I do. I'll pray, too."

"You will?" She brightened.

"Does that surprise you?"

"You did say you hadn't been to church since—"

"Yes, well . . . maybe it's time I did something about that, too."

"Yes, Michael," she pleaded, "please pray. Pray that we will be able to accept and live with whatever comes out of this." He nodded, but she felt compelled to add, "You might not get the same answer I do."

"I told you I would respect your decision, Emily. I think the Lord would be more prone to speak to you. Whatever happens, I will not regret this time we've shared. I can only hope we will be blessed with more."

Tears came to Emily's eyes and she turned to look straight ahead. Michael touched her chin to make her face him.

"I love you, Emily. I love you more today than I would have ever thought possible the day you left me. I have learned so much from you, and I want you to know that I respect you, and I admire you."

Tears trickled down her face. Michael bent forward to kiss her cheek, lingering a moment to breathe in the essence of her, to taste the salty moisture of her skin.

Emily touched his face as he drew back to look at her. "I love you too, Michael. Whatever happens, you must remember that."

He nodded carefully and Emily felt a longing for him that reduced her to panic. "I must go," she said firmly. Michael nodded again, understanding what she meant. He felt it, too.

"I'll see you soon." He opened the door and put one leg out of the car. "I can't say for certain which day, but I'll get in touch with you."

Emily nodded. "I'll be waiting to hear from you."

Michael got out and closed the door, standing with his hands in his pockets as he watched her drive away. The memory that came back to him was painful. As clearly as if it had been yesterday, he could feel himself standing on the porch of his apartment, watching her go. He wondered if her leaving now would be as tormenting as it had been then. He could only pray that this was the beginning, not the end.

CHAPTER SIX

EMILY DROVE TOWARD HOME in a tearful daze, then made a detour. Knowing the children were long asleep, she parked behind the Provo temple and stared at its spire, mulling over the impact of all that had happened. The reality of what lay before her brought on a bombardment of emotion as painful as the pounding she had felt earlier in the day. She didn't know how long she sobbed in solitude, but the kitchen clock said twelve thirty-five when she shuffled wearily through the back door. Quietly she checked on the children and pressed soft kisses to three small foreheads. She prepared for bed and slipped between the covers, certain she hadn't disturbed Ryan until he turned over abruptly and startled her.

"Where have you been?" He sounded more angry than concerned.

"Didn't Penny get you some dinner?"

"Yes, she made sloppy joes. Bret and all the kids were here. She said you went to the mall, but it's been closed for hours."

"I'm surprised you noticed."

"What do you mean by that?"

"Sometimes I feel that you don't notice me at all."

He was silent for a long moment. "It's too late to fight, Em. I just want to know where you've been."

"I . . . came across an old friend. We were talking. That's all."

Again there was silence. Emily wondered if he might connect her getting Michael's book autographed yesterday to being out with a friend today.

"You could have called," he said finally. Either he hadn't thought deeply enough to make the connection, or he didn't care.

"Yes, I could have. I'm sorry," she said, but she didn't mean it. Coming home late was common for Ryan, but he never called.

"Well," he said tersely, "just so you're home." With that he turned over and went to sleep.

Emily awoke feeling more physically drained than when she'd gone to sleep. Ryan was still sleeping soundly and she remembered it was Saturday. For a long while she lay staring at the ceiling, wheels of confusion spinning through her mind. Squeezing her eyes shut, she prayed silently until Amee's call interrupted.

"Mommy! Mommy! Get me!"

Emily hurried to wrap the child in her arms and relish her nearness after nearly a full day's absence.

Amee was barely dressed and put into the highchair when Alexa cried herself awake and Emily began the diaper changing, dressing routine again. Allison appeared and turned on Saturday morning cartoons after a proper greeting and catching up with her mother. While Emily fixed the baby's cereal and fed it to her, Allison got the Cheerios and milk and headed back to the T.V. When the babies were fed and playing, Emily glanced at the kitchen and decided that she was in no mood to cook breakfast.

"Allison, would you mind keeping an eye on the babies? I think I'll rest a little more."

"Sure, Mom," she replied, intermittently giving Amee a spoonful of Cheerios and feeding the baby one at a time.

Relieved to find Ryan still sleeping, Emily reached under the bed to find *Crazy's Day*. She nearly got back into bed to read, but instead went to Allison's room where she found an unmade bed to crawl into—alone. The book quickly absorbed her, and she was hardly aware of reality until she heard Ryan's voice.

"Is something wrong?"

"No," she answered dryly. "I'm just reading."

He paused, apparently waiting for her to figure something out. When she didn't, he stated, "What's for breakfast?"

Emily normally would have felt guilty for not fulfilling a duty, or apologized for not feeling up to it. She had missed only a handful of cooked breakfasts in ten and a half years of marriage, including three pregnancies and several bouts with viruses. But in that moment Emily encountered a feeling totally foreign to her. She was indifferent. She didn't care what Ryan thought, or even what Ryan did. Her children were cared for, her home would survive some relaxation, and Ryan was capable. After a considerable pause, she turned her attention to the book and said absently, "Try Cheerios. They're vitamin fortified and full of natural fiber."

Ryan gave a disgusted sigh, but she ignored him. When he realized she wasn't going to react the way he expected her to, he subtly scolded, "You know I can't make it through the day without a good breakfast."

Emily looked up at him. With no malice in voice or expression, she calmly observed, "You're not going to work today, Ryan. You're going to Lane's house to vegetate on the couch and absorb television sports. I think you'll survive. I'm tired, and I have no desire to spend an hour and a half in the kitchen just so you can have a hot breakfast, when everyone else in this house is content."

"My," he said with biting sarcasm, "aren't we haughty today."

"No," she replied, managing to stay calm, "I am not haughty. I simply said that I'm not going to cook breakfast."

"Is it really such a big deal? I mean, it's just a little breakfast. It doesn't take that long to—"

"By the time I clean it up and get the dishes washed, it takes a significant part of my morning. But you're right, it's not such a big deal. That's why I think you'll survive on Cheerios."

Ten minutes later Ryan left the house without breakfast,

slamming the door on his way out. Emily sighed and continued to read, ignoring the possible consequences of yesterday's excursion that still lay before her. She was glad for Ryan's absence, and for the first time she consciously realized that in his absence she felt peace and tranquility, while in his presence she was often uptight and on edge.

Emily did laundry and played with the children. She tried several times to call Penny, wishing she were home. There was so much to tell her that she couldn't talk about with Ryan around.

Knowing that she needed groceries, she looked through the checkbook but found little to buy them with. They wouldn't get a paycheck until Tuesday. With the hope that putting it off would prove they had enough to get by, she did other things, thinking she could borrow milk from Penny if they got desperate. And maybe she could figure out something else to do with tuna and macaroni for Sunday dinner, even if Ryan didn't like it.

While the babies napped, Emily and Allison shared a game of checkers and dressed Barbies. Then Emily continued to read, realizing that it was a good book, personal bias toward the author excluded.

In the late afternoon Penny came by, peering through the door with a grin.

"I've been wondering when you'd show up," Emily said.

"It's been one of those days. I haven't had a minute." She plopped onto the couch.

"That's probably because you're catching up from spending the last two days here." Emily smiled. "Thank you. You can't know what coming home to a clean kitchen and sleeping children meant to me."

"Oh, yes I can." Penny leaned forward expectantly. "How did it go?"

"Allison," Emily said quietly, "have you got something you could do in your room for a while? Penny and I need to speak privately."

"Okay, Mom." Allison jumped to her feet. "I was gonna ride my bike, anyway."

"Good idea. It's a beautiful day for that. Be careful."

Allison left and Penny shook her head. "I wish I had a few children who were that easy to get along with."

"She is a blessing," Emily agreed. "But I dare say Amee and Alexa will make up for it. They already do."

"Now tell me," Penny insisted, ignoring any other topic.

Emily set the book aside, wondering where to begin. Penny watched her and didn't miss the subtle smile teasing the corners of her mouth.

"Emily!" she insisted.

"It was an . . . interesting day."

"You spent the whole day with him, then?"

"Yes." Emily didn't know whether to sound proud or guilty.

"Well, tell me! I can't stand it."

"We . . . just walked around the mall, and talked. I guess you could say we kind of . . . caught up on everything that's happened over the years, and . . ." Emily became distant until Penny nudged her.

"Is he married?"

"No."

"Did you tell him about you and Ryan? I mean . . ." Penny trailed off into silence.

"I wasn't going to, but . . ." Emily's voice turned sad. "He knows it all."

"And?"

"And what?" Emily wondered why Penny seemed to expect what had happened, when she could still hardly believe it herself.

"He bought me a sweater," Emily said proudly, grateful for the distraction. She hurried to the bedroom and pulled it out from under the bed.

"Ooooh," Penny teased as her friend returned with a shopping bag from one of the more elite stores in the mall.

"It was on sale. He spent fifteen dollars." Emily dumped the contents of the bag onto the floor. Along with the sweater and receipt came an array of tumbling money, falling over the floor like an offering from heaven. Penny gasped, but Emily's first reaction was anger. She quickly moved her hand over the bills and coins to mentally tally that this was the change from the fifty-dollar bill he'd used to purchase the sweater. When the reality settled in, Emily felt choked up. The suppressed emotion of the entire drama began to surface and she looked up at Penny, saying in a cracked voice, "And I was wondering how to buy groceries to get by until Tuesday."

"You always told me that answers to prayers come in strange packages." Emily gathered the money while Penny held up the sweater to examine. "It's nice. You're not going to put it in your cedar chest, are you?"

"No," Emily said and started to cry as the reality took hold. "Oh, Penny. I don't know what to do. I'm so confused and afraid and—"

"Emily." Penny put the sweater aside and wrapped an arm around her. "What happened? What's wrong?"

Emily fought for control of her emotions, knowing she would never make it through the coming days if she didn't. "Penny," she sighed, exhausted. Their eyes met in a familiar bond of friendship. "He asked me to . . . to . . . leave Ryan; to . . . marry him."

Penny gasped, then gave a squeal of delight. "Emily, that's wonderful. You could—"

"It's not wonderful!" Emily stuffed the handful of money into the shopping bag along with the sweater. "Do you realize what kind of decision that puts on my shoulders?"

"As I see it, there's no decision to make. I think Ryan's had more than a fair chance."

"Whether he has or not, I can't do anything without a lot of fasting and prayer. Frankly, I'm scared to death. Either way, this is not going to be an easy thing to face, Penny."

"Oh, Emily," Penny laughed, "I can't believe it. What woman wouldn't give her right arm to have such an opportunity to escape a miserable marriage?"

"It's not as easy as that, Penny. You should know me better than to think I could just up and leave my marriage. This is not some magical happily-ever-after thing. I'm talking about a decision that will affect many lives. I would always have to live with the consequences of divorce."

"But at least you'd be happy living with them," Penny observed.

"There is no point arguing, Penny. Michael and I agreed that I have to fast and pray about this. There is no way I can know the long-range effects of my decision, but the Lord does. I have to trust Him."

"Yes, you're right," Penny admitted grudgingly. "But promise me you'll at least stop and consider yourself for once. You have a right to be happy, Emily." She leaned forward and quoted scripture. "Man is that he might have joy."

Emily put her arms around Penny, feeling a glimmer of peace. "What would I do without you, Penny?"

"I hope you never have to find out," she replied. "I don't think I'd do so good without you, either. I wonder if you realize how much the little things you let me do for you lift my own spirits."

"Well then," Emily grinned slyly, "you'd best not get too enthusiastic about Michael Hamilton. If I marry him, I'll be moving to Australia."

"Australia?" she gasped. She might as well have said Siberia. "What? The kids too?"

"Of course the kids too," Emily chuckled. "I'm sure he's aware that I'm now a group package." Emily shook her head dubiously. She still couldn't believe this. "I think I'd better go to the store, Penny, or we'll be eating tuna casserole again, and Ryan may kick me out before I get a chance to leave him."

Penny laughed and headed for the door.

"Penny," Emily added, "thank you again for all your help the last few days. However this turns out, I'm grateful for the time I had with Michael."

"It was my pleasure," Penny smiled, then added tensely,

"Australia?"

Emily nodded. Penny shook her head and left Emily to briefly close her eyes and tell herself this wasn't a dream.

When evening came and Ryan still hadn't returned, Emily began to get concerned. It wasn't like him to stay so long after she knew the game had ended. She nearly called to find out if he'd left, but decided she didn't want to look like a nagging wife. He still hadn't come when she was ready for bed, but she took the opportunity of being alone to offer a long, deep prayer—something she found difficult when Ryan was in the room, even if he remained quiet. She read until she was exhausted, then finally turned out the light around midnight.

Minutes later, she heard the car pull in and Ryan unlocked the back door. Emily lay staring at the ceiling while he tinkered in the kitchen, apparently getting a snack that she knew he'd not clean up after. When he finally came to bed, he moved close to Emily and leaned over her.

"Are you asleep?" he asked loudly enough that she couldn't possibly have slept through it.

"No." She wanted to ask where he'd been, but in truth she didn't care. The realization left an empty ache inside as she wondered how long she had been indifferent. How long had she been existing by habit?

"Hey, Em, I'm sorry about this morning. You know, you are pretty good about cooking breakfast. I wasn't being fair. Most of the guys said their wives almost never cook breakfast." He actually sounded humble.

"You told the guys we were arguing about breakfast?" Though not surprised, Emily did feel irritated. Ryan didn't answer, apparently figuring it was obvious. "Well, if the rest of them rarely get breakfast, why am I so awful for taking a break once in a while?"

"You aren't."

"Next time, think about that before you get down on me."

After some silence he said warmly, "All right, Em. I'm sorry."

Emily wondered why she felt angry. She usually felt so warm

toward his apologies and signs of humility. But his doing it now seemed like nothing more than an obstruction thrown into her path of decision. It was too bad he hadn't come home drunk; then she could have left him easily. The thought surprised her, and she willed herself to stop such nonsense. The last thing she wanted was to see Ryan slipping further down on the ladder of life.

"You feeling any better?" he asked, touching her face.

"I'm all right," she replied, trying to get Michael Hamilton out of her head. Ryan bent to kiss her, and she felt a degree of warmth in it. Emily knew he wanted to make love, but everything inside of her protested. It wouldn't be right—not when she was torn this way between two men. She already felt as if she'd somehow betrayed Michael simply by accepting Ryan's kiss. Until she made a decision, she knew she had to keep her distance.

Emily turned her back and sensed Ryan's disappointment, but she was grateful that he didn't prod her for reasons. In the darkness she cried silent tears, contemplating the emotional and spiritual vacuum that made her intimacies with Ryan seem almost sordid. She could see now it had been that way for years. What should have been a beautiful, sacred union had somehow lost its power to enhance their relationship.

Emily made every attempt to be the perfect wife on Sunday, certain that it would ease some of the guilt and confusion. To her surprise, it not only failed in that respect, but it seemed to make Ryan all the more . . . She couldn't define it. What was he? Complacent? Self-satisfied? Too comfortable? Could it be possible that she was trying too hard?

She ended a twenty-four hour fast Sunday evening, and Monday morning she stayed in bed an extra half hour, with three choices of cold cereal left on the counter. It seemed a silly thing, but Emily almost considered it a test. Though what exactly she was testing, she couldn't be certain.

On Tuesday, Emily brought out her painting for the first time in years. She set it up in the dining room and made a delightful mess while experimenting with the oils in between changing diapers and feeding babies. Ryan came home to no dinner and total disarray. Emily didn't apologize. She and Allison picked up the mess and made macaroni and cheese for dinner— something that Allison loved and Ryan hated.

Emily fasted again on Wednesday. She finished *Crazy's Day* and cried, then she read from the latest *Ensign* and cried more. Again Ryan arrived to a disorderly home, grilled cheese sandwiches, and canned soup. Thursday and Friday Emily painted. She used the remainder of the money Michael had left her to buy some oils, and found great satisfaction in using nap time to enhance a painting she had started years ago, working from a photograph she'd taken in Australia. While she painted, Emily pondered the memories associated with the photo and felt a peaceful warmth toward Michael. She began to believe her destiny was with him. She felt such peace that she sat down and cried. If she had known where to find Michael, she'd have called him and told him to get her a lawyer.

Saturday marked an entire week without cooking breakfast, which was the issue that began the argument. By mid-afternoon, Emily and Ryan had yelled and argued over everything that had ever been misunderstood in the past ten years. Allison went to her room and stayed there. Emily took care of the babies and finally got them down for naps, while Ryan followed her around the house, doing his best to illustrate that all of this was her fault. He made it clear that he didn't know what had gotten into her, but he would not put up with it. He said he didn't work hard all week so he could have pathetic meals when she cooked at all, and a house that he could barely walk through for all the toys and clutter.

Emily cried, pleaded, and attempted every direction she knew to work out their disagreement and get him to see where she was coming from. She tried to listen to what he said and reflect it, but it always backfired. She always came up short. Even in this final attempt to save what little was left of their marriage, she just couldn't make it work. Finally, like an overused appliance, she simply shut down. She said nothing, did nothing.

Ryan finished his current tirade and looked at her hard, expecting a retort. Quietly she said, "If I am so awful, Ryan, why don't you just leave me and find someone who can give you what you want?" Emily almost felt despair in knowing he never would. She firmly believed that even if he did go, he'd never find anyone as patient with him as she had been.

"I didn't say you were awful." He sounded insulted.

"You didn't have to. You've been making it clear for years exactly how you feel about me. But I'll tell you something, Ryan Hall. It's me that's not going to put up with it any more. One of these days, you might just wake up and find me gone. Then you're going to wish somebody was here to fix you a grilled cheese sandwich."

Emily walked out the back door and straight to Penny's house. "I don't want to talk about it," she announced to her friend, who was washing dishes. "I just want to use the phone."

Emily made an appointment with her bishop and was in his office at nine o'clock the next morning. She had begun another fast, and left home fifteen minutes early so she could sit in the car and pray without interruption before approaching this interview.

She hadn't intended to spill it all to the bishop, but once the tears started the words followed. She fully expected, and felt she deserved, chastisement for spending time with Michael, but the bishop surprised her with a completely different approach to the problem.

"Perhaps you're just too good a wife, Emily," Bishop Wright said gently.

"I'm sorry?" She leaned toward him, certain she'd heard wrong. Or perhaps he had transposed words to say it differently from the way he meant it.

"Emily, I must confess that finding myself in such a position is very humbling in moments like this. We've been friends for a long time, so I feel I can admit to you that I've never considered

myself a wise man. But what I am feeling right now is. . . .
Well, let me put it this way. I know, because you've told me,
that you study the Book of Mormon avidly. What happens
when the people become too comfortable?"

"They grow in pride and rebellion, and . . ." The systematic
reply caught in Emily's throat as she began to perceive what he
was getting at.

"You know as well as any dedicated member of this church,"
the bishop continued, "that trials and difficulties will humble
and strengthen a person. I think perhaps it's hard for a person
who is meek and humble to find proper balance, especially
when self-esteem is suffering."

Bishop Wright shifted in his chair and deepened his gaze on
her. "From what you have told me, I assume that your relationship with Ryan has likely not been conducive to your self-
esteem, and perhaps that has put you into an unfortunate cycle
of believing that you have to be everything for him in order to
be a good wife. If we did everything for our children, they
would not grow up able to care for themselves." He paused for
emphasis.

"If you are too good a wife, you're not giving Ryan a chance
to grow and appreciate what he's got. I'd say that what has been
happening this past week or so is a good start for you to make
some necessary changes. Set your priorities in order, Emily. See
that your home is orderly; but if taking time for yourself leaves
some clutter, so be it. See to your family's needs, but remember
that the emotional and spiritual temperature of the home is
much more important than whether or not the toys are picked
up, or whether a meal took fifteen minutes or two hours to prepare.

"Take time to replenish yourself, and instead of worrying so
much about what you can do to be a good wife for Ryan, or
what you can do to help him come around, ask yourself what
you can do to be the person you are striving to become. Stay
close to the Spirit for guidance and set an example, but don't
think you have to justify or apologize for being human and

having needs."

"Are you saying I've been handling this all wrong for ten years?" Emily asked pointedly.

"I think what I'm saying is that there is a season for every purpose. Perhaps these years have been an important part of the process of growth for the two of you. But now that certain lessons have been learned by trial, maybe it's time to try a different approach. Perhaps you are entering another season of your life.

"Emily, you are the kind of woman that the Lord holds in the highest esteem. Like all of us, you have your weaknesses, but you are aware of them and I know you try. Don't be hard on yourself; remember your worth in the eyes of God, and demand that kind of respect while you give honest love in return."

"Sometimes I wonder if I still love him. I feel so detached at times."

"I heard it once said that to learn to love someone, you must serve them. Taking into consideration all I have just said, keep that concept in mind and see if it doesn't bring some positive results. And I want you to keep me informed, Emily. I'm here if you need me. It's my job, or so they tell me," he added with an easy chuckle. "Is there anything else?" he asked, indicating he'd said what he felt was needed.

"Sometimes I . . ." Emily hesitated and bit her lip. "I feel so guilty, because my attitude and my feelings toward him are so . . . uncharitable."

Bishop Wright contemplated her statement for a long moment. "Your behavior is a natural result of the circumstances. If Ryan has treated you unfairly, he must suffer the consequences of his actions, while knowing he is still loved unconditionally. I would suspect that much of his behavior is a result of his own insecurities. It's a delicate situation, but I think with the help of the Spirit, you have the capability of handling it."

Emily's heart ached when she thought of Michael. She attempted a smile and looked down at her cold, clasped fingers, toying nervously with her wedding rings.

"Now, is there anything else?" he asked again.

Emily thought for a long moment. The answer to her dilemma was very clear. She felt grateful for the obvious answer to her prayers, the defined guidance, and the first lack of confusion she'd felt since this had begun. But realizing what still lay ahead, she felt afraid and unsure. And yes, she had to admit that when she thought of Michael, she was disappointed. Looking at the bishop with tear-filled eyes, she asked softly, "A blessing perhaps?"

Tears ran steadily over Emily's cheeks, soaking into the collar of her blouse, as the bishop placed his hands on her head and uttered words that only the Lord would have understood in regard to her circumstances. When it was done he handed her an ample supply of tissues, and she left his office with the realization that he'd said nothing at all about Michael Hamilton. No chastisement. No admonitions. She could only believe that he had given her the counsel he'd felt prompted to, and by his silence concerning Michael was expressing faith in her to handle the situation properly and put it behind her.

Emily returned home to find Ryan entertaining the children and seeming to enjoy it. With nearly two hours until meetings began, she went to the bedroom and locked the door. After a lengthy prayer of gratitude and a request for strength and guidance, Emily sat on the bed to write Michael a long letter. She considered her words carefully and stopped more than once to weep over them. But there was peace when she folded and sealed the letter, writing on the envelope: To my first love, forever.

With the letter tucked safely away, Emily washed her face and resigned herself to taking on life with a fresh attitude. She went to the front room and bent over her husband. He looked up in surprise.

"You all right?" he asked.

"I'm fine." She smiled. "I'm sorry about the way I've been lately. I'll try to do better, but I want you to know that I've got to do more for me. I think I can be a better wife and mother if I take some time for me, and that may mean some changes. Does that make any sense?"

"I think so," he said tonelessly.

"I'd like to talk later," she added. "It's important."

"All right," he agreed easily.

Emily touched his face and put a kiss to his lips. "I love you, Ryan," she said. "I hope one day you will realize how much."

Emily went to the kitchen to prepare some chicken and rice that could be left in the oven through church meetings. She cried a few more stray tears. Yes, she told herself, she did love Ryan. Twice now, she had sacrificed Michael Hamilton for his sake.

CHAPTER SEVEN

MICHAEL GLANCED FROM HIS WATCH to the billowing clouds below. Knowing this would be the final stop of his tour made him impatient to get there and get it over with. This entire promotional escapade had started out as an enjoyable prospect, but an unforeseen interruption, in the form of Emily Ladd, had just made it tiresome.

The plane landed and Michael hurried through the Las Vegas airport. Different city, different faces, same tedious routine. Through all the traveling and hotels, all the patronizing smiles and scribbling signatures, Michael's mind was in a house in Orem, Utah. He didn't know what it looked like, and could only identify it by an address on a worn deposit slip in his pocket. But he could well imagine her there, and much of what he imagined made his stomach churn.

Emily. His sweet Emily was living in silent pain, and Michael could do nothing but pray that she would be willing to put the pain behind her and find a new life with him. How could she not accept his proposal? He'd asked himself that question a thousand times in the days since he'd seen her. But he recalled all too vividly the confidence he'd once felt in being the right man for her—a confidence that had been shattered mercilessly. He truly wondered if he could take such rejection again.

With his commitments finally completed, Michael returned to his hotel room amidst the glare of the city lights. He lay far into the night, hoping, fearing, praying. When he'd first

promised Emily he would pray, he hadn't counted on how difficult it would be. Those first words uttered to God were strained
and guarded, but gradually it became easier to express his
desires. Not wanting to sound selfish in the eyes of his Maker,
Michael had to stop and look at all he had to be grateful for,
and make certain he expressed that as well. Then, as the praying
became more frequent and open, Michael also had to stop and
look at the reasons he had severed his relationship with God,
and the reason he was now willing to reestablish it. Facing up to
the sense of betrayal and the ache of bitterness was nearly as difficult as the reality of what had caused them.

Being a writer, Michael had always tried to think of words
to describe Emily and the way he felt about her. The word that
kept coming to his mind now was "poignancy." It had all started out so beautiful, so perfect. But it had ended in a pain so
astounding that Michael still had trouble comprehending it.
And now—now, when the pain had finally settled deeply
enough to hardly be felt, Emily Ladd had come back into his
life. Seeing her, touching her, talking with her, could be nothing
but joyous. But even that pleasure was edged with pain—the
pain of her suffering, and of his being so helpless to change it.
And fear. There was an ever-present fear that it would start all
over again and leave him still with nothing but . . . poignancy.

Trying to be positive, Michael concentrated on the good.
He carefully led his mind through each of the memories that
gave him hope. He felt confidence in recalling the feelings that
had led him to Emily; they were much like those that had led
him to BYU in the first place.

Michael had known for years that he wanted to attend college in the states. He didn't know why, exactly; he just knew.
And the events that led him there left no doubt that he had
been divinely guided. When he found the right college, it just
felt right. And when he found Emily Ladd, he felt the same
way.

Emily was not only beautiful, with the character he had
always dreamed of in a woman, but she made him feel utterly

alive and good about himself. He believed from the start that he had been led to BYU just so he could find her. There was an intangible rightness about their relationship that made Michael certain their being together was no coincidence. And through the months, as that relationship had developed into something he considered as perfect as this earth could offer, he'd gotten every impression that she felt it, too.

Michael recalled that first date, when he'd finally mustered the courage to ask her out on a second. But not before they faced what he considered an important point.

"I'm not a member of the Church, Emily," he'd told her gravely, though he didn't apologize.

"I know," she stated as if it were nothing. "And I'm not an Australian."

Michael smiled, then chuckled. "Does that mean you'll go out with me again?"

"Only if you ask me. I'm a little old-fashioned that way."

The following Saturday was the best Michael had seen in more than three years of living in Provo, and it ended with Emily inviting him to church. Of all the Mormons he'd associated with, Emily was the first to extend the offer. For the first time, Michael was included in the social and spiritual aspects of an ethnic group from which he'd always been excluded.

Meshing into Emily's religion was as simple as meshing into her life. It was easy to be with her, to talk to her. From that first date in September until their return from Australia in July, only her four days in Idaho during Christmas vacation had kept them apart. They did everything together, and as far as Michael could see, they were as close as two people could be and still remain chaste.

Looking back at the issue that had come between them, Michael truly felt he'd been wronged. That was where the bitterness came in. His initial fear in asking Emily out had been the difference in their ethnic backgrounds. He knew that Mormon girls wanted to marry Mormon boys, and the significance of temple marriage was something he'd been well

rehearsed in. But he'd been honest with Emily from the start.
She knew he wasn't a Mormon, and she loved him anyway. If
he'd had any doubts on the subject, Emily had dispelled them
when her mother casually mentioned that Michael wasn't a
member of the Church. Before Michael could open his mouth
to respond, Emily broke into a warm, eloquent speech about his
undying support of her beliefs, making it clear that to Emily, it
didn't matter.

But Michael's fears came around to slap him in the face. He
had no warning beyond a subtle uneasiness that had come
through their phone conversations during the month she'd
spent in Idaho. Michael felt certain her return would put everything straight. He bought a ring and made reservations at their
favorite restaurant. Then she walked in and told him she was
putting some other man on the opposite end of the scale, with a
lead weight Michael couldn't compete with.

The week following was the worst of Michael's life. He barely saw or talked to Emily, and when he did she seemed
depressed and aloof. He told her every day that he loved her,
and she always told him the same, with a fervency that deepened his hope.

On a hot afternoon, Michael answered his door to find
Emily standing on the porch. She looked different. He felt
scared.

"Come in." He motioned and stepped aside, as if she were a
stranger. He closed the door and leaned against it. She turned
hesitantly to look at him and tears filled her eyes. Her chin
quivered. She bit her lip.

"Emily." He heard his voice crack.

He saw her pull back her shoulders, heard her draw a deep
breath. "I've fasted and prayed, Michael. I've never prayed so
hard in my life. I don't know if you'll understand this, but I
know you've studied the concept, because we've discussed it. I've
been extremely confused and upset, but I've made my decision
and . . ." She glanced down and Michael felt a knot gathering in
his throat. "I feel peace, Michael. An undeniable, unquestionable peace.

There is no doubt that what I am doing with my life is what the Lord wants me to do." She squeezed her eyes shut and tears trickled out as she said it. "I'm going to marry Ryan."

Until those final words came out, Michael held onto a heart-pounding hope that it would be him. But once she said it, the world fell away. He felt hurt and afraid and alone, but they all culminated together in anger. He was angry at the feelings that had brought him to this place, and the feelings that had drawn him to Emily. He was angry at God for doing this to him, to her, to them.

And he was angry at Emily. He wanted to accuse her of leading him blindly through a relationship only to leave him high and dry. He wanted to tell her she was being a fool, that he hoped she ended up miserable—as miserable as he was going to be without her. But something inside him couldn't find the will to be harsh with her. As she stood there crying, he had more of an urge to just take her in his arms and force her to stay with him. But he couldn't bring himself to even touch her. If he touched her now, he doubted he could ever let her go. All his thoughts and emotions came together in a pounding frustration. His fist hit the door behind him and he groaned. Emily winced and turned away.

"I'm so sorry," she cried without looking at him. "I don't know what to say. It's so difficult, but . . . I . . . know it's right. Somehow I . . . just know. Maybe one day we'll understand, Michael. But for now . . . I . . . I . . . can only hope that you will forgive me, that you . . . will try to . . . understand why it has to be . . . this way."

Michael didn't understand. And he didn't want to try. He just wanted to die.

"So," he said, hating the coldness in his voice, "what now? Are you going to finish school here, or—"

"I'm not going to finish," she said, and his anger deepened. "At least not yet. I'm going back to Idaho in a few days . . . to stay. And after that . . . I just . . . don't know yet. It depends on . . . a lot of things."

"I see," Michael said in a tone that belied the tears beginning to burn in his eyes. "So, that's it, eh?" He thought of hurtful words but bit them back. Emily turned slowly toward him and he felt the tears spill. Michael shoved his hands in his pockets and looked away. He couldn't bear it. He just couldn't bear it!

"I should go," she said quietly, wiping at her face in an attempt to dry it. "I have to get back and . . . well, it's not important."

Michael could do nothing but mechanically open the door. Emily walked toward him and reached up to kiss his cheek where she accidentally caught a tear with her lips. He watched her lick it away, and heard her say as if from a distance, "Goodbye, Michael. I can't thank you enough for all you've done for me. I'll love you forever."

Michael couldn't return the good-bye. He just looked at her a long moment, hanging onto a small hope that she might take it all back. He wanted to get down on his knees and beg for mercy, but he just followed her out to the porch. She looked at him again, then headed down the steps. Michael pushed his hands into his pockets and clenched them into fists.

"I love you, Emily Ladd," he said. She turned back and fresh tears filled her eyes. His vision of her blurred, and when he blinked to clear it she was getting in the car. He saw her glance back once, then she was gone.

Michael didn't know how long he stood on the porch, feeling like he had turned to stone. When he finally managed to walk inside and close the door, he felt the stone crumble into millions of unfixable pieces. Unwillingly he went to his knees. His arms came over his head and anguish rose from the depths of him, twisting like a dagger from the inside out.

The turmoil continued for days. He barely ate. He hardly slept. She might as well have died for the way he mourned. He cried like a baby until he thought he couldn't cry any more. But somehow more tears always came. He kept remembering the famous words that it was better to have loved and lost, than never to have loved at all. But he cursed those words. He would far prefer to have never known that Emily Ladd existed, than to face up to what was happening to him now. The only thing that had ever come close was his father's death. But even then, he couldn't remember hurting like this. It was a nightmare. He believed his life was over. It even crossed his mind to end it all, but he knew such madness as taking his own life was not in him. He respected life too much, even as desecrated as his seemed to be.

Michael lost count of the days. When he finally looked in a mirror, he groaned. He couldn't remember the last time he'd taken a shower. He convinced himself that he had a life to live, and attempted to push all the raw feelings away. He distracted himself with loud music and hard work. He cleaned up and cleaned the apartment, then he went out to get groceries and try to orient himself to the term that would begin soon. But everywhere he went, all he could see were memories. Why did she have to be so completely involved in his life? He couldn't go anywhere without remembering a time when she had been there with him.

Three weeks into the fall semester, Michael looked at his life and realized that he was lost. His grades were going to be awful. He'd gone nowhere but to the grocery store and classes since she'd left. He wished he drank so he could get drunk. But he had to admit he was grateful for knowing it wouldn't do any good, so he could avoid the hangover.

He found himself resenting Mormonism and all it represented. What could be so important about temple marriage, that it could catapult him into this anguish? He wondered if he should have joined the Church, if only to make her stay. But he'd meant what he said to her. He was a man of integrity. On the other hand, what good was integrity, or anything else, without Emily?

It wasn't until he got the announcement in the mail that the reality sank in, and everything that was bad got worse. There was no picture, for which he felt grateful, but the words clearly stated it. Michael scanned down to the date and looked at the calendar. He looked back at the words near the bottom of the announcement: *Marriage solemnized in the Idaho Falls LDS Temple.*

Michael shoved the announcement back in its envelope and stuck it in the bottom of a drawer. He was on the next plane to Australia, hoping it might somehow put distance between himself and the reality.

On the flight over, he analyzed what had become of his life. He felt sick. And if there was any question, the verification came when his mother saw him walk through the door.

"Good heavens! What happened to you? You didn't start taking drugs or something, did you?"

"No, Mother." He tossed his bag down. "I'm stupid, but I'm not that stupid."

"What happened?" she insisted. "Why aren't you in school?"

"I quit school." He walked past her and threw himself into a chair. "I dropped out."

"You did *what?*" she gasped. And he couldn't blame her.

Katherine appeared from the hallway. "I did hear you," his sister observed. "What are you doing here?"

"He quit school," LeNay reported. She directed a soft voice to Michael. "What happened? Does it have something to do with Emily?"

Michael glared at his mother, then at Katherine. Then he reached for the closest tangible object, which happened to be a porcelain vase. With little thought he threw it across the room, where it shattered against the wall. He didn't remember exactly what he said after that; only that it was all said in a heated anger that finally vented what he'd been feeling since she'd left him. He ranted about Mormons and their narrow-mindedness. And about Emily; how unfair and cruel it all was. He cursed her to a life of misery equal to what he felt now, and he cursed God for toying with his life in this way. And when he couldn't think of anything to say that he hadn't already said twice, he disappeared into his room and locked the door.

Over the next several days he picked idly at the food his mother sent to his room, and refused to talk to anyone. But he did keep an eye on the calendar. He'd left the announcement in Provo, but the date and time were as clearly etched on his mind as the photograph of a bad dream. He calculated the time difference from Utah to Queensland, and when he realized that Emily was married, he stared out the window and saw nothing.

The hours wore on, and the real torture began when he lay back on his bed and comprehended that it was Emily's wedding night. Some other man was holding her, sleeping with her, making love to her. The pain was beyond what he could bear, and the silent tears he shed didn't begin to relieve the pressure.

It wasn't until weeks later that Michael convinced himself that Emily was probably happy. She wouldn't have married this guy if she didn't love him. The important thing, he told himself, was her happiness. He repeated the thought enough that by Christmas he had almost begun to function again. By April he finally found the courage to go back to Provo with the determination to finish his goals. If nothing else, he was not going to let her keep him from being what he wanted to be. It was all he had left.

In a mechanical state of mind, Michael completed his schooling and received his second degree. Without allowing himself to feel anything at all, he left Utah for good, as if he'd closed the door on a piece of his life that would never be requited.

Ten and a half years after Emily Ladd married another man, Michael's plane touched down in Salt Lake City. Memories immediately assaulted him, but he felt a fresh determination to face up to them and get on with his life. Outwardly he had stopped wallowing over Emily years ago. He'd dated and lived a normal life. But his mother and sister sensed the truth—and deep inside, he knew the truth. He'd never gotten over it, and it was time he did. He felt certain that Emily was happy, and figured he had a right to be the same.

Michael purposely drove his rented car to all the places

they'd shared together, and was relieved when he didn't feel like crying. Finally, he was at peace.

As he settled into the autograph signing, he began to recall why he'd liked Utah. The people were friendly and open, and he realized that much of his bitterness toward Emily and the Church had dissipated. It seemed he'd barely gotten used to the idea when he looked up to see her there. At first he wondered if he was hallucinating. But there was no denying the reality of the way she felt, the scent of her. It was all so familiar.

Looking back to that moment, Michael couldn't believe that her being there was any more coincidence than the circumstances of their original meeting. But his initial reaction of pure joy was soon tempered by reality. What Michael learned about Emily's marriage brought all the bitterness rushing back to the surface, hitting him between the eyes.

And now, here he was, hours away from the reckoning of his life—again. The only thing that alleviated his inner turmoil was prayer. As Michael dedicated himself to it, he found peace imagining a life with Emily. He thought about her children and felt added peace, envisioning himself as a stepfather. It just felt right.

By Sunday evening he finally found the courage to call her, certain he had finally met his destiny. These years had humbled and refined him. Perhaps now he would be worthy of her.

CHAPTER EIGHT

THE PHONE RANG while Emily was changing Alexa's diaper. Allison answered it with a loud "Hello," then added a moment later, "It's for you, Mom."

Allison set the phone down and Ryan asked, "Who is it, Allie?"

"I don't know. He just wanted Mom."

Amee picked up the phone to jabber a long line of nonsense before Emily took it from her with a gentle, "No, you let Mommy talk." Amee screamed and Emily motioned to Allison, who distracted the toddler with a freshly-baked cookie.

"Hello, Emily." Michael's rich voice sent a flood of divergent emotions shooting through her. "How are you?"

"I'm fine," she said after a slight delay. "How are you?"

"Better now," he said. Emily squeezed her eyes shut. If he only knew.

"Sorry about the dramatics. Amee loves to talk on the phone."

"I enjoyed it," Michael chuckled.

Emily glanced toward Ryan and breathed easier when she saw that he wasn't paying attention. "Where are you?" she asked quietly, relieved that the television was buffering the sound of her voice. Alexa, in her lap, whined in protest.

"Las Vegas," Michael reported. Emily could barely hear him, so she set Alexa free to crawl. "It's a lovely place," he said with sarcasm, then added solemnly, "Did you know they have a temple here now?"

"Yes, I knew."

After a moment's silence he said resolutely, "I'm flying into Salt Lake City in the morning. Can I see you sometime tomorrow?"

"That would be fine."

"I'm not certain when I'll get to Orem. Is it all right if I just . . . stop by and—"

"That would be fine," Emily repeated, purposely interrupting him. If she felt any concern about Ryan finding out, she reminded herself that he ought to be told what was happening. Her conscience required it.

"Emily," he said with intensity, "I . . . I've been praying."

"So have I." She tried not to betray the emotion rising in her throat.

"And?" he pressed gently.

"And . . ." she hesitated and added in an unnatural tone, "that's about it."

"You can't say," he guessed, "because you're not alone."

"That's right," she stated.

"We'll talk tomorrow, then."

"That would be fine," she said again, wishing she could think of something more original.

"I love you, Emily," he said with an edge of desperation that wrenched her heart.

"I know," she replied, hearing her voice quiver. "And the same to you."

"I'll see you tomorrow."

"That would be fine," she said still again, feeling like a broken record. "Take care," she added with sincerity.

"You too," he replied. She hung up, attempting to appear normal.

"Who was that?" Ryan asked absently.

Emily couldn't lie, but she knew now was not a good time to approach the subject. "I'll tell you later," she said, which brought a deeper spark of curiosity into his eyes, but he said nothing.

The opportunity to talk to Ryan seemed to purposely evade Emily through the evening. But as he finished his breakfast Monday morning, she felt a strong urge from within that seemed to say: *Tell him now!*

Logic told her this wasn't a good time, but the prompting became stronger and she spoke as he put his hand to the door-knob to leave for work. "Ryan, I . . ." He looked at her expectantly. "About that call I got last night, I . . ."

She hesitated and he glanced impatiently at his watch. "Emily, can it wait? I—"

"No," she insisted, "it can't. It was Michael Hamilton on the phone." He looked disoriented. "The writer," she clarified.

"The Australian?" His voice raised a pitch in apparent distress. "What did *he* want?"

"It's a long story, actually," she admitted. "I know you need to go, but we have to talk about it when you get home. I just wanted you to know that he'd called. I don't want you to think I'm trying to keep something from you."

"Oh, that ought to make my day," he said with sarcasm and left abruptly.

An hour later Penny sat at a barstool, leaning over the counter while Emily washed the breakfast dishes. "I just can't believe it."

"Believe it," Emily said with no betrayal of her true emotion. "It's right and I know it's right. I told you what the bishop said. I have to try. I can't give up on Ryan if the Lord believes in him enough to make it clear that I should stay. But at least I have some hope. I have a direction to take, some guidance. And I feel at peace." She sighed and added, "Disappointed and discouraged, but at peace."

"I still don't believe it. What are you going to tell Michael when he shows up?"

"Exactly what I told you."

Penny made a noise of dismay. "You're going to break his heart, Emily."

"Yes, I know. Again. I don't particularly want to think about that."

"When is he supposed to be back?"

"Today sometime."

"I suppose I should get home," Penny said without enthusiasm. "I ought to be sewing. I promised Heather I'd finish her dress for the dance this Saturday."

"First big date, huh?" Emily smiled. "I can't believe she's sixteen already."

"Neither can I, but mostly because I don't want to be old enough to have a daughter who's dating. Next thing I know she'll be married, and I *refuse* to be old enough to be a grandmother. Speaking of Saturday, I'm having a yard sale. Got anything you want me to put out?"

"I don't know. I'll check before then."

"Well, I'll be off now and—"

"Penny," Emily pleaded, "I don't want you to go. When he comes, I don't want to be alone. We shouldn't be alone. Can you sew over here? I just did some mending, so the machine is set up."

Penny smiled. "I think I could do that, but only if you feed me some of that leftover chicken."

"It's a deal."

"I'll be right back."

Penny returned in five minutes and spread her project over the dining room table. Emily put in laundry and straightened the house. After sharing lunch, Penny helped put the babies down for naps and returned to her sewing. Emily picked up toys, then went to the basement to put clothes in the dryer.

When the doorbell rang and Emily apparently hadn't heard, Penny went to answer it. She had to put her brain on hold a moment to convince herself that Emily was really turning down life with this adorable man, who was standing on the porch holding a dozen red roses.

"Excuse me." He glanced at the house number near the door. "I'm looking for Emily Ladd . . . I mean, Hall. Emily Hall."

Any doubt was dispelled when Penny heard the accent.

"Come in." Penny gathered her wits and stopped gaping. "I'll get her." She motioned him inside and closed the door. "Please sit down."

"I'm all right." He glanced around quickly, not surprised by the coziness of his surroundings. "Would I be wrong to assume that you're Penny?"

She grinned. "That's me."

"I've heard nothing but good about you." He offered a hand and she shook it eagerly. "I'm Michael Hamilton."

"Yes, I know. I suppose I can say the same about you. I'll get Emily. I think she's just downstairs putting . . ."

Emily came around the corner with a laundry basket against her hip. "I'm right here." She set the basket down without taking her eyes off Michael. His eyes bored into hers, obviously searching for the answer Emily feared voicing.

Michael willed his heart to slow down after its reaction to just seeing her. He studied her intently, hoping and fearing what her decision might be. He couldn't recall ever finding her so completely unreadable.

"Hello." He smiled quietly.

"Hello," she replied, then nodded toward Penny. "I see you've met. I asked Penny to stay so . . ."

Her words faltered, but Michael nodded his understanding. As Emily's guard melted slightly, he looked deeper into her eyes and caught the reality.

"Oh, no," Michael muttered, hearing it echo silently back to him as verification of something he didn't want to hear. "Emily, please don't tell me that . . ." Now his words faltered.

Penny slipped quietly out of the room and they were alone. Emily looked at the floor and sighed. "Excuse me just a minute."

"Wait," Michael said. "These are for you."

Emily took the roses and felt his hand brush hers for a lingering moment. "Thank you. They're beautiful." Tears welled up and she turned away. "I'll put them in water and be right back."

Instead, she handed them to Penny and went to the bedroom to dig out the letter. Uttering a quick prayer, she returned to find Michael settled into the corner of the couch, his ankle crossed over his knee. He watched her closely as she sat beside him and held out the letter.

"Read it now," she said quietly.

With hesitance, Michael put on his glasses and took the envelope. He glanced at the words written there, then looked intently at Emily while he broke the seal.

"I read *Crazy's Day*," she said for lack of anything better to say. "I loved it."

Michael made no comment as he adjusted his glasses and began to read in silence. It took all of his concentration to keep from visibly crumbling as memories mingled with the moment like ocean waves crashing over a carefully-molded sand castle. When he finally looked up, silent tears were streaming down Emily's face. All he could do was stare at her.

"I doubt there is anything more I can say," she mumbled.

"It would seem that you've covered it pretty well." Michael took off his glasses and held them while he put his forehead into his hand. A minute later he put the glasses in his pocket, followed by the folded letter.

Every justification or apology Emily could think of had already been expressed in the letter. The explanations were complete, but the emotions had only begun. She could see a silent torment in his eyes that matched her own. The intensity of the moment seemed unbearable. All she could do was hang her head forward and attempt to keep the tears silent.

"Where are the children?" he asked, his voice barely steady.

Emily was grateful for the distraction. She sniffled and wiped a hand quickly over her face. "Allison is in school. The babies are asleep."

"I was hoping to meet them." He chuckled tensely and began to chew his thumbnail. The irony was unbearable. He'd been hoping to take them home with him. Part of him just wanted to break down and cry. He simply hadn't counted on this. But what could he do? He'd told her he would respect her decision. And he'd told her that the Lord would be more likely to speak to her of his purposes. He had to believe that was true. But he wondered why. He wanted to ask her, but he knew she didn't know any more than he why they had been brought back together this way, only to be torn apart—again. If this was a test of faith, he felt certain he'd already failed.

Michael tried not to feel the emotion, but the numbness was beginning to dissipate in the silence. He watched Emily attempt to hold back what he knew must be fierce pounding in her head by the torment in her expression.

Michael came so abruptly to his feet that Emily gasped. She expected him to say something, but he only stood rigidly, hands deep in his pockets, eyes squeezed shut. A horrible sense of *déjà vu* enveloped them. She could almost taste the reality of that hot afternoon in his apartment when she had come to tell him good-bye. Then, just as now, she had sensed the volatile emotions threatening to erupt, while outwardly Michael appeared as hard as marble. The thought of confronting those emotions was terrifying, but Emily realized that living with them unvented would only make it more difficult to deal with. Perhaps that was the very reason Michael had spent the last ten years unable to let go.

"Michael." She mustered the courage to stand and touch his arm. He said nothing, but his eyes fell upon her with a distinct expression of torment. Emily drew back her shoulders and inhaled deeply. "We can't say good-bye without talking this through. Not again."

Michael gave a cynical little laugh and looked toward the ceiling. "I don't get it," he said with barely-concealed fury. "What is wrong with me?" He hit a hand against his chest. "Not once, but twice, I get jilted for some *imbecile* who treats you like dirt." He looked directly at Emily. "What is wrong with me?"

"It's not like that, Michael." She attempted to console him. "You don't understand. It's—"

"You're right." His voice rose in quiet anger. "I don't understand. I've been trying to understand for over ten years, and I still do *not* understand!" He groaned and clenched his fists. "What is wrong with me?"

"There is nothing wrong with you, Michael," she declared emphatically. "But I need you to understand. These feelings I have are—"

"Yes," he interrupted with a lifted finger, "I've heard a lot about *your* feelings. But what about . . ." Michael stopped when he saw the anguish in Emily's eyes.

"What, Michael?" she asked and he looked down. "What about your feelings?" she guessed, and his eyes turned sharp. When he said nothing more, she persisted. "I've told you before that your silence at our last good-bye has haunted me. If you've got something to say, say it now. Don't stand there and suffer in silence like you have criticized me for doing."

Emily could see the rage building in his eyes and felt urged to provoke it further, if only to free him of it. "Don't walk away from here a martyr, Michael Hamilton. You're the one who has to live with this. If you feel you're being wronged here, you'd best speak up."

"And what difference would it make?" he asked hoarsely. "If I told you that I believe with all my heart and soul that you and I are supposed to be together, would it make you leave him?" Emily turned pointedly away and he added cynically, "No, I didn't think so. But since you asked, I'm going to tell you how I feel. If I had told you back then, maybe I'd have gotten over this by now. Or maybe it would have made you stay. You can't imagine how many times I have analyzed what I might have done to make you stay, but somehow I always knew it wouldn't have made any difference. As far as I can see, my feelings are the last thing to be considered. I guess you have to be a Mormon to get the right messages, because I sure as hell am not getting them."

Emily finally found the will to protest. "Michael, you know better than to think that—"

"Do I?" he interrupted. "I'll tell you what I know. I know

God sent me to BYU for a reason, and I still believe that reason was you. So, you tell me, Mrs. Hall. You look back at what we shared, the rightness of it, and tell me what it was all for."

"I don't know, Michael," she said softly. "I can't answer the questions of your heart. I can only tell you what I must do according to mine."

Michael gave an anguished sigh and pushed a hand into his hair.

"I understand your bitterness," she said quietly, then immediately regretted it as his eyes turned angry again.

"Oh, *no you do not!*" He grabbed her arm and pulled her close enough to feel his heated breath. "You have *no idea* what it's like to stand where I stand; to love someone so completely and still want to—"

Emily's eyes widened as he cut his sentence short. His expression filled with guilt and she realized what should have been obvious. "If you're angry with me," she said, "why don't you just come out and *say* it? Stop beating around the bush and just let me have it. Say it," she challenged while her heart pounded with fear. "Say what you wanted to say the day I told you I was going to marry Ryan. Go on, Michael," she nearly shouted, "just say it."

"Okay, fine!" He spoke through clenched teeth. The words had echoed through his mind so many times that he knew them like scripture. "You want to know what really makes me angry?"

Emily nodded stoically.

"My biggest fear from the moment I met you was that you would reject me because of our ethnic differences. Before I asked you out a second time, I stated it point-blank. Then, and many times after that, you made it clear to me that our differences didn't matter."

He pointed a finger at her, and she began to tremble as she faced a reality she'd never considered before.

"You sat next to me and told your parents that my not being a member didn't matter to you; that my support of your religion was all you could ever want. You told me you wanted to be my wife, that you loved my home, my life. You accepted me into your world so perfectly. You loved me, Emily." He took her upper arms into his hands. "And then you had the nerve to walk through my door and slap me in the face with temple marriage."

Unbearable pain rose in Emily's throat. She clamped a hand over her mouth and squeezed her eyes shut, but Michael shook her slightly, forcing her to look at him.

"How dare you?" he rasped through gritted teeth. "How dare you take me so completely into your heart and then toss me aside? If you were so determined to have a temple marriage, why did you even go out with me twice?"

"We both know the answer to that," Emily sobbed in her own defense.

"You might," he insisted, "but I don't."

"I loved you, Michael. I had no way of knowing—"

"Did you or did you not lead me on, Emily?"

"Yes," she had to admit, "I did. I was selfish and thoughtless, and you have every right to be angry with me." Emily swallowed hard and knew she only had one real defense. "I was wrong, Michael." She lowered her voice. "And I'm sorry! If we could go back, maybe we would have done it differently. But I do know that all I ever tried to do was what God wanted me to do. I don't know what God has in mind for you, but I know he wants me here. I apologize with my whole heart for the hurt I've caused, but you've got to forgive me and get on with your life."

Michael let go of her and stepped back as if he'd been slapped. While Emily attempted to absorb and sort through all he'd said, a thought occurred to her. Before she stopped to ponder it, the words slipped out.

"Maybe it wasn't me, Michael."

"What do you mean?" he asked quietly.

"The reason you came to Provo, our relationship, your feelings. Maybe it was all for some . . . greater purpose."

Michael's eyes narrowed as he began to perceive what she

was implying, but he couldn't begin to comprehend its significance.

"Michael," Emily continued, gaining confidence as her words seemed to make sense, "maybe God has something else in mind for you."

He chuckled dubiously while she attempted to dry her face with the flat of her hands. "What would God possibly have in mind for me if it isn't you?"

"I don't know." She shrugged her shoulders and sat on the edge of the couch. "Maybe he's been trying to tell you all these years, and you just weren't listening."

Michael sat down. Whatever she was trying to tell him made no sense as far as he could see. He figured it was nothing more than a futile attempt to console him. He turned to meet her gaze, and the reality descended. The anger had been vented, but nothing had changed. He still loved her, and she was still telling him good-bye.

If Michael had stopped to contemplate his reaction, even for a moment, he might have talked some sense into himself. But it was pure, impulsive desperation that drove him to take her in his arms and kiss her.

Emily found her lips beneath his and wanted to pull away, but what little sensibility she had been clinging to fled quickly beneath Michael's display of affection. His kiss turned warm and moist. Nothing within her power could keep her from responding. With no thought of anything beyond the moment, she reached her arms around his shoulders and pressed a hand into his hair. He must have kissed her hundreds of times, but never like this. Never in her life had she been kissed like this. He drew her closer, held her tighter. Her bruised and aching conscience gave way beneath the pressure of the moment, and she allowed herself to completely and utterly enjoy it.

Michael asked himself why he was doing this. He knew this moment would only torture him with its memory of empty promises. His mind began to protest, telling him she was another man's wife and always would be. But how could he resist the way she responded, the way she clung to him? Was she as starved for affection as he? His mind began to wander, and he was grateful they weren't alone in the house. He couldn't imagine himself, or Emily, doing anything to bring more pain into their lives. But then, a moment ago he would not have imagined himself holding her this way, kissing her like he'd never kissed any woman before.

The ecstasy turned to irony, and Emily sobbed in the midst of his kiss. Michael pulled back sharply. "Emily. I'm so sorry. I shouldn't have done that. I—"

Emily put gentle fingers to his lips. "Hush," she whispered. "It's all we have."

Their eyes met, and Michael's little remaining composure shattered. He felt the tears coming and pressed his face to her shoulder to hide them.

Time flew and stood still as they held each other and cried. Emily felt a desperate need to never let him go. The warmth of his embrace replenished her strength, and the evidence of his love and sustenance made her long to just lose herself in him and put the past behind her. But she knew without doubt the direction her life must take—and Michael Hamilton would not be a part of it.

"I'm so sorry, Michael," she muttered, attempting to put her emotion under control.

The phone rang and shattered the moment. Michael looked up abruptly.

"I'll get it," Penny called from the kitchen.

Seeing the phone in the hall, Michael quickly wiped his face and attempted to appear normal.

With her back to them, Penny answered the phone with a soft "Hello."

Emily met Michael's melancholy expression as they quietly listened but barely heard.

"She's kind of busy right now. Can I have her call you back, or . . . All right. All right. I'll get her."

Penny turned to Emily with her hand over the mouthpiece.

"It's for you."

"Who is it?" she asked, noting something significant in Penny's eyes.

Penny cleared her throat tensely. "It's Ryan. He's very insistent."

Emily glanced carefully at Michael, who swallowed hard. She rose to take the phone from Penny and cleared her throat with effort.

"Hello," she said, proud of herself for the normality in her tone, wishing Michael couldn't overhear. "I'm fine. Why?" She paused to listen. "Everything is all right. Yes, we can talk when you get home." She paused again. "I love you, too." Her voice cracked slightly. "Thanks for calling."

Emily hung up the phone and turned to Michael. "That's the first time he's called from work in years, unless he's wanted me to do something for him. He said that . . ." she attempted to control her emotion ". . . that he was just sitting there and had this awful feeling that something was wrong."

"Maybe it will be better for you now," Michael said calmly.

"For all of us, I hope."

Michael didn't look anxious to leave, so she sat back down beside him.

"Don't let him treat you badly, Emily," he said. "You mustn't put up with it."

"I'll do my best." She tried to smile. Her eyes met his deeply. "And you, Michael. You've got to put this behind you. You can find someone." He turned away and closed his eyes, not wanting to hear, but Emily continued. "What woman wouldn't want a man like you? You're handsome, talented . . . and rich." She attempted to lighten the mood, but it only sank further as she continued. "And sensitive, and warm, and . . ." Her voice trembled. "You're a good man, Michael."

"Apparently not good enough for you." His voice was edged with bitterness, but she couldn't blame him.

"Maybe it's the other way around." She tried to smile. "I dare say you've broken many hearts."

"I just pass it on."

"Michael, I can't blame you for being bitter. I know how you must feel after—"

"No, Emily, you do not. I'm sorry, but you have no idea how I feel."

"You're right," she admitted. "I probably don't. But this is not easy for me, either."

"Then why do you . . ." He held up his hands. "Never mind. I don't want to hear it. I can't." Emily's tears welled up again and he took her hand. "I'm sorry, Emily. I understand why it has to be this way. At least I think I do. It's just so . . ." His voice broke ". . . hard."

"I know," she agreed, putting her head on his shoulder to cry.

Michael just held her in an attempt to offer comfort, for himself as much as for her. If only he could hold her forever.

CHAPTER NINE

MICHAEL SAW PENNY come into the room before Emily looked up, startled by her voice.

"You're not going to believe this." Penny bit her lip nervously while Emily wiped the back of her hands over her face. "Ryan just drove up."

Emily looked to Michael in panic. "He *never* comes home this time of day."

"Does he know?" Michael asked.

"Not yet." Emily wrung her hands nervously. She expected Michael to leave, or at least look like he was on his way out. But he crossed his legs and folded his arms, making it clear that he intended to stay. Whether she wanted him to or not.

"Uh . . ." Penny said quietly, "I think I'll just go on home and—"

"You stay right where you are," Emily insisted. "No," she corrected, pointing to a chair, "sit down. The last thing I need is to be caught here alone with Michael."

"Good point," Penny said and dutifully sat, arranging herself to look as if she'd been there for hours.

Emily hurried to the back door to meet Ryan, reminding herself that she had nothing to hide. She'd had every intention of telling Ryan the situation. If nothing else, she was grateful she'd mentioned that Michael had called.

"Who's here?" he said before he closed the door. Emily hesitated.

"There's a car out front," he added tersely. "Who's here?"

"Michael Hamilton," she stated, then went on before he could question her further. "He's on his way back to Australia. He came to say good-bye."

Ryan's eyes bored into her, as if he were beginning to perceive that something wasn't right. He pushed past her and went to the living room with Emily close behind.

"Hello, Ryan," Penny said, just as she always did. But his eyes were fixed on the man seated casually at one end of the couch.

"Hello, Penny," Ryan replied without looking at her. Then he said tersely to Michael, "I don't believe we've met."

Michael came slowly to his feet but said nothing. While his first instinct might have been to belt this guy in the jaw, he instead had to acknowledge something he'd not expected. First of all, the tiny wedding picture he'd seen did the man no justice. Ryan Hall had dignity and a commanding presence. He had a look so conventionally handsome that Michael might have imagined one of his fictional heroes to appear much the same way. If not for the things Emily had told him, Michael would have no reason to dislike him. But there was a fury in Ryan's eyes that marred his image. And Michael knew it had to be confronted.

Emily sensed the rage building silently. She stepped between Ryan and Michael.

"Ryan," she said carefully, "this is Michael Hamilton. Michael," she swallowed, "my husband, Ryan."

Michael gave a barely detectable nod. "You're a writer," Ryan stated tonelessly.

Emily was hoping this encounter would remain in small talk. Then Michael folded his arms and spoke. "Actually," he said, "I'm more accurately the man your wife left so she could marry you."

"Is that why you're visiting my wife while I'm away?" Ryan retorted.

"Did you want the truth?" Michael asked, almost smugly.

"Or would you like me to paint an illustrious picture of fiction? I'm rather good at that."

"I would prefer the truth." Ryan didn't seem impressed by Michael's approach.

"Good. I ran into your wife the other day at the mall, and I asked her if she's happy."

"I hope she told you that she is." Ryan chuckled without any trace of humor.

"No." Michael put his hands behind his back and pushed his face forward slightly. "She told me the truth."

Emily sighed, suddenly wanting to be anywhere but here. Ryan's eyes shot her a blatant question, and she felt certain he needed to hear what was being said. Facing the full depth of their problems would not be easy, but perhaps facing them head on would bring about more progress, however painful.

"What exactly did you tell him?" Ryan demanded quietly.

"The truth," she stated firmly.

"Which is?"

Emily didn't know how to answer. She turned to Michael for support and felt relieved to find it.

"I think that's something the two of you should discuss privately," Michael said, his affection all too apparent. He turned his gaze to Ryan and added, "Now that she's decided to stay."

Emily expected Ryan to question her again, but his gaze only hardened on Michael. "What are you implying, Mr. Hamilton?"

"I'm not implying anything," Michael stated. "I'm telling you that Emily was considering my offer."

"And what offer is that?" Ryan asked, his voice a study in quiet fury.

Michael looked to Emily in question. He didn't want to make the situation worse, but he wasn't about to leave here without being certain that Ryan Hall knew exactly where he stood. Michael would not live alone, while this man lived in complacency. He wondered how far to take it. Despite Emily's obvious nervousness, her eyes gave him undeniable approval.

With confidence he looked back to the man he envied more than any other on earth.

"I asked her to leave you and spend the rest of her life with someone who loves and appreciates her for the incredible woman she is."

Emily watched anger crease Ryan's brow and draw his lips tightly together. He turned to her, and she perceived something in his eyes that made her afraid. But she drew up her chin and said with courage, "You can get angry if you want, Ryan, but it will not change the facts. Michael's telling you the truth."

"And you were actually considering . . . leaving . . . with *him?*" Ryan sounded insulted.

Emily felt an urge to buffer the situation. Her instincts tempted her to smooth it over and tell Ryan it wasn't as bad as all that. She had just been caught up in the excitement of it. Perhaps saying such things would take away the tightness in his jaw and the brewing anger in his eyes. But instead, recalling the bishop's advice, she said firmly, "Yes, I considered it very seriously."

A warmth began to fill Emily as the anger in Ryan's eyes melted into shameless fear. A heavy silence fell over the room. Emily glanced at Michael, but he was watching Ryan, a combination of empathy and pain etched into his expression. She turned back to Ryan and felt the confusion hovering over him. His shoulders slumped and Emily wanted to hold him. But Michael's presence held her back, and she could only watch Ryan helplessly.

Michael observed the two of them, husband and wife, plainly seeing the realizations dawn. But all he could feel was the devastating reality of being on the outside—again. He suddenly wanted to escape from all of it.

"I should be going," he announced. Emily looked toward him abruptly, feeling torn. He stepped toward her, not caring about anything except facing up to a final moment with Emily. Setting his fingers to her chin, he sensed Ryan's tension, but decided the man should know exactly how Michael felt about

Emily. If nothing else, maybe it would keep him on his toes in the years to come.

"You're the most wonderful woman in the world, Emily Ladd."

Emily closed her eyes, but she didn't expect the quick kiss upon her lips.

"Take care of yourself, and be happy. I'll write."

Michael turned to Ryan and impulsively decided that some good faith couldn't hurt. With purpose he extended a hand. Ryan looked at it dubiously, then he reached out to accept Michael's firm handshake.

"She loves you very much, Mr. Hall. If I were you, I'd remember that." Michael dropped Ryan's hand and nodded toward Penny, who sat silently observing the drama. "It was a pleasure meeting you, Penny."

"And you." She smiled warmly.

Michael looked again at Emily. "If you ever change your mind . . ." he said. And abruptly walked out the door.

Emily looked at Ryan and felt a brief sense of panic. "I'll be right back," she muttered and ran after Michael. "Wait," she called as he opened the car door. She stopped on the walk. "Come here," she said. He immediately closed the door and walked around the car to stand close to her. "You will write?"

"I'm a writer," he said, but neither of them smiled. "I told you I would. But will you answer my letters?"

Emily nodded firmly. "But I'm not keeping any secrets, Michael. Don't put anything on paper that you wouldn't want anyone else in my home to see, and don't expect anything different from me. Of course, I will keep them private, but it's a matter of . . ."

"Principle. Yes, I know. I can honor that."

A moment of silence brought tears to her eyes. "Thank you for what you did in there. I intended to tell him, but . . . you made it easier."

"Well," Michael glanced toward the house, "at least he'll know you weren't making idle threats."

Emily nodded and sniffed.

"Emily, I have to tell you. I don't know if I am so misdirected, or what, but I . . . I felt so right about it—about us. I really believed that you and I were supposed to be together."

"If you must know, there was a moment when I believed it, too. But we have to trust the Lord. Only He knows what's in store for us."

"If it doesn't work out, Emily." Michael took her hand. "If he doesn't change and you—"

"Please don't, Michael. I have to be positive."

He looked down and shuffled the toe of his boot over the concrete. "I know."

"And I want you to promise me that you'll try. Try to find someone, Michael. You can. Pray about it. He'll help you."

Michael nodded feebly and decided enough had been said. He squeezed her hand once more, then brought it to his lips. "I love you, Emily. I will love you forever."

"And I will always love you." She reached up to kiss his cheek. He closed his eyes to absorb it. "Good-bye, Michael."

He looked at her long and hard, but couldn't bring himself to say it in return. He just got into the car and drove away, wondering if he would ever get over this.

Emily watched until Michael's car was out of sight, praying in her heart that the anguish would be worth it for all of them.

Ryan moved to the window when Emily ran out the door, solemnly observing the farewells. Beside him, Penny said softly, "Kind of puts a whole new perspective on life, doesn't it?" He turned and walked toward the back of the house as Emily approached the front door.

"You all right?" Penny asked her friend.

Emily slowly closed the door and leaned against it. She sighed and swallowed the fresh tide of emotion. It was time to put J. Michael Hamilton and all her fears concerning him in the past, and dedicate herself to a future with Ryan Hall.

"I'll be fine," she finally said, glancing around to notice that Ryan wasn't in the room.

Penny attempted to lighten the mood. "Boy," she chuckled, "daytime soaps have nothing over on you."

Emily laughed softly, but it turned to another sigh. "You don't watch that stuff any more than I do."

"I don't have to. I was at your house this afternoon." Penny gathered her things to leave. "Call me later if you need to talk." Emily nodded and held the door for her.

She found Ryan sitting at the dining room table, staring at the roses Penny had arranged in a glass pitcher. She sat quietly beside him and waited for a reaction. She'd never seen him so thoughtful. Without looking at her, he said flatly, "I assume he brought the flowers."

"Yes," was all she said.

He chuckled tensely and his eyes grew distant. "It was the strangest thing," he mused. "I was just sitting there at work, and I started thinking about what you said this morning before I left. Then I got to wondering about that night you had been out late, and . . . and out of nowhere I had this kind of . . . panic hit me." He shook his head. "I just had to call you. But even after you said you were all right, I couldn't get rid of the feeling. I had to get home."

"Maybe that was an answer to my prayers." Emily put a soothing hand over his.

He looked to her with deep questioning in his eyes, and for the first time in all their years together he said with conviction, "Talk to me, Emily. Tell me all of it. I have to know."

Emily drew a deep breath and looked directly at him.

"You already know that Michael and I were very close in college. When you returned from your mission, he and I were seriously discussing marriage. He was hurt when I told him I'd decided to marry you. I didn't see him again until last week, when he autographed his book for me. He wanted to get together and talk."

Emily saw the fear return to Ryan's eyes, this time edged with a touch of anger. She wondered for a moment how it might have felt if she were trying to tell him she was leaving.

The thought made her grateful for her decision.

"I didn't want to meet him," she continued, "but I did. Before you jump to any conclusions, I want you to know that we stayed in public. I did nothing wrong. I was only late because I drove around, alone, to have some time to think."

Ryan leaned back and folded his arms. "About what?"

Emily set her clammy palms on the table. "About his offer."

He chuckled breathily. "I still can't believe it."

"The important thing is that I turned him down. I'm still here."

Ryan's eyes narrowed. "Emily, are you really so . . . so . . . unhappy here, that you would . . ." He didn't seem to want to finish.

Emily felt afraid, but reminded herself that the worst was out. And he wasn't showing the anger that normally created distance between them. He appeared now to be more humble than she'd ever seen him.

She leaned forward. "Ryan, I have come to realize there is much in our relationship that leaves me unfulfilled. Perhaps if you had taken the time to listen more, it wouldn't have been such a surprise to learn what you did today. Michael was right. Much of the time I am unhappy. But I'm staying, Ryan."

She wondered if she should tell him the real reason—that it was the Spirit guiding her to stay. But knowing his present status in the Church, she decided to keep religion out of it.

"I'm staying because I know this is where I'm supposed to be. I respect the vows we share. I love you, and I believe we can make the necessary changes for both of us to be happy."

Ryan's expression became unreadable. The tension in him relaxed, and she decided impulsively that she might as well have the entire truth out in the open. She wasn't going to live with any guilt.

"I'll probably never see Michael again," she said, wincing at the ache her words produced, "but he asked that we keep in touch through letters. I agreed, but I made it clear where I stood. Any exchange between us will be as friends alone; but if the truth be known, I need his support. We care for each other very much. And I guess you should know . . . he kissed me before he left."

"I saw that," he said peevishly.

"No," she corrected, "before you came home."

This made Ryan's eyes go wide.

"That's all that happened, Ryan. You have the full story. I'm not going to live with any secrets. I'm going to talk to the bishop about it, just so I know it's all taken care of. I am putting it all behind me from this moment forward. I am accepting Michael as a friend, and I am dedicating myself to you as my husband. But there are going to be some changes. If this marriage is going to work, it will take some hard work from both of us."

Emily waited for a reaction, but she was totally unprepared for the question he asked.

"Do you love him, Emily?" Ryan's voice was edged with fear.

Knowing she couldn't lie, Emily attempted to deflect his question. "I'm staying, Ryan," she said. "That's all that matters."

"I understand," he said softly, "and I'm grateful. But I have to know. Do you love him?"

While emotions threatened to erupt, Emily's mind repeated a lie over and over, as if she could bring herself to tell him no. But the word wouldn't form in her mouth. She knew she had to tell him the truth, but she couldn't hold back the tears that accompanied it.

"Yes," she muttered and closed her eyes tightly. "I love him." As difficult as it was, she was grateful to have acknowledged her feelings.

Ryan said nothing. After several minutes of silence, Emily got up to start dinner. She moved the roses to the bar to make room for the meal, pausing to inhale their fragrance and rearrange them slightly. With a certain sense of peace, she decided that everything would be all right.

Michael drove two blocks before his tears blinded him and

he had to pull over. His knuckles turned white where he gripped the steering wheel; he pressed his forehead against it, wondering if the throbbing would ever cease. He couldn't believe it. He just couldn't believe it. But unconsciously, he did something he hadn't been able to bring himself to do the last time this happened.

"Please, God," he muttered aloud. "Please, help me understand. Help me cope. I can't live through this again. Please," he nearly sobbed, "please . . . help me."

Michael didn't know how long it was before he could put the car into drive, and he was equally unaware of the turns he made or the signs he passed. But his heart began to pound when he turned a corner and saw the Provo temple looming above him, some distance up the hill.

As if he knew what he was doing, Michael turned in at the entrance gate and drove through the parking lot twice before he found an empty space. Turning off the ignition, he leaned back and folded his arms, staring intently toward the magnificent white edifice, its golden spire rising before a background of mountains.

For nearly three hours Michael sat where he was, watching the people come and go, dressed in their finest, carrying little suitcases. They were all ages and all kinds, but they all looked like Mormons. He'd gotten so he could pick one out from a distance. He wondered what really went on in there. What was so wonderful about it that these huge parking lots were always filled? What made these people so eager to be there, to marry there? And what about it had kept Ryan Hall away all these years, and left Emily so miserable?

Attempting to ease the stiffness in his back, Michael got out of the car and stuffed the keys in his pocket. Slowly he ambled up the walk and around the building to the east side. He remembered coming here with Emily, and he sat on a bench they had shared more than once to look at the words etched in gold: *House of the Lord. Holiness to the Lord.*

Again Michael stared and wondered. There had been a time

when his resolve on religion had been firm. He clearly remembered telling Emily that his life was good and he saw no reason to change it. Now the thought made him groan aloud and press his face into his hands. After Emily left him, he had felt nothing but bitterness for years, and religion was the furthest thing from his mind. God had betrayed him . . . and now it was happening all over again.

Michael was confused about a lot of things, but he wasn't so stupid that he couldn't figure one thing for certain: his life was not good now. It hadn't been good for many years. He felt suddenly chilled from the inside out, and bolted abruptly to his feet. Thinking of what his exposure to Mormonism had done to his life, he felt the bitterness rise like bile in his throat. He stuffed his hands into his pockets and walked briskly back toward the parking lot, wondering what on earth he was doing here in the first place.

He felt angry and miserable as he got into his car and slammed the door. He wondered what Emily was doing now; a number of possibilities flashed through his mind, all of which made him want to die inside. The anger melted into pain, pounding into his chest like an ice pick.

Determined to get away from this forsaken place, Michael gritted his teeth and turned the key in the ignition.

Nothing happened.

He tried again.

Not a sound.

"Oh, this is too much," he groaned, slamming his fists against the steering wheel. Anger welled up and engulfed him like a familiar companion. He wanted to throw something, or hit something, or just die. There was a time when he never would have believed that a man could feel such complete despair.

As he succumbed to desperation, Michael's grip tightened on the wheel as if it were a lifeline. Instinctively the anguished words came from deep in his throat.

"Please, God. I can't do this alone. I can't. I'll do

anything. *Anything!*"

A calm thought appeared in his mind like the first tiny star glittering against an otherwise black sky. The words were so simple and meaningless that he almost ignored them. Again Michael said through gritted teeth, "I'll do anything."

And again the answer came: *Then just get out of the car.*

Michael hesitated, then stepped out of the car as if guided by an unseen force. He ambled up the sidewalk, while thoughts raced through his mind. Maybe he could make a call and get a cab, or perhaps get someone to jump the battery.

He found himself standing before the temple's tall glass doors, and felt his heart pounding in his ears. He couldn't go in there. He was well aware of the requirements to enter the temple, and he simply didn't qualify. Yet people were walking past him and going in as if it were nothing.

With little thought he stepped onto the mat, and the door swung open automatically. How strange that he would recall the scripture, "Knock, and it shall be opened unto you."

So far, so good. Nobody seemed bent on kicking him out. He stopped and looked around. In front of him was another set of glass doors, and beyond them he could see a desk where recommends were being checked. Well, he knew he couldn't go past there. But he stepped out of the traffic to look beyond that desk to a large lobby, finely decorated, where people were sitting about.

To his left, a staircase descended beneath an immense painting of John the Baptist baptizing Christ in the River Jordan. He paused for a moment to absorb its beauty. Then, turning to the right, he found what appeared to be a waiting room.

Seeing a pay phone shocked him back to the moment. He was searching in his pocket for a quarter when he felt a hand on his arm and turned to see an elderly woman, dressed in white. She smiled warmly and he could almost imagine a guardian angel.

"Are you waiting for someone, young man?" she asked kindly.

"Uh . . ." Michael stammered, "uh . . . no, I was just going to use the phone. My car won't start, and—"

"Oh, dear." She furrowed her aging brow. "Would you like me to call someone to help you or . . ."

He shook his head and managed a smile. "No, thank you. I'll just make a call, if that's all right."

Michael glanced once more past those doors and went into the waiting room to use the phone, but every call he attempted got no answer or a never-ending busy signal. Frustrated to distraction, he left the waiting room. He nearly went outside, but felt compelled to stop once more and look as deeply into the temple as possible from this point of view.

Thinking back over the years, he felt a familiar ache. That's how it had always been since he'd come to Utah. He was always on the outside, looking in. He'd been the non-member at a Mormon university, where the social life and activities centered around something he couldn't be a part of. Emily had drawn him into that world, and he had felt comfortable there. But then she had turned him out, and he had felt more out of place than before.

All these years, while Emily had been married and raising a family, Michael had been alone. He'd felt it keenly this afternoon, standing in her front room. Everything about her life excluded him. And now here he was, torturing himself by standing here, gazing into a world he could not enter, wondering what had brought him here. He contemplated what it might be like to actually walk through those doors, flash that little white card, and move on to what Mormons called the closest place to heaven on earth.

For a moment the discouragement crowded into his head, pushing away what little peace of mind remained. Then, out of nowhere, Emily's words of earlier that day came back to him. At the time they had sounded trite and insensitive, but in that moment they gave him warm goosebumps. "Michael," her voice whispered in his memory, "maybe God has something else in mind for you. Maybe he's been trying to tell you all these years, but you just weren't listening."

Michael turned and walked out the door, suddenly feeling more afraid than he ever had in his life. There was something happening here that he didn't understand, and he wasn't certain if he wanted to. A thousand feelings washed over him as he walked briskly back to the car, but rising above them all was the pain that came with the reality of his loss. God had led him to Emily, then taken her away—twice. It wasn't fair, and it hurt as he imagined only hell could.

Absently he got into the car and turned the key in the ignition. It wasn't until it turned over and roared to life with little coaxing that Michael leaned back wearily and wondered if he was going crazy.

Convincing himself that he was, Michael backed out and drove away, determined to put all of this out of his life once and for all. With any luck, he would never have to come back to this wretched place again. He longed only to be home, away from Mormons and their bizarre ideas. It was time to start over. If only he could.

CHAPTER TEN

OVER THE NEXT FEW DAYS, Ryan was quiet and politely aloof. Emily let him be, sensing that perhaps he was soul-searching. She prayed that whatever he found would bring positive changes.

While the maple tree in the yard began to bud with the coming of spring, the roses Michael had brought opened to a full bloom and filled the air around them with brilliant fragrance.

Emily began to establish a new routine for herself. It was a balance between her old, overly-dedicated self and the drastic opposite she had become the week before. She went about her home and church duties with an open mind and a light heart, and she began setting aside the babies' nap time to paint.

The day the roses began to wilt, Emily put on the sweater Michael had bought her and felt a peaceful nostalgia. She thought of him and wondered how he was dealing with all of this. She had a desire to write to him, but realized she couldn't until he did first; she didn't have his address. But she kept a prayer in her heart for him and decided it would have to do for now.

Ryan came home early and found her painting while Allison had the babies out for a turn around the block in their double stroller.

"It's nice," he said, looking over her shoulder at the scene finally taking full shape on canvas.

"Thank you," she said brightly.

"Where did you get the sweater?" he asked.

Emily smiled up at him. "You noticed." She returned to her painting. "Michael bought it for me," she reported as if it were nothing. "It was on sale."

Ryan sat beside her and watched her face while she dabbed green into the cluster of trees rising over the hills. "Emily," he finally said, "what's he got that I haven't got?"

Emily stopped painting but left her brush poised. To try and compare them was like comparing spring to fall. They were both good, but too different in all respects to even attempt an analogy. Emily pulled the brush away and looked at him.

"There is only one difference that matters."

"And what is that?"

"He makes me feel my worth." Emily was tempted to expound, but decided to let Ryan figure it out himself.

"Maybe you should tell me more about him," Ryan continued to Emily's surprise. "I know you were close, but you hardly ever mentioned him. Obviously there is more to the two of you than I realized. Tell me about him, Emily."

Emily wasn't certain of his motives, but she sensed something good about this. She continued to paint while she told Ryan how she had met Michael Hamilton, and described their experiences together. She told him about her trip to Australia and what a memorable adventure it had been. He had known she'd gone, but until this day he'd known nothing more.

Allison came back to ask if they could go around the block a few more times. With permission she was off again, leaving her parents with some much-needed quiet time.

Emily told Ryan how she had avoided even thinking about Michael all these years, and the way her decision had come to haunt her when the marriage became difficult. She repeated recent events in more detail, shedding silent tears as she told him that she knew her choice many years ago had been right, just as she knew her decision earlier this week had been the proper one.

When Emily stopped talking, Ryan stood and took the

brush out of her hand, setting it aside. He touched her chin and looked into her eyes. "I love you, Emily. I can see now that perhaps I helped close a door to your past that should have been left open. Maybe I was afraid of it. I don't know. But I do know I'm a very lucky man. I want to thank you for giving me another chance."

Emily held him and cried until Allison came back with the babies. Ryan ordered a pizza to be delivered and told Emily to keep painting.

The roses finally wilted and looked pathetic. Emily sighed and gathered them for a trek to the outside garbage can, past Ryan who was pulling weeds. He watched her throw them away. Their eyes met and exchanged a new warmth.

The following Sunday, Ryan went to church. Emily fought with her emotions through the entire day, but managed to keep them under control except when she knelt alone in prayer to pour her heart out in gratitude.

A letter arrived from Michael the following day.

Dear Emily,

I've been thinking about you a great deal. I doubt
that would surprise you. I hope everything is well there.
Mother sends her regards.

I realized through my journey home, that it's autumn
here while it's spring there. I somehow found that
significant.

Take care and write soon.

Love, Michael

The conciseness of the letter made Emily certain of his present heartache. If he could say nothing he wouldn't want read by others, it seemed that he could say very little.

Emily immediately sat down to write him a long letter, telling him of the things happening between her and Ryan. She added trivialities about her painting, her church work, the children, and a little about Penny. Then she called the post office to find out how many stamps it took to send a letter to Australia, and she put the babies in the stroller and walked down the street to mail it. When the babies went down for naps, Emily began to read *Verity*, and thoroughly enjoyed it.

As the days passed, Emily felt a degree of regression. A tendency to feel discouraged settled in, but she kept close to the scriptures and reminded herself that changes didn't happen overnight. Ryan was a proud man, and there were likely difficulties that ran deep. It would take time. As long as she could feel any improvement at all, she could keep going.

A month after Michael left the country, Emily stopped to tally the changes and decided they were good. Ryan had twice taken Allison out to spend time with her, and one Friday evening he impulsively called Penny and asked if she could watch the children while they went out to eat. It was only at Burger King, but they were out and they were together. Emily couldn't ask for more.

Ryan continued going to church, though he often left before priesthood meeting. Again Emily looked only at the positive. At least he was going. There were days when he was much like his old self, distant and insensitive. But there were others when he was attentive and considerate. Whenever Emily expressed a need to talk to him, he seemed willing, even eager. Discussions of their difficulties brought on natural disagreement, but on a few issues, Emily felt him becoming more flexible.

Assessing the changes in Ryan, Emily had to credit part of it to whatever miracle had induced his bout of panic during a timely moment. And perhaps Michael's intrusion had made Ryan begin to value her as he should. If another man was so eager to have her, perhaps he figured he should stop and take notice. He admitted once that realizing how close he'd come to losing her was frightening. Emily felt that all of it, combined with heeding her bishop's advice, was making things come together in a way that gave her real hope.

Letters arrived almost weekly from Michael, and gradually they became more relaxed. He told her about his horse racing business, and a little here and there about the novel he was working on. Emily's letters to him were filled with details of her life, as well as subtly-maneuvered positive advice for him to get on with his.

June was pleasantly warm, and Emily was beginning to feel that she had found the true essence of happiness. The reality struck her one morning as she looked out the window to notice how the maple tree in the yard was fully green with summer. She attended the temple that day and came home feeling a spiritual high. Everything in her life seemed good, and the peace left her feeling close to heaven. She baked cookies, and Allison took a plate of them to an elderly lady on the corner. The joy of service continued to fill her as she painstakingly prepared Ryan's favorite chicken recipe and put the house in order.

Ryan came home with a smile and a warm, "Hi. Something smells good." After the usual exchange of small talk, he sat at the desk in the corner of the dining room to look over the bills and start writing out checks. He remained silent, but from the kitchen Emily sensed the signs of tension rising. She tried to ignore it and not let it affect her as she set the table and put dinner on.

"It's ready," she said brightly, then called Allison to the table and put Amee in her highchair. Ryan finally turned grudgingly from the desk when Emily said gently, "We're ready to bless it now."

Ryan ate in silence, paying little attention to the meal. Emily tried not to feel hurt, but she couldn't help thinking that he'd have commented if she'd served hot dogs.

While Emily washed dishes, Ryan called to her, "Hey, Em. Could you come here a minute?"

Emily sighed and picked up a towel. If he wanted to talk about money, she'd rather not. But she approached him with a cheerful, "What is it?"

"What is this check for?" he asked curtly, pointing out the amount in the register.

Emily thought a moment then said, with a conscious effort to not apologize, "It's for Allison's lunch ticket. I pay it once a month. You know that."

"Okay, fine," he answered, an undercurrent of tension in his voice. "But maybe we could save money if she took lunch from home."

Emily looked right at him. "You don't."

"Emily, I work very hard and—"

"And Allison works hard in school," Emily interrupted calmly. "If I didn't pay for school lunch, we would have to spend at least that much more a month on groceries to compensate. This way she gets a hot, balanced meal."

Ryan stared blankly at the check register until he found another point to make.

"Are you sure you need to spend this much for groceries? I can't believe the percentage of our income that goes for food."

His tone implied that she was doing something wrong, but Emily swallowed and took it at face value.

"Groceries are expensive, Ryan. I use coupons and I budget carefully. I can honestly say that I could do no better, unless you want to start eating a whole lot differently."

"I just can't believe it costs this much to feed a family."

Old habits provoked anger and a desire to suppress it, but Emily calmly forced herself to call him on it.

"Are you implying that I'm not handling the grocery budget correctly?"

"I didn't say that," he shot back.

"I asked what you were implying."

"I just said that I can't believe it costs that much to feed a family. I wasn't implying that it was your fault."

"Then whose fault are you implying it is?"

"Em, I don't want to fight about this."

"Neither do I, but I'm not going to stand here and feel

guilty for doing the best I can with what you give me."

"Nobody said you had to feel guilty."

"Then how should I feel? Perhaps you should try buying the groceries for a month and see if you can do any better."

He laughed as if the idea was ridiculous, then added in the same tone, "I have no doubt of that."

"Of what?"

"That I could do better."

"You have no idea what you're talking about." Emily heard the anger in her voice but couldn't help it. If there was one thing she could do well, it was hunting grocery bargains.

"Forget it, Em." He pushed an impatient hand through the air. "Sorry I brought it up."

Emily closed her eyes to force a measure of reason into her mind. The tactic was common. After making implications so subtle that she couldn't respond, he insulted her with humor to make it sound teasing, then changed the subject to leave her opinions disregarded and her feelings invalidated. Like a million times before in her married life, Emily had to stop and ask herself: *Am I imagining this? Am I crazy?*

Consciously she tried to steer her efforts toward compromise. "Ryan," she said gently, "if the finances are so stressful, why don't you let me help with the bills? I could take some of the load, and I might even enjoy it."

"Thanks, Em, but I think I'd better keep it under control." Another implication.

"Ryan, you know I took finance classes in college, and I did well. I lived on my own for quite some time. I'm perfectly capable of handling household finances." Emily wished she hadn't said it when the hundred times it had been said before came back to her in silent echoes.

Ryan looked up at her with patronizing eyes. "Emily, I'm well aware of the grades you got in college. You've reminded me a thousand times. But the real thing is different."

Emily ignored his gross exaggeration and gave him another point. "Don't you think I should be aware of what's going on? If something were to happen to you, I wouldn't know what was what. We should share the responsibility of the finances. That's what marriage is about."

"If I make the money, I'm going to see how it's spent. Housewives were not intended to determine such things."

Emily's mouth fell open and tears of humiliation stung her eyes. There was nothing subtle about that. She recalled countless times he'd made such statements, but the progress of their relationship had made her forget just how bad the situation could be.

Help me, Father, she uttered silently. A moment later she opened her mouth to speak.

"Do you hear what you just said to me?" The strength of her tone caught his attention. "Do you have any idea how degrading your attitude toward me can be? And the sad thing is that you don't even realize you're doing it. It could slap you in the face, and you still wouldn't recognize it. The problem here, Ryan, is not the money, or the groceries, or anything else we could think to argue about. The problem is that we argue in endless circles, and it never gets either of us anywhere. I don't know how you end up feeling when we fight, but I feel *worthless!*" She pushed her hand through the air abruptly for emphasis. "And I won't stand for it any more. I am a daughter of God, and a darn good wife, and I will not allow you to treat me as anything less."

Emily felt proud of her assertiveness and the way it left Ryan silently stunned. She was surprised at the next thought that entered her mind, but when it didn't go away, she added with quiet vehemence, "Stop and think about it, Ryan. Listen to yourself more closely, and you might figure out why I nearly accepted Michael Hamilton's offer. You wouldn't have been eating chicken divan for dinner tonight if I were in Australia."

Emily turned and walked back to the dishes, feeling triumph in the argument for the first time ever. Ryan said nothing the remainder of the evening, until she crawled into bed and he uttered a quiet, "Dinner was nice, Emily. It's my favorite."

"I know," she stated and kissed him quickly on the lips. "Good-night," she added and turned over to go to sleep, feeling better about herself than she had since Michael told her she looked like a million bucks.

The next morning Ryan went quietly to work, and Emily spent the day in good spirits. At dinner, she stared at her husband in disbelief. He had come home thoughtful and distant, but in a positive way that didn't leave her feeling excluded. He complimented her on the Hamburger Helper he was eating, then said to Allison, "I've been thinking that maybe this summer we ought to take a vacation; just go somewhere and see something we've never seen before. What would you think of that?"

"Oh, could we?" Allison beamed. "I want to go to the Grand Canyon. Laurie says it's so enormous you just can't believe it."

"The Grand Canyon sounds nice. What do you think, Emily?"

"Can we afford it?"

"I've been putting a little away. I think it would be a worthy investment."

Emily had no idea there was money put away anywhere, but she wasn't concerned about her ignorance in that moment. She just smiled at him. "I think it sounds wonderful."

"Good," he concluded. "Maybe we can make plans during family home evening next week. I'll find out when my vacation is scheduled."

Emily continued to eat, wondering why she was being so blessed. When they had held infrequent home evenings in the past, Ryan had either declined joining or been grudgingly involved. Now he was suggesting they have one, and actually promoting a family vacation—something they had never done.

The surprises continued when Emily went to the bedroom after the children were put to bed and the dishes done. In the center of the bed was a sack, and a card in a pink envelope bearing her name. Ryan came in to look over her shoulder as she opened it.

"I had an urge to buy you something," he said, "so I stopped at the mall on my way home. That's why I was late. I had trouble finding just the right thing."

Emily smiled as she read the card. It was more funny than sentimental, but it clearly said that he appreciated her.

"What were the requirements for just the right thing?" she asked slyly while she picked up the sack and began to open it.

"It's kind of a . . . truce." He sprawled himself over the bed, leaning on his elbows to watch her, eager anticipation in his eyes.

Emily realized it was a T-shirt and smiled as she lifted it out, wondering what the significance might be. She didn't know what she'd expected, but holding it up, she felt touched in a way words could not express.

"I found it at the Missionary Emporium," he announced in reference to the flag covering the front, with the bold red word above it: *Australia.*

"I love it." Emily grinned, then she held it against her and laughed. "I just love it!" She bounced onto the bed and hugged him. "Thank you, Ryan. It's the perfect truce."

He laughed and hugged her tightly, then his expression sobered.

"Emily, I've been thinking a lot about what's been going on here, and . . . what you said last night. I can see there is a great deal I've been neglecting. I want to make some changes, and . . ."

Emily saw moisture gather in his eyes and her heart swelled with unspeakable joy, even before she realized what he was going to say.

"Emily, I think maybe you were right about . . . well, I'm not excited about it, but I think that maybe some counseling would be good for us."

Emily couldn't believe it. "Oh, Ryan." She touched his face. "I'm so grateful to be here . . . with you . . . now."

Tears squeezed out the corners of his eyes. She couldn't recall ever seeing him cry before, except during his father's funeral.

"And one other thing," he said, as if he had a mental list of requirements to check off. "Last Sunday in priesthood meeting, they mentioned a temple preparation class." Emily held her breath. "I think I'd like to go."

She could only hold him, her eyes squeezed shut while her mind filled with a silent prayer of inexpressible gratitude. Her life was rich and full.

They made love with a candle burning, and Emily's joy was complete. For the first time in years she felt a full unity with her husband, and was reminded of the scriptural description of marriage. They were truly one in all things.

Emily prepared the finest breakfast she'd made in weeks. While she watched Ryan eat it, her joy only deepened. She was falling in love with him again. Just to look at him she felt fluttery inside, and she found she didn't want him to leave.

"What are you looking at?" he grinned.

"You," she answered as if it were perfectly normal. Ryan reached over the table and kissed her in a way that brought memories of their intimacies rushing back. Emily giggled and rubbed the goosebumps from her arms. Ryan winked at her and settled back to his breakfast as she forced herself away to begin washing dishes. She stopped to turn on the little cassette player on the shelf above the sink, then started to dance while she wiped off the counter and put the pans in the sink to soak. Ryan brought his dishes to the sink and stopped to watch her with a dubious grin.

"You're a strange woman, Mrs. Hall."

"I know, but you love me anyway."

He went into the bathroom to brush his teeth and Emily followed, recalling something she wanted to ask him before he left. "Amee's birthday is Sunday," she said.

"I remembered." He put toothpaste on the brush. "You showed me that little doll you bought her. I thought I'd pick up something else, maybe today on my lunch hour."

"She's only two. I doubt she'll notice much what she gets, but I wondered if we could all go out for ice cream or something tomorrow, since we can't on Sunday. Allison would enjoy that, even if Amee doesn't appreciate it. What do you think?"

Ryan held up his finger to indicate that she should wait until he rinsed his mouth. "I told Lee I'd help the Simpkins move tomorrow. Elders quorum project."

Emily smiled. It only verified the changes in him. "Well, maybe afterward."

"How about tonight?" he suggested. "I don't think I'll have to work later than five. We'll make an evening of it."

"All right," Emily grinned. "I'll see if Penny is busy. Maybe if she watched Alexa we could enjoy it more."

"Sounds good." He kissed her, tasting like toothpaste. Emily went to answer Alexa's cries from the bedroom as Ryan left for work.

Penny had one of those "I don't want to be at home" days, and loitered around Emily while she ambitiously cleaned her house and caught up the laundry. Her new T-shirt started a conversation about the incredible changes in Ryan. Penny had to admit that Emily had been right. She concluded that the entire thing was miraculous.

Mid-afternoon, Ryan called.

"Is something wrong?" Emily asked, fearing he'd have to work late.

"Oh, no," he chuckled. "I just called to tell you how much I love you. I'll be early. Give the girls a hug for me."

"I'll do that," Emily replied dreamily and hung up the phone.

Penny went home when the children returned from school, then came back to get the baby at five o'clock. At six, when her own family was fed, she returned to Emily's house to find them still waiting and Allison getting impatient for her father to come home.

"He'll be here any minute," Emily assured her, then absently went to answer the phone while Penny got Amee off the kitchen counter where she was exploring the butter dish.

"Hello," Emily said, nodding gratefully toward Penny. "Yes, this is Mrs. Hall."

Emily's heart began to pound as a voice on the other end said in clipped tones, "This is the Orem City Police Department. Your husband has been in an accident. He is on his way to Utah Valley Regional Medical Center to assess the extent of his injuries. We would appreciate it if you could get there as quickly as possible."

Once Emily found her voice, she quickly said, "Thank you," and slammed down the receiver so carelessly that it slipped and fell to the floor. Emily ignored it and grabbed her purse, fumbling impatiently for her keys with trembling hands, breathing sharply.

"What is it?" Penny asked, replacing the phone. "What's happened?"

"Ryan's been in an accident," Emily barely managed to say.

"Good heavens!" Penny gasped, her eyes wide.

"I'm going to the hospital. I . . . I don't know how long I'll be." She finally found the keys. "Will you—"

"Yes," Penny insisted, "everything will be fine. Hurry up."

Emily turned to Allison, who stared in disbelief. She could hardly console her daughter when the fear she felt within told her she had no idea what to expect. Despite her sense of urgency, Emily took a moment to embrace Allison and touch her face. It was the best reassurance she could offer.

All the way to the hospital, Emily asked herself questions without answers. Why had the Orem police called to tell her he was going to the hospital in Provo? Could it be because Orem's hospital wasn't equipped to handle serious injuries? This made her heart pound faster. She thought of all the changes in their lives and wondered why something like this had to happen now. She had images of Ryan spending the rest of his life paralyzed, or . . . She couldn't think of that. She had to be positive. He would be all right. The Lord would not have helped them come so far to have something like this happen now!

Emily parked the car and ran through the two sets of

automatic glass doors of the emergency room. She rushed to the desk.

"I was told my husband is here. Ryan Hall."

"Just a minute." The nurse turned to another and spoke quietly before reporting. "There is a thirty-three year old male en route. If you were called, it's likely him. If you'll just wait a minute, or . . ." An ambulance pulled up on the other side of those glass doors. "That's it."

Suddenly all was chaos. Emily was barely aware of the medical team rushing toward the door as paramedics wheeled a gurney in, meeting somewhere near where she stood and moving on through another set of doors with perfect synchronization, relaying information back and forth, barking orders, and leaving Emily with a nightmarish image of her husband, lying motionless in the midst of it, battered and bloody. For a moment she just stood there and absorbed the quiet bustle of activity. She turned helplessly to look around her and saw the nurse approaching.

"If you'd like to come with me, Mrs. Hall, you can wait in here where it's—"

The paramedic who had driven the ambulance came back through those doors with the empty gurney, and Emily put up a hand toward the nurse.

"Excuse me," she said. The paramedic slowed his pace and gave her a kind expression. She wondered how often his job called for patronizing concerned relatives. "That was my husband you just brought in, and . . ." She walked beside him. "Could you tell me . . . I mean . . ."

They went through the automatic glass doors where he paused near the back of the open ambulance, speaking with measured, informative words. "He was hit broadside. They figure the other driver was drunk. He was wearing a seat belt, but he was hit pretty hard. It took the extrication team quite a while to get him out of the car. I'm afraid I can't tell you much more than that."

"And the other driver?" she asked in concern.

"She was dead when we got to her," he reported. "It seems she ran a red light; must have been going pretty fast. Sorry I can't tell you more."

"Thank you," she said quietly and walked back inside to find the nurse, who was busy again behind the counter. She looked up to see Emily and guided her to a place where she could wait.

"Is there anything I can get you?" she asked gently. Emily shook her head, wondering if everyone was being so nice to her because they knew it was bad.

An overpowering weakness forced her head back against the wall as she replayed the scenario in her mind. She wondered why she was so calm, when everything inside of her wanted to scream and tear her way into that room so she could somehow give him her life's breath. She turned naturally to prayer, but the numbness engulfing her made even that feel disjointed and obscure.

Horrid images flashed through her mind of the scene described by the paramedic. She closed her eyes to be free of it and could only see Ryan being wheeled past her. The evidence told her that this was much worse than she had expected. The fear was indescribable.

Emily expected to wait. Emergency rooms had a reputation for that. But always before it had been for stitches or a broken bone. Sitting here now was like being on the edge between life and death. But it hardly seemed more than a few minutes before Emily looked up at the doctor standing above her.

"Mrs. Hall?" She came to her feet unsteadily, but he urged her back to the chair with a hand on her arm while he took the seat beside her.

"I'm sorry," he said quietly. "The damage was too extensive. There was nothing we could do." Beyond that, Emily only heard distant mumblings; something about arrangements for the body and getting some information.

"I'm sorry?" she heard herself say.

"I asked if there is someone we can call for you or—"

"No, thank you," she said, "I'll be fine." As soon as he offered some words of compassion and walked away, Emily wondered why she had said that. She couldn't begin to think how she was even going to get to the car, let alone handle whatever she was supposed to take care of before she left.

That same nurse approached, and Emily felt some relief. At least they weren't going to leave her alone. But coming right behind her were faces that soothed like a balm to her soul. Bishop Wright and his wife, Launa, sat on either side of her, each taking a hand.

"How is he?" Launa asked gently. Emily looked up at her, disoriented and distraught. Launa added carefully, "Penny called us. We figured you could use some company. Is it bad?"

Emily turned to the bishop, as if doing so might give her strength. It seemed forever before she mustered up the courage to say it.

"He's dead."

Emily was barely aware of the sharp glance that passed between the two, and the gentle arms that came around her. Her keenest awareness was the reality that voicing those words brought back to her. The emotion came and she crumbled into Launa's arms, oblivious to anything but the pain.

It wasn't until later that Emily realized the bishop had given the hospital all the information they needed after Launa found Emily's wallet in her purse. Bishop Wright identified the body and made arrangements with a mortuary. Launa drove Emily home while the bishop drove Emily's car. They didn't leave her until she was safe with Penny, who took over efficiently and helped Emily to bed, where she cried herself into exhausted oblivion.

Emily woke and knew it was late morning by the way the sun filled the room. Her first panicked thought was that she'd overslept and forgotten to get breakfast for Ryan before he . . .

A groan came from the depths of her and she curled around a pillow. Penny's hand on her shoulder brought her to some semblance of coherency, and she leaned back against the headboard. Looking down at herself, she realized she'd slept in pajama pants and the Australian shirt she'd been wearing yesterday.

"How are you?" Penny asked quietly. Emily could only shake her head and attempt to fight back tears that came from an endless source. Penny took her hand, seeming to know that the only thing really helpful was her silent presence.

"Is Allison . . ." Emily tried to ask, but her mouth felt like cotton. Penny provided a glass of water from the bedside table.

"She's playing with the babies. Bret and I told her. She cried a little, but I don't think it's hit her yet."

Emily nodded. "Has anyone told Ryan's mother?"

"Bishop Wright called her last night."

"Good. I'm glad I don't have to do *that*." Their eyes met. "Oh, Penny," she sobbed, "I can't believe it. I just . . . can't believe it."

Penny put her arms around her and let her cry. A few minutes later, Allison peered quietly through the door and Penny moved aside. Emily opened her arms and Allison flew to take refuge there. Penny left them alone to share their mutual grief.

CHAPTER ELEVEN

A NETWORK OF SUPPORT was quickly formed, with Penny at its head. She supervised the meals brought in, and the babysitters that periodically took the children out. She kept the house clean and spent every spare moment just being there, urging Emily to talk it out, to feel it and face it.

Emily was grateful to Penny for all of it, but mostly for the mediating she did between herself and Ryan's family, none of whom had ever believed she was good enough for him. Penny went with Emily to the mortuary and seemed to know exactly what to say and how to handle all the details. In the back of Emily's mind she was concerned about the money, wondering where she stood, hoping the life insurance would be sufficient. But all of that seemed irrelevant for the time being, and she tried not to think about it.

Through it all, Emily felt a deep gratitude for the many ward members, most of whom came and went silently, giving of themselves and their time to help where it was needed. While Emily mourned and put most of her conscious effort toward helping Allison deal with her father's death, she was aware of the food provided and the help with the children. But the team of women that came in to give the house a thorough cleaning was as much of an appreciated surprise as the team of men who came in to mow lawns, pulls weeds, clean out the garage, fix a leaky faucet, and repair a broken window.

All of this left Emily humbly grateful to her Father in

Heaven, despite her lack of understanding as to why it was happening at all. Her time in prayer was more abundant than ever before in her life, but still the reasons eluded her. It wasn't until the viewing that the answers began to jell.

She had expected that seeing her husband's body would be painful and disturbing. But there was a peacefulness about Ryan's appearance, and the signs of the accident had been well disguised. Courageously she touched him, and peace enveloped her with undeniable verity. There was only one reason Ryan had been killed: it was his time to go. His progress would continue on the other side.

In that moment, too, she felt an overwhelming gratitude for the events in her life and the guidance of the Spirit that had allowed Ryan to pass on in happiness and in a better gospel standing than he had enjoyed for years, rather than hardened and bitter because his wife had left him.

The funeral service added to Emily's peace, and gave her hope that she could face the uncertainty that lay ahead. She knew the adjustments in her life would not be easy, but she had to believe that somehow everything would be all right.

The morning after the funeral, Allison left with her grandmother who was returning to her home in Idaho. Allison would stay for a week and return with Ryan's brother and his family when they passed through on their way home to Arizona. Emily felt it was a good opportunity for her daughter, who barely knew Ryan's mother. And perhaps Allison could help buffer the shock for the rest of the family. Emily was concerned for Allison, but felt the diversion would be a good transition for them both. Summer vacation was too long, anyway.

Emily spent much of the morning at Penny's house, until she pulled one baby or another out of something at least a hundred times and recalled why she and Penny always visited at her house these days.

"I'll be over to check on you in a while," Penny called from the kitchen, where she was loading her dishwasher.

"I'll be fine. Take your time," Emily called back as she

herded the mischief out the back door. She ambled slowly up the walk toward home, trying to ignore her mounting dread. Looking at the house and yard, a recently familiar ache rose in her. Everything looked the same, but in her heart the emptiness cried out.

Emily calmly swallowed the emotion and sat on her front lawn to let the babies play in the fresh air. It quickly became too hot, so under much protest she took them inside for lunch and naps. The quiet of the house made her miss Allison. She glanced at the clock. Gone four and half hours, and she already ached for her daughter's company.

Needing a distraction, she went to the bedroom, perhaps hoping to find something to read or some mending that needed doing. But all she saw was evidence of Ryan. His computer with papers scattered about as if he'd used it last night. Trivial masculine items strewn over the dresser, his shoes in the corner, his pillow on the bed.

She went to the medicine chest in search of an emery board, but before she found it she came across Ryan's razor and shaving lotion. She opened the lotion and inhaled its fragrance, scolding herself for doing it when her senses were overwhelmed with vivid memories. As she set the bottle back on the shelf, she realized that a dab had stuck to her nose. Even after she washed it off, she could still smell a freshly-shaved Ryan. She slammed the medicine chest closed and went to the phone.

"Help," she said to Penny with a teary voice. "I can't stand being alone here. I'll come to your house and do your work if you'll come over here and tend my babies."

"My work is nearly finished," Penny insisted. "I'll be over in ten minutes."

The next morning Emily lounged around the house and played with her babies, wearing the freshly-laundered Australian shirt. She thought it funny how the article had become a comforting reminder of both Michael and Ryan, though the ironies could almost be unnerving if she stopped to think about it. Recalling that evening before Ryan died, the way he'd made

such a point of planning for the future and taking steps to rectify the problems, made Emily wonder if subconsciously his spirit
had known what was coming.

Penny continued to hover close by and help where needed.
Emily began to wonder how Penny's home and family were sur-
viving.

"It's good for them to learn to get along without me," Penny
insisted, handing Emily the mail. "There's a letter from
Michael." Penny sat to thumb through a magazine while Emily
opened it with trembling hands.

She had hardly thought of Michael through the drama of
these past days, but now that it was over and life had to be
faced, there was an undeniable comfort in knowing that he was
there. Unfolding the letter's pages, she wondered if he still
might hold a place in her future, though contemplating it too
deeply seemed impossible for the time being.

Eagerly she read:

My dearest Emily,

I was so glad to hear another good report from you. As
time passes, I have to admit that I share your peace in the
situation.

Emily felt tears well up, and Penny handed her a tissue as if
she were a programmed robot. Dabbing at her eyes, she
continued.

I am happy to report that I too am doing better. I did
something I should have done a long time ago. I went to
church. This might sound funny, Emily, but I realized the
reason I hadn't found anyone to replace you. Perhaps it's
because I hadn't looked in the right place. So, I went
like you suggested. And guess what? I met someone!

The irony hit Emily between the eyes. She wanted to pick

up the phone and call Australia this very minute to beg him not to get involved with anyone. Not now—not when there was a chance that one day she could be free to love him again. She might well have called if she'd had his phone number; but she convinced herself it was just as well. The bill would likely devastate her.

Carefully she swallowed and continued to read the letter. It was full of his intrigue with a woman named Jenny, who was twenty-eight and had a college degree in Australian history. She wrote children's books, and she was a Mormon.

Emily folded the letter carefully and went to the desk in the corner of the dining room to stuff it into a drawer. She distracted herself by digging out the file folder marked BILLS. An intangible fear crept over her as she idly thumbed through the imposing stack of papers. Her stomach churned as she recalled her argument with Ryan just a week ago.

With a sigh she sat down and pulled out the calculator. It was time she started applying her knowledge to find out exactly where she stood.

"What did the letter say?" Penny asked, coming behind her.

"Not much," was all she answered.

"Oh, you're not going to do that," Penny said with disgust, eyeing the stack of bills.

"No one else is going to do it." Emily opened a credit card statement and gasped. She'd seen the bill come each month but, at his request, had never opened it. He told her he used it to buy gas for the car so he could keep track. Of course she'd believed him. The balance was nearly a thousand dollars, with an appalling interest rate.

"I'll fix some lunch," Penny offered. But Emily lost all appetite as she dug through the files in search of receipts that might be evidence of exactly what that credit card had been used for.

It wasn't difficult to find the folder of neatly-filed receipts. At least he was organized. But the reality sickened her. While she had been struggling with a grocery budget and eating leftovers most days for lunch so they wouldn't be wasted, her husband had been eating out. She found evidence to account for nearly every day of every month, where he had apparently often paid for himself as well as someone else. He had occasionally mentioned the people at work that he shared lunch with, but she had assumed he meant grabbing a sandwich from the snack bar or a hot dog at Seven-Eleven—not going to expensive restaurants. She had offered to fix him lunches, but he was never interested. Emily was furious.

"If he weren't dead, I'd slap him silly!"

"Come again?" Penny leaned out of the kitchen.

"Never mind." Emily had almost forgotten she wasn't alone. Stuffing the receipts back out of sight, she went through the remainder of the bills.

The utilities were no surprise. Their house payment was the same as it had always been. She felt some peace to look at a recent statement and realize the equity they had built in ten years by paying a little extra here and there. That could help. There was a dentist's bill that was staggering; Ryan had needed a crown last winter, and Allison had some work done. They still owed the hospital money from the percentage the insurance hadn't paid on Alexa—or was it both babies? Emily doubted that Amee had been paid off before Alexa was born. The car Emily drove was paid for, but the one Ryan had been killed in had over three thousand dollars owing. She hoped the insurance was sufficient to cover that.

Insurance! Panic pressed Emily to find the life insurance policy, while she realized that since Ryan would no longer be working, the medical benefits for the family would cease. She prayed they would all stay safe and healthy. Recalling the episode at the hospital, Emily dreaded getting that bill and hoped their policy covered emergency care. Finally locating the life policy, Emily looked it over. A dreaded reality began to sink in.

No longer able to bear it alone, Emily went to the kitchen and handed the policy to Penny. "How would you interpret that?"

Penny looked it over and shook her head in disbelief. "I'd say you better start looking for a job."

Emily started to cry. "I can't, Penny. I can't leave my babies. They need me."

"Calm down." Penny reached across the bar and took her hand. "Getting upset won't help. You've got to think rationally."

"There's got to be another way. I've got to pray about it, and I've just got to believe there is another way."

"For now, you just take it one day at a time, and whatever happens, I'll be here." Emily sighed at Penny's assurance and wiped her tears. "Who knows?" Penny gave a teasing smile while she put two bologna sandwiches on plates and cut them in half. "Maybe Michael Hamilton will come back and. . . ."

She stopped when Emily scowled. "Did I say something wrong?"

"Let's just say that I think Michael's out of the picture."

"But you just got a letter from him and—"

"A letter to tell me that he met someone."

Penny rolled her eyes in disgust and pushed a plate across the counter.

"I'm not hungry," Emily insisted.

"Eat anyway. You're going to need your strength."

"I said I wasn't hungry."

"Shut up and mind your manners. I'm going to bless the food."

After lunch Penny announced, "I've got some errands to do. I'll be back in an hour. Why don't you take a nap or something while the babies are sleeping? You look tired."

"Good idea," Emily agreed and lay down on the couch as soon as Penny left. When she was almost asleep, a knock at the door startled her. She jumped up and smoothed her hair, hoping it was someone in the ward dropping by for a visit.

Emily opened the door to a woman she'd never seen before, and wondered at first if she was a new Avon lady. For a brief moment they just looked at each other while Emily absorbed her appearance. Dressed tastefully in expensive clothes, the woman was slightly heavy and likely in her mid-twenties. She had long, brightly painted nails, too much makeup, and her hair looked like it had just been styled professionally in the last twenty minutes. But when she smiled, her face was kind and sweetly pretty. In her hands she held a box.

"Mrs. Hall?" she asked guardedly.

"Yes."

"My name is Kathy Gibson. I worked with your husband for the last four years."

Emily didn't know whether to feel joyous or leery at the prospect of visiting with a stranger about her husband, who had been gone less than a week. But she politely opened the door further.

"Come in."

"Thank you." The woman stepped inside. "I hope I'm not intruding or anything."

"No." Emily motioned toward the couch. "Please sit down."

"I was at the funeral," she said gently, "but I didn't think that was an appropriate time to talk to you. I know this must be terribly difficult for you. All of us at work are having a tough time with it. I just can't imagine what you must be going through."

Emily wanted to say something, but she couldn't without making it evident that she was about to cry. So she just bit her lip and attempted to convey with her expression that she appreciated the sympathy.

"Anyway," Kathy Gibson continued, "I cleaned out his desk yesterday and found some things I thought you might like to have. There were some pictures and a few personal items." She offered the box and Emily took it with reluctance.

"Thank you." Emily placed her hands on it, knowing she couldn't possibly open it now without falling apart.

After a length of uncomfortable silence, Kathy spoke again.

"He really was a nice man, Mrs. Hall. We all miss him. He worked hard and we could all depend on him."

At first Emily found the words comforting, but as Kathy went on, something incongruous started filtering through.

"He was always so fun, full of laughs. And he liked to talk to anybody about their troubles. We could always count on him to listen. I know he helped me through some really difficult things I've had to face. Of course, he probably told you all about that. He spoke of you often, always telling me what a good relationship the two of you had, and how close you were. Every once in a while when I was having a bad day, he'd take me out to lunch and offer some words of encouragement."

Emily's heart began to pound and her throat went dry. If her discernment hadn't told her this woman was being genuine, she'd almost believe it was some kind of game. Were they talking about the same Ryan Hall? She wanted to ask some questions, but her voice became lost somewhere in a pool of hurt and confusion.

It was nearly a relief when Kathy Gibson spoke again. "And of course he was always a perfect gentleman. Even when we'd stay late or sit in the car and talk, he never once made me feel uncomfortable. Why, the very day he was killed he had stayed late to help me talk through a problem." Kathy stopped, apparently distressed by Emily's expression. She cleared her throat tensely. "Well, like I said, you probably knew all of that. I just wanted to tell you how much we're all going to miss him, and let you know that we're thinking of you."

Emily could only nod.

"Oh," Kathy added, "we all wanted to pitch in and get flowers or something, but we had this little conference and decided that flowers were pretty useless and you'd probably get too many of them anyway. But we thought maybe you could use a little extra cash to help you through." She reached into her expensive leather purse and pulled out an envelope.

Tears came to Emily's eyes. Even this painful surprise visit had brought the answer to a prayer.

"We all gave what we could." Kathy sounded a little choked up herself. "There's nearly three hundred dollars in there. We hope you can use it."

"Yes," Emily finally found her voice, "I'm sure we can. Thank you. Tell them all thank you . . . for me."

"Oh, and Ryan's last paycheck is in there, too."

Emily nodded gratefully, and Kathy Gibson came to her feet.

"Anyway, we want to wish you the best, and let you know that we're thinking of you. If there's anything we can do, let us know."

Emily wanted to ask if they could pitch in to pay off the credit card bill Ryan had chalked up, taking them all out to lunch and listening to their troubles. But she only said, "Thank you. We'll be fine."

Emily didn't know how long she stood leaning against the door after her visitor left. She tried desperately to reconcile what she'd just learned with the man she had known as her husband. When it all came together, she gritted her teeth and groaned with anguish, impulsively throwing the box across the room where it hit the wall. She heard glass break, and the contents spilled over the floor as tainted reminders of the reason she'd thrown it.

Amee began to cry, awakened by the unfamiliar sound. Emily groaned again and knelt to pick up the mess, knowing she couldn't set Amee free while it remained.

There were a couple of cassette tapes, partial packages of Certs and Tums, a pencil holder Allison had made in kindergarten, the pen his father had given him for high school graduation, and several chocolate kisses. Emily found the source of the broken glass as she turned over a picture frame to find the front cracked severely but still intact. At least she didn't have to vacuum up glass, but seeing the ugly crack over the five-by-seven print of their wedding portrait wrenched a heavy sob from her throat. The sobbing worsened as she found a handful of snapshots, mostly of the children at various ages. But to her surprise there were a couple of her, one from high school and another from their honeymoon.

Amee's cry became more demanding, and Emily stuffed the contents haphazardly into the box, barely able to see what she was doing through her tears.

"What is that?" Penny's voice startled her.

"It's the stuff from Ryan's desk at work," she mumbled tearfully. "Some woman brought it by while you were gone."

"Why is it all over the floor?"

"Because I threw it!" she nearly screamed.

Penny's eyes widened. "All right," she murmured as Emily shoved the box at her and went to get Amee.

"You cry, Mommy?" Amee muttered, touching the tears as Emily carried her to the front room. "Mommy cry?"

"Yes, Amee. Mommy cry." She set the child down to play and added to herself, "Does Mommy do anything else these days?"

"Might I ask," Penny said quietly, "why you threw the box?"

"Whether you do or not, I have every intention of telling you." Emily wiped her face dry with her fingers.

"Good." Penny leaned forward eagerly, and Emily repeated the essence of the visit.

"So," Emily concluded, "what would you make of that?"

"The money's nice."

"Yes, the money is nice. But it won't pay off that credit card that he used to help them think he was such a wonderful guy. I wonder if it's him they miss or his generosity with plastic money."

"I don't blame you for being upset," Penny said gently.

"You'd better believe I'm upset." She stood and began pacing with clenched fists. "I can't believe it. While I'm struggling here at home, eating leftovers, can't even afford a hot dog at Der Weinerschnitzel once a week, he's out to lunch—with a woman! The man comes home late on a regular basis, treats me like a door mat, ignores me, patronizes the children, lives in his own silent world, while at work he's full of laughs, always willing to listen." She raised her voice in mocking sarcasm. "Caring and encouraging. Ooooh! I wonder how many of those nights he came home late, he had been sitting in a car talking to Kathy Gibson, and then he . . . he . . ." The anger melted down to the pain at its source. "He came home and . . . ignored me, made me . . . made me . . . feel like I was *nothing!* Where was *my* encouragement?"

Emily drew a deep breath and continued. "She said he had stayed late to talk to her the day he was killed." She shook a finger at Penny. "He told me he'd be home early so we could go out together . . . as a family. He could have called. He shouldn't have been with her, for any reason. If he had come home when he was supposed to, he would not have been the one in that intersection."

Emily clenched her fists and looked toward the ceiling. "How could you do this to me, Ryan Hall? After all I gave you, how could you leave me to face this alone?" Her voice rose to a shout. "If you were still alive, I would kill you!"

Emily clamped a hand over her mouth and fell to her knees. Penny rushed to her with a protective embrace.

"Oh," Emily sobbed, "I can't believe I said that. What's wrong with me, Penny? How can I miss Ryan so much and be so angry at him?"

"He was changing, Emily," Penny soothed, "but he had a long way to go to rectify the mistakes he'd made. No one can blame you for feeling resentful, having to bear the brunt of those mistakes."

"What did he think he was doing?" Emily cried. "Did he really believe that spending time alone with another woman was so harmless?" Emily shook her head. "Listen to me. Didn't I do the same thing with Michael? Didn't I—"

"Hold it. Hold it." Penny took Emily's shoulders and forced her to look up. "Don't start judging yourself here until we lay out all of the facts. Yes, you did see Michael, and if you want to get technical, it probably wasn't the most proper thing. But you were the one being ignored and neglected, Emily. Ryan drove you away. And I know how ridiculously guilty you felt after you saw Michael, because I heard it from your own lips, several times. Now Ryan, on the other hand, chooses to spend time and money on another woman—time and money that should have been spent at home, with a wife who was always there for him, always trying to be the best for him.

"I realize I don't have the right to judge, but I'm going to say this anyway. I know for a fact that, despite all of your unhappiness, you would never have allowed yourself to get into a position with Michael where trouble could have started. But I wonder what Ryan might have done if you had treated him half as bad as he treated you. Did he think that his long talks with this woman would have ended there if he had felt lonely or hurt? The man was being stupid. He was married, and he was asking for trouble; trouble that would have come back to hurt you in one way or another."

Emily pressed her forehead into her hands. "Oh, Penny, it doesn't matter anyway. He's gone," she cried. "If he were here we could talk about it. He was changing. But sometimes I . . . I feel so . . . confused. When I think that just a few months ago I nearly left him . . ." She put a hand over her mouth and cried a full minute before she continued. "I . . . I just . . . want to die."

"But you didn't leave him, Emily. You did the right thing. You stayed." Penny lifted Emily's chin to look at her. "He died a happy man, Emily, because you loved him. Despite all his faults, you still loved him."

Emily cried helplessly until Amee nuzzled into her lap. "Mommy, you cry?" Emily laughed through her tears and held the child close.

While Emily gained control of her emotions, Penny contemplated the part Michael Hamilton might play in this drama. Despite what Emily had repeated from his last letter, she couldn't help wondering if his knowing of Ryan's death would make a difference.

"Emily," she said thoughtfully, "have you written to Michael? Don't you think he should know that—"

"No," Emily snapped. "If he's finally found someone, the last thing he needs is to be burdened with my troubles."

"It might make a difference if he knew."

Emily had to admit that the same thought had crossed her mind. But at this moment, however painful, she couldn't bring herself to intrude on whatever he might be finally making of a relationship. She'd hurt him so badly, not once, but twice. She just couldn't do it again.

"I'll write him one of these days," Emily said, if only so Penny would drop the matter. Then she carefully pushed thoughts of Michael away. There was enough pain without contemplating that her opportunity to be with him had come too late.

CHAPTER TWELVE

NOTHING MORE WAS SAID about Michael Hamilton. A letter came from him the following week and Emily stuffed it, unopened, in the drawer with the other. She was too absorbed in financial realities to even have the motivation to look at it. Ten unopened letters later, including something in a parchment envelope that could only be a printed announcement, Emily began to believe that life could not possibly get worse.

Penny's family left for a week to attend a family wedding in Montana. To Emily it seemed like the longest week in her life. By the time Penny returned, Emily doubted she could ever live without her.

At the first possible opportunity, Emily began to tally her problems to her friend over the phone. "All right," she said to Penny, "the life insurance covered the funeral expenses and the hospital bill from the accident. And I had enough to pay the bills for a month or so. Now the bills are all a month behind, and there is less than two hundred dollars left in the bank after I spent the bare minimum to get Allison ready for school. I'm afraid to spend the rest for fear of anything that might come up. Like the need to eat, perhaps."

"Maybe you should get some help from the Church. That's what they're there for, you know, to assist in times of need."

"Yes, I know. I've thought about it, and if it comes to that I will. But even if I did, it would only be temporary. I've got to face the reality of having to make a living, and it just breaks my heart to think of leaving the children."

"You can leave them with me," Penny offered, not for the first time. "My rates are good," she added, while Emily knew she would do it for nothing and not begrudge it.

"I know, Penny, and I appreciate it, but—"

"Yes, I know. It's hard no matter how you look at it. I wish I could do more."

"You've done so much already. I've just got to keep praying. Maybe I should fast."

"Wouldn't hurt," Penny muttered. "I mean, you're already nearly down to skin and bone these days. What's another day?"

"Oh, hush," Emily scolded. "I can't help it if I don't have an appetite."

"Speaking of appetite, how is Allison adjusting to school?"

"Not very well. I expected the first few days to be difficult, but it's been nearly three weeks now. Her teacher called me again yesterday. Same old thing. She's despondent, won't hardly do anything. Penny, I'm so worried about her. I just never dreamed all of this would affect her so badly."

"How does she act at home?"

"She's quiet, but she always was. I've tried to talk to her about it, but it's just like I told you before. She says she misses him and won't say anything else. If I could afford it, I'd take her in for some counseling before it gets any worse. I could probably use a little myself. As it is, I just have to hope she pulls out of it."

"Does her teacher seem concerned?"

"She's keeping an eye on Allison, and says she'll keep me informed. In the meantime she feels it's best not to give the problem too much attention, and hopefully it will pass. Sometimes I think if I had a way of giving her some compensation it would help, but I can't afford to take her anywhere or do anything. I can't even afford to get her a coat for winter, and she really needs another pair of jeans. Maybe that's where the savings will have to go. And she's invited to a birthday party a week from Saturday. You know, for Ashley. It's one of those 'you gotta be cool to be there' parties, and Allison's just sure that if she can't give the ultimate gift, what little social life she has left will be doomed. What can I do, Penny?"

"I don't know, but watch out. The mailman is coming up the street."

"Oh, great." Emily's voice reeked of sarcasm. "Just what I need—another overdue bill. Hold on." She set the phone down and stepped onto the porch to get the mail.

"Well?" Penny prodded after she came back to the phone.

"Nothing much. Just a shutoff notice from the power company. Emergency number one. Penny, I can't live like this. I've got to do something, but I just don't feel right about this job business. I've prayed about it, and I feel like I'm supposed to stay at home. What I need is a miracle."

"Emily," Penny said cautiously, "hit me if I'm being presumptuous, but even if Michael is going to marry someone else, do you think it's possible that you could, well . . . you know, get some help? He'd probably jump at the chance to help you. I did get the impression that he was rather fond of you, and you said he had an endless supply. I mean, Australian money does work here, doesn't it?"

Emily's admission followed a lengthy silence. "I must confess that it's crossed my mind. It just seems so . . . so . . . I don't know."

"Pray about it. You'll know what to do. What did he have to say when you told him what happened, anyway?"

"I haven't told him," she admitted.

"What?!" Penny's appalled shriek hurt Emily's ear. "What do you say in those letters? 'Hi, I'm fine. How are you?'"

"I haven't written to him. I suppose I should."

"Chances are he'll notice sooner or later. What has he said?"

"I don't know. I haven't opened the last few."

"Emily!"

Emily briefly put some distance between the receiver and her ear. "Oh, mind your own business," she half teased. "I'll write to him this week, I promise."

The sarcasm returned to her voice. "Oh, great. Call waiting. What a blessing. It's probably a bill collector. I'll call you back."

She pushed the button on the phone and lifted it again quickly. The conversation that followed made her wish that she didn't own a phone, though she doubted it would make any difference. At this rate, it would be turned off before the month was out.

As soon as she hung up, Emily dialed Penny's number again but there was no answer. She paced frantically, wondering how she was going to face *this*.

Alexa woke up and Emily quickly changed her diaper then tried Penny again. Still no answer. She immersed herself in some mending to try and keep her mind occupied, but she got little accomplished, wondering how long Penny would be gone. The minute Penny returned, Emily had her on the phone.

"I need you to come over here, Penny. You're not going to believe this unless I tell you to your face."

"Is it bad?"

"It's worse than bad."

Amee woke up and was taken to the potty. By the time Penny arrived, Emily had busied both babies with a bowlful of crackers that they were crumbling on the carpet as much as they were eating.

"All right, let's have it." Penny sank into her accustomed spot on the couch.

"Well, you know how I told you I was checking to see if I could get a second mortgage on the house to tide me over, at least until the babies got a little older."

"Yes."

"Well, that was a lawyer on the phone."

"A lawyer?" Penny squealed.

"Yes, a lawyer." Amazed at her own calmness, Emily wondered if she was becoming accustomed to despair. "He informed me that when this house was purchased, Ryan had his parents co-sign on the papers. I knew that. They have never once had to compensate. We've made every payment dutifully, and only paid late fees twice in ten years."

"All right," Penny urged the story along.

"Well, it seems that Ryan didn't bother to put my name on any of the papers. So, guess what? The house isn't mine. It belongs to his mother."

Penny bent her head forward but kept her eyes peeled on Emily, hoping this was a joke and that any second Emily's expression would betray it. But the hardened lines of concern only deepened around Emily's eyes as she continued. "Now you know as well as I do that Ryan's mother was never terribly fond of me. I don't know where she got her prejudice and I never cared, but I have a feeling this is not going to go well." Emily came to her feet. "I'm going to call her right now and get it over with."

Penny could only hear bits of Emily's side of the conversation, but she had a good idea of what had transpired when Emily slammed down the phone and huffed back to the couch.

"I can't believe it." Emily slammed her fists into the cushion, then stood again and began to pace. Amee acted afraid of her mother's mood, so Emily softened her voice and picked the child up to soothe her. "Do you know what she had the gall to say to me?"

"Do tell," Penny said with disgust.

"She told me that considering the way she knew I treated Ryan, I should be glad that she's going to let me live here at all."

Penny gasped. "The way you *what?*" she shrieked, then softened her voice when Amee acted frightened. "The way you treated Ryan?"

"That's what she said."

"All right, so she's a little off. But she is going to let you live here?"

"Oh, of course. And she's considering it a huge favor that she will graciously let us stay for twenty dollars a month less than the house payment would have been. Isn't that so kind of her? I just lost ten years of equity in my home, and she acts like she's doing me some big favor."

"Emily, it's a long shot, but Bret's brother is a lawyer. I'll call him and see if there's anything you can do."

"Well, that's something. I guess it can't hurt to try, but I have a feeling I don't stand a chance."

"You could just not pay the rent," Penny said brightly. "What's she going to do? Kick you out?"

"It wouldn't surprise me," Emily groaned, dashing Penny's attempt to lighten the mood.

Amee relaxed and wanted to get down. She began running back and forth from the front room to the dining room, coaxing Alexa to crawl and chase her. It was a common game that made the babies giggle, and Emily couldn't help smiling as she observed them.

"Hang in there, Emily," Penny said gently. "You know we all have a lot to be grateful for."

"Yes, I know."

"And they say it always gets darkest just before the light."

"Yes, I know that, too. But how much darker will it get first?" Emily said, unable to conceal the cynicism in her voice.

"The scriptures say that the Lord doesn't give us more than we can bear."

"Yes," Emily chuckled humorlessly, "but the Lord's opinion of what I can bear might be a lot different than mine. I know that from experience."

"Well, there's one bright spot. You used to tell me that you believed the Lord shows his love by the trials he sends. He really must love you, Emily." Penny's smile was partly teasing, but Emily had to admit she felt some peace in it.

From the other room they heard a familiar thud, followed by Amee's bawling. Emily rushed to get her. "I swear she does that a hundred times a day." The words caught in her throat as she saw little Amee's blood-covered face. "Penny!" she screamed. For a moment, she couldn't move.

As always, Penny calmly took over. She shook Emily gently. "It's all right. I'll get a towel."

Emily scooped Amee into her arms and was immediately

provided with a dishtowel that she used to find the source of the bleeding, a deep vertical cut through the child's eyebrow. Penny handed Emily a wet washcloth to use as a compress and said calmly, "I've got your purse, and I left a note for Allison to go to my house and stay there when she gets home. Heather will be there. I'll put Alexa in her car seat. You hold Amee. I'll drive."

As she had been hundreds of times before, Emily was grateful for Penny's help, and for her ability to remain in control. She could swear that Penny's presence in her life had been a foreordained gift from heaven. Her friend was just too good to be true.

As they drove toward the Orem hospital, Emily murmured, "I'm glad we don't have to go to Utah Valley Hospital. I don't think I could stand the memories." She looked down at the weeping Amee in her arms and the blood spattered over her pink shirt. Emily tried not to cry, but she couldn't hold it back. She wondered if anyone on this earth cried as much as she did.

"You all right?" Penny asked.

"A little shaky, but I'll be fine." She looked over at Penny severely. "What did you say about it getting darkest just before the light? How much darker can it get?"

After a considerable wait at the hospital, Penny volunteered to shepherd Amee through the stitches while Emily stayed in the waiting room with Alexa. Emily could hear Amee screaming and was glad she didn't have to be there. She probably would have passed out.

Now that she felt certain Amee would be all right, a fresh reality seeped in. She began to hear the question drum over and over in her mind: *How am I going to pay for this?* She wondered if they should have gone to a doctor's office instead, but it was too late to worry about that. They'd had no way of knowing how serious it was. There was no insurance, and there was no money except what she had in the bank; and that already had a long list of possible uses. She could only pray that somehow all of this would come together, and decided in that moment to begin a fast. She needed it desperately. Perhaps it would help her come to some kind of decision.

Amee slept in Emily's arms through the short drive home. Allison came running out of Penny's house to meet them.

"What happened?" she asked with a panic that made Emily's heart ache. She knew Allison was thinking of the night Ryan had been killed.

"Amee just hit her head. She's going to be fine. How are you?"

"I'm all right."

"School go okay?" Emily walked into the house to put Amee in her bed while Allison followed, staring curiously at the stitches.

"Yeah," Allison answered indifferently.

"Any problems?"

"No."

Emily laid Amee down and gave Allison a searching gaze, but it went unnoticed.

"I think I'll do my homework," Allison said and went to her room.

Emily sighed and went to find Penny, who had put Alexa into the high chair with a pile of Cheerios and was cleaning the blood off the floor.

"Would you mind staying here while I go pick up Amee's prescription and get a couple of things at the store?"

"No problem," Penny said easily. "Do you need any money?"

"As if you have so much to give."

"I can't pay your bills, but I have a ten in my purse I won't miss too badly."

"Thanks, Penny, but I'll just stop and get a little out of the bank. I've got to pay that power bill anyway. I guess I'm going to have to break down and find the cloth diapers I used for Allison. I can't keep buying disposables. Doesn't that sound fun? I get to wash diapers now, too."

"I'll help you." Penny smiled. "And if you won't hit me, I'll get you an appointment with the bishop so you can get some food in the house. It looks like Old Mother Hubbard lives here."

"Maybe she does." Emily couldn't help smiling. Perhaps that was the answer, at least for now. They wouldn't starve, and there could be worse things than washing diapers. At least Amee was potty-trained now. That would make half as many diapers as a month ago.

"What were you going to fix for dinner?" Penny called as Emily headed for the door. "I'll get it started."

"See if I have another box of macaroni and cheese. I'll hurry."

The bank drive-through had long lines, so Emily decided to go inside. She waited in line only a few minutes but still felt nervous. Maybe it was the lack of money in her account that put her on edge. The teller counted out the precious cash and passed over a receipt.

"Thank you," Emily said and turned to leave. But the computer-printed numbers she read turned her back immediately.

"Excuse me, but there must be a mistake. This says I have over a thousand dollars, and on my last statement it was only—"

"Just a minute." The teller tapped keys and waited for something to appear on the screen. "There was a deposit made on September sixth. A thousand dollars."

Emily chuckled dubiously. "You don't understand. Nobody put that money in my account. It must belong somewhere else. Somebody must be missing a thousand dollars. It's a mistake."

"Is there a problem?" A woman who was apparently a supervisor stopped to ask. The teller briefly explained, and the woman concentrated on the screen for a long minute. "No," she stated, "there's no mistake. I remember that deposit."

"How could you remember a deposit?" Emily chuckled again in disbelief. "It was over a week ago. You've probably seen thousands of deposits."

"But only one that came from. . . ." She looked at the teller. "Where was it? New Zealand or—"

"Australia," interjected the teller in the next booth. "I took the stamps home to my son. He loved the one with the aborigines on it." Emily's mouth went dry. She didn't know whether to laugh or cry.

"And the deposit slip looked well worn," the supervisor added. "Does that help?" she asked politely.

"It certainly does," Emily said tersely. "Thank you." She walked away, commenting to the teller on the way out, "I've got a lot of Australian stamps you can have," then adding under her breath, "And the letters attached to them, as well."

Emily sat in the car for at least five minutes before she remembered where Michael had gotten that deposit slip. For a moment, pride made her angry—at herself for being stupid enough to give it to him, and at him for thinking a thousand dollars could take away her grief. Then she realized that he wasn't aware of the grief, and she had to admit that it was an answer to her prayers. Was Michael Hamilton acting as an instrument in God's hands to care for her from a distance?

The money would definitely help, but she decided that for now she would pretend it wasn't there. She wouldn't use it until she absolutely had to. Perhaps it would cover Amee's bill for the stitches and keep the utilities going for a while. Knowing it was there added a measure of peace. Still, a thousand dollars wouldn't even cover a month's living expenses. It helped, but it didn't alleviate the problem by any means.

Emily sighed and went to the power company, but found it closed. She didn't want to put cash in the night payment box, so she decided to pay it tomorrow. After picking up Amee's prescription, she went to the grocery store and carefully bought what they needed to barely get by for another day or two. She gazed longingly at the disposable diapers, but passed them by.

At the check-out the bill was higher than she'd expected; she was glad she hadn't paid the power bill or she wouldn't have had the money to cover the groceries. She would have to get more out of the bank in the morning. She wondered if they could find a used coat at D.I. that Allison wouldn't be mortified to wear. And selfishly, she hoped that Allison would get a cold or something so she couldn't go to that stupid birthday party, and they wouldn't need to get a gift. She canceled the wish for a virus, recalling that such a thing required luxuries like tissues and cough medicine, not to mention the added stress. *Please,* she prayed in her mind, *at least keep us healthy.*

Emily walked in the house and put her purchases on the counter. Penny was sitting at the bar grinning.

"What's so funny?" Emily scowled.

"Well, I had a great time while you were gone." Emily put away groceries while Penny talked. "I had just put the water on to boil for the macaroni when the doorbell rang. It was Launa Wright with a casserole and a plate of cookies." Emily stopped with her arm in the fridge. "Casserole's in the oven. She said she had made a big one for her family, and figured what little you and the girls would eat wouldn't amount to anything."

Emily reminded herself that she was fasting, but she could heat some up tomorrow for her lunch. She briefly squeezed her eyes shut with a grateful sigh. Just to know that someone was thinking about her helped. That made two blessings today.

"And then," Penny announced triumphantly, "Susan stopped by, wondering if you could by chance use these." Penny produced a bag of disposable diapers and Emily gasped. "She said she only used one or two out of the bag before she realized they were too small for Jamie, and they'd been sitting there for weeks while she wondered what to do with them. Then, just a while ago, it came to her that you have a baby this size." Emily sat down and started to cry. "I'd say that's a pretty good indication there's light somewhere."

"Yes," Emily agreed, dabbing at her tears, "even if I only make it one day at a time, I suppose I'll make it. I just hope I can survive the stress."

"If you think you can make it a while on your own, I'd better go fix my family some macaroni and cheese."

"Bret hates macaroni and cheese."

"I know, but it'll keep him humble."

"As always, thank you, Penny. Sometimes that phrase sounds like a broken record. I'm always thanking you for something."

"It's my pleasure," Penny smiled. Then she was gone.

Allison enjoyed the casserole and cookies, but she mentioned the upcoming birthday party three times before she finally went to bed. Emily could only say they would do the best they could. She hadn't kept Allison ignorant of the situation they were in, but it was difficult for a nine-year-old to comprehend the full spectrum of how much money it took to run a household. She thought of that thousand dollars and wished it could be used for something besides bills. Something frivolous—like Christmas for her children.

Amee fussed through the evening and into the night, finally falling asleep around two. Emily woke to get Allison off to school, feeling groggy and unenthusiastic. She put on her Australian shirt and felt dismayed to see that it was beginning to look worn. Had she used it so much?

During the time Emily normally showered, Amee was fussing more than usual over her breakfast, and Allison was running too late to help. With Allison finally off to school, Emily looked around and wondered how the house had gotten to look so bad since yesterday afternoon when it had been in fairly decent condition. The few dishes from dinner and breakfast were left on the counter, along with baby bottles and some Kool-Aid that had spilled. Toys were scattered everywhere, and the general clutter looked worse than usual.

Emily went into the bathroom to brush her teeth and hair, deciding she'd have to wait until nap time for a shower. She was disgusted by how dirty the bathroom looked, and decided that cleaning it might at least give her a sense of accomplishment that would urge her through the rest of the house. She put bowl cleaner in the toilet, then squirted what was left of the bathroom cleaner into the tub and began scrubbing. Amee started to cry, and she rinsed off her hands to go check on her. A few story books solved the problem, and Alexa played contentedly with some big Legos that had been Allison's.

Emily returned to the bathroom to finish her scrubbing, and was nearly ready to rinse the tub when the phone rang. She sighed and went to answer it, then wished she hadn't when Ryan's mother asked sweetly how she was doing. Mrs. Hall then proceeded to inform Emily that the rent was due. Emily had no strength to protest, but she called Penny the minute Ryan's mother decided she couldn't afford these long distance calls.

"I can't take this, Penny," Emily insisted. "I know you must be sick of me grumbling all the time. Laman and Lemuel didn't murmur any more than I do, but honestly, if I couldn't pour my heart out to you, I'd go insane."

"Just keep pouring," Penny urged. Alexa started to fuss and Emily put her in the highchair with some measuring cups and a cracker. "That's what I'm here for," Penny continued. "Besides, maybe one day you'll be rich, and I'll have something horrible happen to me, and you can return the favor."

"Huh!" Emily exclaimed doubtfully. "Even if I were in a position to help you, I could never repay what you've done for me."

"You're not supposed to repay it, you're supposed to pass it on. Someday you'll have more to give. Right now you're the one who is allowing others the opportunity to be blessed by giving."

"You always make it sound so right, so easy." Emily looked out the window and noticed the leaves on the maple tree were beginning to change color. The evidence of summer's passing brought an inexplicable sadness to her heart.

"By the way, how's Amee?"

"Doing better. She's a little whiny at times, but not as bad as I expected. I just hope she . . . oh, great." Her voice turned sarcastic. "Call waiting. I suppose I'd better check it."

"Go ahead. I've got laundry to put in. Talk to you later."

Emily pushed down the button and let it up again.

"Mrs. Hall?"

"Yes."

"This is Brian Millner. Penny called me last night and told me a little about your situation."

"Yes," Emily responded, already feeling doom over this.

Amee started to fuss, and Emily sat her at the bar with a half-empty carton of yogurt.

"Well, I must say it doesn't look good." He proceeded with a long legal explanation of why Emily had no rights to the house since her name wasn't on any of the papers associated with it. Despite the changes Ryan had begun to make before his death, there were moments like this when she felt bitterness for the circumstances that had left her to face such things.

Emily listened quietly, occasionally making a noise to indicate she had heard. A knock came at the door, but she knew she couldn't interrupt this conversation. Stretching the cord to its limit, she pulled the door open absently. The lawyer's words disappeared somewhere in the distance.

Michael Hamilton was standing on her porch.

CHAPTER THIRTEEN

EMILY HASTILY SURVEYED MICHAEL from head to toe, if only to convince herself that she wasn't hallucinating. His hands were deep in the pockets of well-worn jeans, topped by a faded BYU sweatshirt. His hair was slightly longer than when she'd seen him last, combed back off his face in the usual manner and hanging over the top of his collar. On his feet were slip-on canvas shoes and no socks. He looked so natural standing there, that for a moment she was reminded of how it felt to have him drop by her apartment to see if she wanted to go to a movie.

Emily couldn't begin to know how to react. She was almost grateful to be on the phone so she could think about it a minute. After staring at his expectant face for a long moment, she motioned him inside and closed the door. Turning away from him to attempt to concentrate on the phone call, she caught the picture of her messy house and wanted to die of embarrassment. Her heart was pounding, but she forced her mind to listen to the voice on the other end of the phone.

"I'm sorry, Mrs. Hall. It seems there's little to be done. My suggestion would be to perhaps rent another home and avoid any run-in. I've seen families get pretty heated over such things."

"I'll have to think about that," she said, wishing Michael couldn't overhear, while her mind played through the impossibility of the lawyer's suggestion. She couldn't possibly come up with the deposits necessary to move, even if she could find a place. And living here in this ward, with Penny next door, was the only thing helping her through this.

"I'm truly sorry," he said again.

"Well, if there's nothing we can do, we'll just have to live with it." Emily felt tears come and hurriedly wiped them away. With her back to Michael, she almost forgot he was there. Why now? Of all the lousy timing!

"If there is anything else I can do, Mrs. Hall," he offered, "just let Penny know, and I'll be glad to help."

"Thank you," she said with sincerity. "And thank you for taking the time to call."

Michael leaned against the door and waited patiently for Emily to finish on the phone. After all the unanswered letters, it was a relief just to see her alive. He'd nearly called her, but felt strongly that he should just come. The long flight over had given him time to consider all the worst possible scenarios.

He was relieved to see that she looked all right, though a little thinner, and the weariness in her eyes had deepened. Her last letter had been so bright and optimistic. The slight uneasiness he felt became more tangible when she discreetly wiped away tears.

Emily hung up the phone and took a moment to gather her composure. She turned to look at Michael and couldn't think of anything to say. So she just stood there, wishing she had taken a shower, that she wasn't wearing sweat pants, that her house was clean, that he wasn't getting married. Or had he already? The last thought sent her into a frenzy of picking up toys. She had to do something, anything, to keep her from feeling what his presence did to her. She was surprised when he bent down to help her. She looked up to meet his eyes and found his face only inches away. She was glad she'd at least brushed her teeth. Their eyes met and she heard pulsebeats in her ears.

"I see you were expecting me." He smiled slyly and nodded toward her shirt. Emily glanced down at the fading Australian flag. The irony tore at her, and she just kept picking up toys.

"I'm glad I heard you talking on the phone. I realize you've lost the ability to write. It's a relief to know you can still talk."

Emily glared at him. Michael couldn't quite figure what was happening here. He wondered if she was somehow angry with him, but he hoped some small talk would ease the tension.

"I like the shirt. Where did you get it?"

After a long silence, Emily figured she had better find the voice to answer him, however difficult.

"Ryan gave it to me." Her voice shook slightly. "It was a . . . a truce offering."

"How quaint," Michael said. He could plainly see that she was upset, and credited it to the phone call. Figuring they weren't going to be able to even discuss the weather until they got past that, Michael asked outright, "Who was on the phone, Emily?"

She wanted to tell him it was none of his business, but she knew from vast experience that there was no evading Michael Hamilton when he wanted the answer to a question. "It was a lawyer, if you must know."

"A lawyer?" He was genuinely surprised. He wondered if things had gone sour again between her and Ryan, but he didn't dare ask.

"What are you doing here, anyway?" she insisted, putting toys into their proper order in the corner while Michael finished picking up the Legos.

"I came to see if you were still alive."

Emily squeezed her eyes shut briefly, not liking the way he'd put that. In fact, part of her had died.

She looked around with some relief at seeing the front room picked up. "Look at that," she said lightly. "The carpet is still there."

"Do you lose it often?" He smiled and stood, returning his hands to his pockets.

"Constantly," she said too seriously and stood to face him. "You could have called."

"I almost did, but I thought dropping by would be more effective."

"You traveled thousands of miles just to drop by?"

"Yeah." He shrugged his shoulders.

Emily thought it was probably to make certain she'd gotten his wedding announcement. She looked to see if he was wearing a ring, but his hand was in his pocket.

"Well, as you can see, I'm alive."

"Good. Do you think it would be tacky of me to take you and your husband out to dinner? I've got some news I'd like to share with both of you."

Emily's eyes grew distant as his words threw her mind into a series of disjointed memories.

"Are you all right?" Michael waved a hand in front of her face and she looked up at him, bewildered and distraught.

"Well?" he insisted.

Emily tried to recall what he'd asked her. She thought how different it would have been if Ryan were alive. Perhaps then, Michael's news of getting married would have allowed everything to settle neatly. As it was, she couldn't even think how to respond.

"Emily," he chuckled, though his brows furrowed in concern.

"Under the circumstances," she finally stated, "that won't be possible."

"What circumstances?" he asked. She didn't answer.

"Why didn't you answer my letters, Emily?"

"I've been busy. I haven't got time for pen pals these days."

"Is that what I am?" He tried not to sound insulted.

"Baby eat bogut," Amee called from the kitchen. Emily panicked. She'd almost forgotten she had children. "Mommy! Baby eat bogut."

"Oh, Amee!" Emily scolded. "You mustn't feed the baby yogurt."

Michael followed Emily, whether she wanted him to or not. He smiled at the curly-headed baby in the high chair, with pink yogurt finger-painted over the tray, up to her elbows, all over her shirt and face, and traces of it in her hair. Emily picked

Amee up and held her over the sink to wash her hands and face. She set her down and dried her with a towel, leaning over to point a finger at her. "Now, don't feed the baby yogurt any more."

Amee disregarded her mother's admonition and looked up at the man standing above them. "Who's 'at?" Amee questioned.

Emily looked up, startled to find him so close. "That's Michael," she said tersely.

"Mikow," Amee said and Michael grinned.

"She looks like Ryan," Michael said lightly. "What happened to her forehead?"

"She fell yesterday. I spent hours at the hospital." Emily turned her attention to the baby and sighed. "Alexa, no one on earth could manage to get so little yogurt spread so far."

Michael chuckled.

"Oh, shut up," she growled at him. "I've got to bathe her. Do something productive. Read Amee a story or something."

Michael picked Amee up and smiled at her while he spoke casually to Emily. "Do you think your husband will come home and beat me up?"

Emily glared at him. "I seriously doubt it."

"Well, he is bigger than I am."

Emily ignored him and gingerly carried Alexa at arm's length to the bathroom. She had no choice but to set her on the floor when she realized the tub wasn't rinsed. It was quickly ready for the bath and Emily peeled the baby down, threw the dirty clothes into a laundry basket that was nearly full, and let the baby play while she finished cleaning the toilet and gathered the dirty towels. She was glad Michael hadn't asked to use the bathroom before she'd had a chance to get there first.

While she bathed Alexa, the reality struck her. Michael Hamilton was in the other room! Was he the answer to her prayers? Was it possible, even if he was committed elsewhere, that he could at least help her financially—more than he already had? She wouldn't have considered such a thought if she didn't know for a fact that his family was one of the wealthiest in

Australia. The money it would take to save her wouldn't amount to a drop in the bucket for a man with his bankroll. It was the asking that could be embarrassing. Perhaps this was a lesson in humility, she told herself. Lesson or not, the flood of emotions was too much to bear. She began to cry as she lathered the baby's hair, noting the baby shampoo was almost gone. At this moment she would feel greatly blessed to have the monthly allowance she had struggled to get by with through her years of married life.

"What did the lawyer say that's got you so upset?" Michael asked from behind, startling her.

"Why don't you mind your own business?" She wiped frantically at her tears with wet hands. "Go read Amee another story or something."

"She fell asleep. I put her in the bed that looked most likely."

Emily sighed. She felt certain that the bedrooms looked as orderly as the rest of the house.

"I guess she was tired. She didn't sleep well last night after those stitches."

Michael closed the toilet lid and sat there to watch Emily's profile as she rinsed the baby's hair. "What did he say, Emily?"

Emily resigned herself to this. She knew better than to avoid the question once he'd asked twice. Almost absently she began to ramble, the same way she might have talked to Penny.

"He told me there is no way I can keep the house. Can you believe it? Ten years of equity down the tube. Just because my name wasn't on the papers, and his parents cosigned, Ryan's mother has every right to it. And she thinks she's being so good to us by allowing us to stay and rent it for less than the house payment. I get so angry when I think about it, I could just—"

"Wait a minute." Michael put up a hand and narrowed his eyes. "Why would Ryan's mother take her own son's home?"

Emily lifted the baby into a towel and looked down at him. She had to stop and remind herself that he didn't know. Their eyes met and locked, his expectant and concerned, hers full of irony.

"Ryan's dead," she stated as if she'd told him what time it was. Then she quickly gathered clean clothes for the baby and went to the front room to dress her.

Michael was so stunned that he couldn't find the motivation to even stand. His chest tightened, and he put a hand there as if it might relieve the pressure. Her statement made several isolated pieces of floating information suddenly settle into a concise puzzle of perfect sense. His mind played through the events of the past several months, ending with the ironies sitting before him.

In the same moment that he felt compassion for Emily's pain, he felt guilt for the way his heart had begun to pound. Emily was free! *Everything* had changed. He didn't have to feel like he was doing something wrong to be here now. He didn't have to penitently force thoughts of her out of his mind. He couldn't believe it! Had they been so carefully guided in God's hands to bring them to this point? He muttered a quick prayer of gratitude for the prompting that had brought him here, and forced himself to his feet. He had to know everything.

Michael found Emily struggling to dress the wiggly baby. Her eyes were distant, her emotions obscure. He briefly wondered what kind of pain she had been suffering and felt an urge to cry on her behalf.

"Emily," he said softly, sitting on the edge of the couch where he could see her, "please tell me what happened."

Emily looked up at him. He had a right to know. For a moment she concentrated on dressing Alexa, a chore that always took great energy.

"It was funny, you know," she began quietly. "He came home one day with all this talk of the future. He wanted to take a vacation, and he . . . well, that was the night he gave me the shirt." She smiled nostalgically and struggled to pull socks over Alexa's feet. "He said he wanted to get me something just right." She glanced up at Michael. They both felt the irony. "He said that he wanted to get some counseling, that he wanted to go to temple preparation classes."

Michael sighed and clasped his hands together, leaning his forearms onto his thighs. He could feel the hope and happiness she must have been experiencing, and it nearly broke his heart to know what was coming.

"We were going to go out for Amee's birthday, and . . ." Emily bit her lip and swallowed. "I got a call, and . . . I went to the hospital and . . ." She paused, toweling Alexa's curls nearly dry, then setting her free to crawl toward the toys that had just been picked up.

Emily looked up at Michael and finished the story with a clinical statement that didn't allow her emotions to get involved. It was the only way she could think about it and not fall apart.

"His car was hit broadside by a drunk driver who ran a red light, going at least sixty, they estimated. It took them a while to get him out of the car. I got to the hospital before he did. He only lived a few minutes after that. His legs and arms were badly broken, his ribs crushed, most of the internal organs were severely damaged, and his spinal column snapped. He didn't stand a chance."

"I'm so sorry, Emily," Michael said, and she knew he meant it.

"Yes, well," she took a deep breath, "it hasn't been easy, but I . . ." She felt the emotion rise again. "I have felt peace over it. If you haven't already figured it out, I guess you should know how glad I am that I didn't leave him. If it was his time to go, at least he went happy and somewhat prepared to face the other side, instead of bitter and . . ." She hung her head. "Well, you know."

Michael nodded, feeling more emotion than he dared voice. "Why didn't you tell me?" he asked softly. "Why didn't you write?"

Emily didn't want to talk about that. Somehow her reasons were even more difficult to face than what she had just told him.

Alexa began to fuss as she pulled toys out in all directions, and Emily glanced at the clock. It was time her little girl had a nap. With no explanation, she went to the kitchen to fix a bottle. Michael followed her.

"Emily! Why do I get the impression that you don't want to talk to me?"

Emily poured milk into the bottle. "They say it gets darkest just before the light. If you didn't bring some light, I don't want to talk to you."

Michael smiled. "I think I could come up with some light of one sort or another."

Emily screwed the nipple on the bottle and Michael followed her back to the front room, where she moved Alexa and began picking up the toys again. Alexa crawled to help her, and Michael impulsively picked the baby up. He hadn't held a baby since his twelve-year-old niece had been one.

"Hello, Alexa," he said while the cherub face surveyed him and wrinkled her nose to expose budding top teeth. Michael chuckled. "My great-grandmother's name was Alexa," he said softly. "She was one of the best horse trainers in Australia. I'll tell you about her sometime."

"Right now she's going to bed." Emily finished her chore and rose to take the baby. "I'll be right back."

Emily put Alexa down with her bottle and took a moment to gather her wits before returning to find Michael leaning back in the middle of the couch, his long legs stretched out and crossed at the ankles.

"Why didn't you write, Emily?"

"I take it you want the truth."

"No," he said with sarcasm, "I want you to coat it with sugar so you won't hurt my feelings." His tone deepened. "Of course I want the truth. I didn't come halfway around the world to see how the weather is."

Emily walked to the kitchen and Michael followed. She was so disconcerted she couldn't stand still. She started filling the sink with sudsy water and piling the dirty dishes into it.

"Why didn't you write?"

Emily didn't answer. She only worked more vigorously, as if it might make him go away.

"Emily," he insisted, "will you stop washing dishes and look at me!" She shook the suds off her hands and turned to him almost defiantly.

"Why didn't you write to me, Emily?"

"What point was there?" she snapped. "The last thing you needed to hear was more of my troubles."

"Oh." His voice deepened. "So you figure you're doing me some big favor by leaving me ignorant on the other end of the world?"

"Maybe."

"Well, it didn't work, did it?"

"I'm sorry you wasted the plane ticket, Michael. But as you can see, I am alive." She turned back to the dishes.

"And hurting," he stated softly.

Emily stopped washing but kept her hands in the water, leaning against the bottom of the sink for support.

"Michael," she said without looking at him, "you've got your own life to live. Too much has changed."

"Some things will never change, Emily. No matter what happens, I will always love you. I came because I felt you needed me."

Emily whimpered and Michael touched her shoulders. "You do need me, Emily," he said behind her ear. "Don't you?"

Michael turned Emily to face him. She wanted to tell him just how badly he *was* needed, but for the moment she could only open herself to feel the relief of his presence. As the emotion began to escape, she found herself in his arms. There was only a moment's hesitation before she allowed it to come, crying like she hadn't since her initial reaction to Ryan's death. With urgency she pressed her wet hands to his back, holding him with a sense of desperation, crying against his chest until the front of his shirt was as wet as the back. She didn't care if he was committed elsewhere. He was here now and she *did* need him.

Michael just held her, relishing a closeness that was no

longer forbidden, but perhaps needed time. Yes, time. Piecing it all together, Michael knew that only time stood between them now.

When Emily finally gained control of her emotion, she drew back and looked up at him, chuckling with embarrassment, wiping at her tears with care.

"Feel better?" he asked gently.

"I think so, but I . . . I could really use a shower, Michael. I didn't get one yet today and . . . would you mind waiting? I could find you a magazine or—"

"I'll be fine," he smiled. "Go ahead. Take your time. My mother's not expecting me home for dinner."

"Even if you left now, I don't think you'd make it." Emily smiled and realized it felt good.

"No, I don't think I could."

Emily moved toward the hall. "I'll hurry, and then I'll fix you some lunch."

"No," he argued, "I don't want you to fix me some lunch. You shower. I'll go get us some lunch."

"Oh, you don't have to do—"

"Emily. Take a shower. I'll be back."

"All right," Emily agreed and hurried to find some clean clothes. As she showered her mind raced wildly, but the most prominent emotion was relief. Michael was here, and she knew he would not leave without making certain all was well.

Emily dressed quickly in comfortable jeans, pink socks, and a faded black sweatshirt that had been Ryan's. She combed through her wet hair and fluffed it a little, applying just a dab of blush and lip gloss so she wouldn't look ghostly.

Emily hurried and expected him to still be gone, but she came into the kitchen to find Subway sandwiches, Cheetos, and large drinks set out on the bar. Michael was leaning on his elbows with the *Ensign* in front of him.

"That was fast," she said. He looked up eagerly.

"You look cute." His eyes appraised her subtly. "Although that shirt could drown you if you're not careful."

"It's Ryan's," she stated, certain he'd already guessed.

"Roast beef," he reported, motioning to her sandwich. "No peppers or onions."

"You remembered." She sat on a stool at the side of the bar to face him.

"Do you want me to bless it or—"

"Go ahead."

He said a simple but sincere blessing over the food, then looked up to say, "Your stomach is growling, Emily. Did you forget to eat breakfast again?"

"Actually, I haven't eaten since lunch yesterday."

He nodded, perceiving the implication.

They ate in silence, except when Emily observed, "This is wonderful, Michael. I can't remember the last time I had one of these."

He smiled shyly and the phone rang. Emily sighed and set down her sandwich. "It's probably a bill collector." She wished she hadn't said it when Michael scowled in a familiar way. She knew he'd be out for more answers. But then, she figured he would find out anyway, and in truth she had to hope he would. However difficult it might be, she had to admit that she needed what he had to offer. The thought made her stomach churn as she picked up the phone.

"All right," Penny said like a suspicious detective, "who is at your house? The car was there, then it was gone, now it's there again. But I missed the coming and going because I have laundry to do. I can't sit by my window and watch your house all day. So, tell me who it is. It's not a relative, is it?"

"No, Penny." Emily glanced toward Michael, who smiled. "It's not a relative."

Michael continued to eat, amusement sparkling in his eyes.

"No, Penny," she said a moment later, "it's not a bill collector coming to take my children as collateral. If you must know, it's an old friend of mine. He just stopped by while he was in the neighborhood. Why don't you come over and meet him? But give us twenty minutes. We're eating lunch. No, we're not eating macaroni and cheese." Emily chuckled. "Good-bye, Penny. I'm going to eat my lunch now." After a long pause she added more seriously, "Yes, I think that's likely true."

Emily hung up the phone and sat down to eat.

"What's likely true?" Michael asked.

"She asked me if I had finally been brought some light."

Michael smiled.

CHAPTER FOURTEEN

MICHAEL LEANED BACK CASUALLY. "So, how have you been, Emily?"

"As if you hadn't already figured that out."

"I would rather not have to figure it out. I'd like you to tell me. Aside from the obvious difficulty of losing your husband, how are you?" The troubled weariness he had seen earlier came back more intensely. "How long has it been?" he added with reverence.

"He was killed in June. It's been nearly three months."

She said nothing more, and Michael wondered if he'd get further by asking questions.

"How is Allison taking it?"

"If only I knew," Emily said in distress. "She won't talk about it at all. She's not doing well in school. She has mostly alienated herself from friends . . . well, let me clarify that. Allison has always been right between the social groups in this neighborhood. To start with, there are a lot of girls one grade older, and even more that are one year younger. But Allison is the only girl on this street in her grade. That's difficult for her. She's mature in her thinking, which alienates her further. The one girl in the area that she has gotten along well with is one of the most popular girls at school, and Allison feels she is often vying for her company. This friend, Ashley, also has a father who is a CPA. Ashley has the best of everything. For the most part, Allison has never seemed concerned with that. I think her attitude about money is good. Let's just say that her father's death has not helped any, considering the lack of compensation she gets elsewhere."

Michael listened with concern, then made a statement that hit a very big nail on the head.

"I take it, then, that the life insurance was not sufficient. There *was* life insurance, wasn't there?"

Emily looked down. "Yes, and it was sufficient to cover the funeral expenses and the medical costs from the accident. I had enough money to pay most of the bills for a month or so."

"And what have you been doing since?" An edge of anger crept into his voice.

"I've managed. The Lord is looking out for me."

"So I see." Michael recalled the prompting that had sent a thousand dollars in the mail, but he wished he had shown up weeks ago.

The phone rang again. "Oh, great." Emily rolled her eyes with sarcasm. "I know Penny wouldn't call again this soon. There's an eighty percent chance that's a bill collector." She walked to the phone, but Michael's hand caught the receiver before she got it.

"Hello," he said easily. "Yes, this is the Hall residence. No, I am not Mr. Hall. I don't think he's available right now. No, I can't tell you how to reach him. If you want to leave a message, I could send it up next time I pray. No, I am not— The man is deceased. You asked if I knew how to reach him and I told— No, Mrs. Hall is not available right now. No, she is very much alive, but she's busy at the moment. Perhaps I could help you. Who am I?"

Emily fought to keep a straight face as she listened to his side of the conversation, but she couldn't suppress a giggle when he said, "I'm from Publisher's Clearing House. I just came by to tell Mrs. Hall that she's won ten million dollars. And how is that nice for you? Well, I'll certainly tell her you called, and I can assure you you'll have your money by next week. It's been a pleasure talking to you, too." Michael slammed the phone down.

"What an *imbecile*. I'm certain every young widow needs someone like that calling to remind her that—"

"He's just doing his job, Michael."

"I suppose. But that doesn't make it any easier for you. So, where is this bill I just promised?"

"That depends on who you were talking to."

"Just how many are overdue?"

"All of them," she said guiltily.

"There's no reason to act like that. If you haven't got the money, you haven't got it."

"Try telling that to one of those imbeciles who is doing his job very well." She folded her arms and penetrated him with a deep gaze. "But I realized just yesterday that I do have a thousand dollars." Her voice turned almost spiteful.

"I wonder where that came from." He feigned innocence.

"I wonder," she retorted.

"But a thousand dollars won't do much good if it's as bad as you say. Where are the bills, Emily?" he insisted.

"I'm not going to tell you right now, Jess Michael Hamilton. I have been eating, breathing, and sleeping money problems for weeks. Unless you are planning to be in Australia for breakfast, I think it could wait an hour."

"Okay," he said softly and reached across the counter to take her hand. "I'm sorry. I'm just concerned that—"

"I know, Michael," she interrupted. "And you will never begin to comprehend how grateful I am. But right now I . . ."

A knock at the door preceded Penny's timid entrance. "Are you still eating, Emily?" she called before entering the dining room. "I won't stay long. I just. . . ." She stopped when she saw Michael, then she grinned at Emily. "Mr. Hamilton." She held out a hand and he shook it. "I believe we've had the pleasure."

"Hello, Penny." He gave a crooked smile that made Emily's heart miss a beat.

"I must say we're glad to see you." Emily nudged her in the ribs with an elbow to keep her from overdoing it. "So, what brings you here?"

"I came to talk to you, Penny," he said. Penny's eyes widened. "Could you perhaps tell me where I might find someone to watch Mrs. Hall's children this evening?"

"And where is Mrs. Hall going?" Emily asked.

"Mrs. Hall is going on a date with an old friend who just happened to be in the neighborhood."

"I don't think I have anything pressing," Penny said easily. "I was invited to a Tupperware party, but I was really hoping for an excuse not to go. I've got more of the stuff than I know what to do with."

"Good. How about seven?" Michael asked Penny.

"Fine. I'll be here."

"What about me?" Emily interjected. "Don't I have any say in this?"

"No," Michael and Penny said together.

"I think I hear my laundry calling." Penny graciously flitted toward the door. "I'll see you at seven, Michael. Oh, by the way," she called back, "I read your books. Keep up the good work. I loved them."

"Thanks. I'll do my best."

Penny cast a sidelong glance at Emily and added, "I love the way he talks."

Michael chortled when she was gone. "This is an interesting friend you have."

"Yes," Emily agreed. Then, opening herself instinctively to the comfortable friendship she shared with Michael, she added more seriously, "She has saved me. You can't believe, Michael, how much that woman has done for me. Through all these years she has been there. Every time I had a fight with Ryan. Every time any little thing went wrong. When my father died. When my mother died. Whenever I was sick, or pregnant, or recovering from childbirth, or depressed. And these past few months . . . Well, she's just incredible. After Ryan died, she was within arm's reach for days. And when everyone else stopped visiting and calling, she was there. She's not let a day go by without doing something to let me know she cares. Friends like that are one in ten million. I wonder sometimes what I have done to deserve such a friend."

"I wouldn't have to wonder about that," Michael said with warmth.

Their eyes met and fused for a lengthy moment. There was so much Emily wanted to ask him. He seemed happy and at peace. Had this Jenny he'd met changed his life? Emily wondered briefly if she might have come to the States with him and was at this moment shopping or waiting in a hotel room. The thought made Emily's stomach churn, but she attempted to ignore it.

"I'm glad you're here, Michael," Emily felt compelled to admit, though the irony still seemed unbearable.

"So am I."

"But," she added, standing to clear off the counter, "you should have called. My college sweetheart is not supposed to show up at my door unannounced. I could really be embarrassed to think how you found me earlier."

"Why?" he chuckled. "I'd far rather see you living real life than have you attempting to impress me."

"I've never been one to put on an act, but I do prefer to take a shower and find my floor before I have company."

"I'm not company," he said candidly, and she wondered if he was implying something. "And besides, I think you would impress me no matter how you looked."

"You're only saying that because you haven't seen me pregnant."

"Not yet," he said, but she missed the intensity in his eyes.

"I do have pictures," she said lightly. Michael made a noise of interest and lifted his hands off the counter so she could wipe it off. Before she moved away, he caught her hand with his.

Emily glanced down at her hand, then up at his face. The emotion in his expression was evident, and for a moment she thought he was going to cry. Tears brimmed too easily in her own eyes, and she looked down quickly.

"Emily." He brought his other hand meekly to her face, but

he said nothing more. She noticed then that he wore no wedding ring. Perhaps there was still a chance. Glancing to his eyes, she saw an undefined torment. Was the irony as difficult to speak of for him as it was for her? Was his commitment to Jenny too strong to let this interfere?

She began wishing he'd let her go, but his grip only tightened. Didn't he realize what his touch did to her? How could she bear it?

"You can't imagine how I have missed you," he said, allowing his thumb to idly explore the texture of her lips.

Emily began losing herself in his eyes, wishing he would kiss her. Knowing it would only make this more difficult, she cleared her throat in an attempt to clear her head. Michael reluctantly let her hand go, and she frantically tried to recall what they'd been talking about. Facing the sink, she said lightly, "Would you like to see some pictures?"

"I'd love it," he said eagerly.

For the next hour they sat on the floor in front of the open cedar chest, looking through photo albums and baby books. Michael appreciated the visual dimension that somehow filled in the holes of his years without Emily, and the life she had shared with her daughters. Most of the pictures were of the children, and he enjoyed seeing how they had changed and progressed.

"They're beautiful children, Emily," he commented with quiet intensity. She agreed emphatically.

When the babies woke up, Michael took an album to the bar and studied it further while Emily saw to their needs. She spoon-fed Alexa while Amee dumped toys in the front room.

"I think you look cute pregnant," Michael said lightly.

"Oh, yes," she agreed with sarcasm, "and I look great in those pictures Ryan was always so eager to take right after the babies were born. Fourteen hours in labor, and he wants pictures."

"Personally, I'm glad he took them. It makes me feel like I didn't miss quite so much."

They heard the front door open, and Michael was quick to notice Emily's expression of panic. "What?" he asked quietly.

"It's Allison." Michael straightened in his seat, sensing her reason for concern. "I don't have to tell you to—"

"No," he interrupted, "you don't."

"Hi, Mom." The nine-year-old with reddish-gold hair braided down her back appeared and started emptying papers out of a pink backpack onto the table.

"How was school, sweetie?" Emily kissed her and glanced through the papers.

"It was all right."

"Did you turn in that book report like you promised?"

"Yes."

"Any problems or . . ." Emily stopped when Allison's gaze fell on Michael, who was pretending to be absorbed in the photo album. Allison looked skeptically toward her mother.

"Allison, this is an old friend of mine, Michael Hamilton." Taking the cue, he looked up and smiled. "Michael, this is my daughter, Allison."

"Hello, Allison. It's a pleasure to meet you."

"Hello," Allison said quietly, glancing at her mother as if to question the accent.

"Michael is from Australia," Emily explained. "I met Michael in college. Remember how I told you I went to Australia before I married your father?"

Allison nodded again, then turned to her mother and asked, as if Michael weren't there, "Mom, when can we get Ashley a birthday present? Her party is next Saturday."

"I don't know, sweetie. Maybe we can go to K-Mart after school tomorrow and see what we can find."

"Do you think we can get something neat?" she asked for the tenth time this week. "I could earn some money to help pay for it."

Emily wanted to tell her now, as she had before, that she would appreciate extra help with jobs around the house, but she didn't have the money to pay her. Allison seemed to have difficulty with that concept, and she was a little too young to be earning money elsewhere.

"We'll do the best we can," Emily sighed.

"Did I hear you say you were going to K-Mart?" Michael shut the album abruptly. "I was planning to go there myself this afternoon; just need to pick up a few things. I left my socks in Australia, for one thing. If you're going, maybe you could pick up some socks for me, or maybe if I go I could pick up a gift for Ashley. Or maybe," he acted as if he'd had a brilliant idea, "we could just all go together. I wouldn't want you to get the wrong color of socks."

"Can we, Mom?" Allison asked expectantly.

"I don't see why not—just as soon as Alexa finishes eating," Emily said. "While I'm finishing here, why don't you go fold those towels on my bed, like you were supposed to this morning." Allison went eagerly to do it. "And don't forget to put them away," Emily called after her.

"And you," Emily pointed a finger at Michael, "don't get carried away with your multi-million pound fortune. There are problems here that money will not solve, and some that could be created because of it."

"Give me some credit, Emily. You should know me better than that."

"Yes," she admitted, "I do. But I had to say it anyway."

"My car or yours?" Michael asked, carrying Amee out the door.

"Amee go to stow," the little girl chattered eagerly.

"I doubt that whoever you rented that car from would appreciate what these two are capable of doing to upholstery." Emily followed Michael down the walk holding Alexa. "Besides, mine has baby seats." She smiled complacently. "They're required."

Michael managed to figure out how to get Amee buckled into the safety contraption while Emily did the same to Alexa. Allison squeezed between the two in the back seat. Emily threw Michael the keys. "You drive."

"Yes, ma'am." He attempted to sound like an American cowboy and Emily laughed.

At K-Mart, Michael picked out some socks that Emily seriously doubted he needed. He wasn't known for being forgetful. They went through the toy department, where Allison stewed and pondered. Emily suggested several appropriate items within a reasonable price range. She knew that Michael would insist on paying for this, and she was not about to promote a frivolous choice.

"How about this?" Michael asked, pointing to a set of Barbie accessories. They were priced three times what Emily would have paid for a child's birthday gift, even if she had the money.

"Okay," Allison said immediately. Michael looked smugly at Emily, who rolled her eyes. He then proceeded to help Allison pick out an expensive gift bag and a birthday card. He added a little junk food to the cart, then asked casually, "Anything else you ladies need?"

"No," Emily said abruptly.

"But you said the other day that when we went to K-Mart you were going to see if they had some baby socks on sale, because Alexa's are getting too small."

Emily could hardly scold Allison for the innocent reminder, but she frowned at Michael as he steered the cart toward the baby department. Emily watched in amazement as he comically pulled socks off the rack and held them up to each of the babies' feet to choose an appropriate size.

"It's too bad they don't have any of these in my size," he said to Allison, referring to some hot pink socks with polka-dot ruffles. Allison just stared at him in disbelief.

Emily quietly observed as Michael picked out six pairs of socks for each of the babies, then he moved on to the racks of little girls' playclothes and chose matching jogging suits for them. He put on his glasses to carefully examine sizes, ignoring prices. Several times he consulted Allison for an opinion, which she gave eagerly.

He ignored Emily's scowl, especially when he announced that it wasn't fair for Amee and Alexa to have something new, if Allison and Emily didn't. Allison looked to Emily as if seeking permission—and what could Emily do but give it? With Michael's encouragement, she picked out a sweater and jeans that cost more than Emily had spent on most of her school clothes combined.

"Now," Michael announced, pulling the wiggling Alexa into his arms so she wouldn't climb out of the shopping cart, "what about Emily?"

"Emily doesn't need anything," she said tersely.

"A new sweater perhaps?" Michael teased. "Or a book?"

"If you're taking Emily out tonight," she said while Allison looked on curiously, "we'd better get home."

Michael decided not to press the issue further. They were loading packages into the car when Emily said, "You told me you wouldn't get carried away."

"And I didn't. If you want to see me get carried away, we'll come back tomorrow."

"You just spent nearly a hundred and fifty dollars, Michael. I don't have that much to my name to live on for the rest of my life."

"You have a thousand dollars."

"That I'm tempted to give back."

He ignored her. "Those socks I needed were sure expensive," he said and closed the trunk. He walked around the car to open the passenger door for Emily. "We will discuss this later."

"You bet we will," she said emphatically, and he closed the door.

"Are you going out tonight, Mom?" Allison asked while she helped unload bags onto the kitchen table.

"Yes, I am, sweetie. Penny is coming to stay with you." Allison glanced dubiously toward Michael as if she felt uncertain about what might be going on. Emily sensed it but didn't know what to say.

"That reminds me," Michael said, cutting tags off of socks.

"I should go to the hotel and get ready. I'll be back at seven."

"Fine," Emily said. "I think I'll go change. Allison, you keep an eye on the babies, please."

"I think she's mad at me," Michael said to Allison, hoping to begin a conversation. But Allison said nothing, the same way Emily said nothing that evening as they drove together toward Provo.

"If you have something to say, Emily, I wish you would say it now so we can enjoy the rest of the evening." Still she said nothing. "Emily," he prodded, "this is not like you. When we were dating, you were usually more than eager to tell me why you were angry with me."

Through the lengthening silence he tried to analyze what might have made her change. It wasn't difficult to guess. "Did Ryan make it so difficult for you to speak your mind?"

Emily looked at him sharply, but the sincerity in his eyes made her face the truth. "Yes, I suppose he did."

"Well, I'm not Ryan. If you're upset about what I did this afternoon, let's talk about it now and get it over with."

"All right. Fine." That was all the permission Emily needed to get the momentum going. "I will be the first to admit that my financial situation is not good, but you can't expect to solve Allison's problems simply by opening your wallet."

"Not good?" he retorted. "Emily, you've got bill collectors breathing down your neck. And I am not trying to solve Allison's problems with money. You said yourself she's had nothing to compensate for her father's death. You can't tell me that what I bought for her today did not lift her spirits. What is the harm in that?"

"She can't expect to get everything she wants."

"If she's anything like you, she gets nothing she wants."

"I have much to be thankful for, Michael. I have a nice home, modern conveniences, and my needs have been met."

"By the skin of your teeth."

"Michael, you cannot waltz back into my life and make it all right with money."

"Listen to me." He held up a finger as he continued to drive. "I may not have been raised with religion, but my mother used the Bible as her handbook in teaching us about life. She bent over backwards to make certain that the money we had did not taint our lives. I always assumed that you knew where I stood on the issue, but just in case you don't, I'm going to tell you. The base of it is this: It's not money that is the root of all evil, it is the love of money. Money is what makes the world go 'round, they say; and you, of all people, know that living without it is not pleasant.

"I have been blessed with access to more money than most people could ever comprehend. But I'll tell you something, Mrs. Hall. I would give up every cent of it in a minute if I had to choose between money and integrity, or money and my belief in God, or money and you. If I had to, I would get a job, any job, and I would break my back to see that you and your children are fed and clothed. Fortunately I don't have to, but that doesn't mean I don't work hard at what I do.

"The scriptures say that any abundance of money should be used to clothe the naked and feed the hungry. My family has never been into fancy cars and expensive luxuries. You know, because you saw it, that we're still living in the home my great-grandfather built. The money that goes through accounts payable at Byrnehouse-Davies & Hamilton goes to care for the boys that have been cared for by my family for a century, and quiet donations to reputable charities. My great-grandfather began a tradition that I uphold of regularly giving aid to the aborigines.

"In short, Emily, I was raised to pretend I don't have money, and to give money away. I hope you know me well enough to know that I live by that for the most part. I am not going to stand by and watch you and your children suffer when I have got the means to do something about it. You have no right to deny me the opportunity to put a minute amount of money to some good use, just because you're too proud to accept it."

He took a deep breath. "Now, I don't believe one afternoon

jaunt to K-Mart is going to ruin Allison's perception of money. I could care less what Ashley gets for her birthday, but I care how Allison feels about what she is giving to Ashley. It might just help her back into some social confidence. The child has lost her father, Emily. Enjoying a birthday party and having something new to wear is not going to hurt anybody. And did you see her face? She's like you. She was more excited about what we got for the babies than she was for herself. And did you see how disappointed she was when you didn't get anything? I couldn't ruin that child with money if it was my major goal in life." He softened his tone. "She's too much like you. Her spirit is strong and sensitive."

Emily looked out the window while she listened to his speech, feeling the anger dissipate into humility. The answer to her prayers had been thrown into her lap, and she was being too proud to accept it graciously.

"I'm sorry, Michael." She turned toward him and swallowed hard. "You're right. I should know you better than that. But a lot has changed in eleven years."

"And a lot hasn't," he insisted.

"Where are we going, anyway?" she asked, purposely turning her attention to the road in order to avoid thinking about the reality. How could she bear getting close all over again, if only to accept his help and friendship, just to have him go back to Australia and marry this Jenny? A nagging certainty told her this wedding was in the making. How long had it been since she'd gotten that announcement? She looked at him as he answered, wishing she could begin to understand why God was doing this to her.

"We are going reminiscing," he announced proudly, but Emily showed no reaction.

Michael parked the car in a central lot on BYU campus, then took Emily's hand to help her out. He didn't let go of it as they went together over the walkway to the rolling lawns beneath the bell tower. They sat on the grass, and Michael related disjointed memories to her as if he were describing bits and pieces of one of his novels. Emily said little. She felt she was being tortured.

She was relieved as they walked back to the parking lot, but Michael went past the car, leading her to the Wilkinson Center where they strolled aimlessly to places they had once gone frequently; then to the bookstore, only to find it closed. When they finally returned to the car, Emily felt exhausted, though she suspected it was more emotional than physical.

"Hungry?" he asked, driving deeper into campus.

"I suppose."

"It's funny," he commented. "Some of it looks so different, while there are things that seem timeless."

"Well put."

He reached over and took her hand to find her palm sweating. Not knowing what to say, he simply expressed a sentiment. "It nearly feels as if the years don't exist, Emily."

Emily gave a phony chuckle and tried to think of something trivial to say. "This car is a little different from your Blazer. What did you ever do with that, anyway?"

"I sold it after I graduated."

"It was nice."

"Emily." Michael couldn't bear it any longer. "I wish you'd tell me what's *really* on your mind."

She looked over at him, and Michael hoped by her expression that they could finally get to the source of her feelings. "I'm hungry," she stated and he sighed.

He pulled the car into the same old pizza place that looked nothing the same. Michael looked at her silently for a long moment, then got out to open her door. He reminded himself that the woman was in mourning. He couldn't expect her to be jubilant and happy. But still, he could swear there was something more.

"Emily." He reached a hand across the table after he'd ordered, and realized she was still wearing her wedding rings. "Is something bothering you?"

Emily made a disgruntled noise and looked away while

Michael fingered the rings. "I'm a thirty-two, no, make that almost thirty-three-year-old widow, with three children." She bit her lip briefly before she looked at him. "And I feel like my life is over."

In the silence that followed, Emily could hear Ryan's reaction to such a statement, echoing through her mind as a merciless reminder of his absence. *Don't be silly, Em.* Or *That's ridiculous, Em.*

Michael's voice startled her back to the present with an impassioned plea. "Why, Emily? Tell me why."

Emily became lost in his concerned gaze, his kind heart, his endless respect for her and her feelings. The thought of living without him tore at her. She closed her eyes and simply said, "I don't want to talk about it right now."

"When do you want to talk about it?" he demanded.

"I don't know," she snapped. "Maybe never."

CHAPTER FIFTEEN

THEIR SILENCE CONTINUED as they returned to the car. Michael drove aimlessly about the darkened campus, around the temple, and through the peaceful streets of Oak Hills. When the quiet became unbearable, he pushed a cassette into the stereo and stopped the car where they could see the lights of the city below. Michael had first kissed Emily in a similar setting, but he felt certain her mind was far from such thoughts now. If only he knew how to find where her mind was!

Emily immediately recognized the Dan Fogelberg song playing quietly from the rear speakers: *Same Old Lang Syne.* She'd heard it hundreds of times on the radio, but now the lyrics came back to her as if they were telling her own story. How could she not relate to the poignant experience of coming across an old love and dealing with the emotions involved? She could almost imagine the thoughts coming straight from Michael's heart:

She gave a kiss to me as I got out
And I watched her drive away
Just for a moment I was back at school
And felt that old familiar pain . . .

The emotions became too much to bear. Emily looked at Michael and found him staring helplessly at her through the darkness. Tears fell as the song ended, and she felt sure its being played was no coincidence. Their college days had been filled with a mutual love of good music, and he had many times used it to express his sentiments. Emily knew she should have been touched, but all she felt now was pain too difficult to face. Without thinking, she turned it to anger.

"Why are you doing this to me?" She flipped the stereo off abruptly. "Why are you torturing me this way? I don't understand!"

Baffled and stunned, Michael attempted to apologize. "I had no intention of—"

"Take me home," she insisted, and he did.

"I'll see you in the morning," he said on the porch.

"What for?" she asked curtly.

Michael wanted to demand a reason for her bitterness, but he only stated, "Because I promised that imbecile on the phone I would send him money. And while I'm at it, I'm going to send your other creditors some, as well."

Emily leaned against the door and folded her arms. "Michael," she said, "there is no reason on earth why you have to feel obligated to pay my bills."

"And what are you going to do if I don't?"

"I don't know, but something will come up. The Lord is taking care of me."

"Did it ever occur to you that the Lord is using me to do that?" Emily looked away quickly, which he interpreted as an agreement. "Sometime when you're feeling a little less proud, you might consider what moved me to put that money in your bank account. It's a story you might appreciate, but I'm certain you realize that money isn't going to last you long under the circumstances. I don't care whether or not you want me here, Mrs. Hall, I am not leaving until I know that you have enough to meet your needs—which might actually include enough for books and sweaters. I will see you in the morning. Good-night."

Emily watched him drive away, then went inside to find Penny sitting on the couch, her arms folded in disgust. "There's no need to tell me how your evening went. What I just overheard wraps it up pretty well."

Emily sighed. "How were the kids?"

"Fine. Allison showed me what Michael bought earlier for her and the babies. The man's a gem."

"The man has too much money," Emily said irritably.

"As long as he spends it to keep you out of misery, I wouldn't be complaining too loudly."

"You're right," Emily admitted, then lapsed into silence.

"Anything you want to talk about?" Penny prodded.

"No, thanks anyway."

"I'll see you tomorrow, then," Penny said on her way out.

"Penny," Emily stopped her, "thank you."

"No problem," she said, and Emily locked the door behind her.

Emily cried half the night and woke up looking like she had. With no idea when to expect Michael, she made certain she got a shower and had the house in order before Allison left for school. While she fed Alexa, a knock sounded at the door. "Come in," she called loudly and heard it open.

"I'm in," Michael announced behind her, but she didn't turn.

"Good morning," she said. "I trust you slept well."

"I hardly slept at all, if you must know."

"That makes two of us."

"What's going on here, Emily?"

"I'm feeding the baby."

"Funny. Very funny."

Emily took Alexa out of the high chair and washed her face and hands. "No, it's not funny, Michael. I have been going through the motions of living for the past several weeks, because my husband was smashed in a car. My life is a complicated mess. I'm glad you're here, Michael. I really am. But I'm dealing with too much here to even have the motivation to act happy, all right?"

"Fine." Feeling helpless and somehow afraid, he allowed logic to take over. "So let's get on with undoing some of this complicated mess. Perhaps we should start by planning an agenda."

"That would be fine, but before you make any plans for me,

I've got laundry to get started and dishes to wash, and I've got to get to the bank and go pay the power bill. If I don't they'll shut it off one day while I'm drying my hair, and I'll have to go out looking like the wicked witch of the west."

"Why don't you just give me those bills, and I'll work on that while you do the laundry?"

"Because I'm not going to let you do it by yourself," she insisted, pulling open a drawer of odd plastic items and setting Alexa in front of it. She turned to give Amee the drink of juice she was demanding.

"I am perfectly capable of taking care of the bills, Emily."

"And so am I," she protested.

"Emily, listen to me—"

"No, Michael, you listen to me. I have spent the last decade of my life in ignorance of my financial circumstances, against my will. When Ryan died, I had no idea in the world where I stood. Your possession of the money is not going to give you solitary control of it. I want to know what's going on."

Michael gazed at her blankly for a moment. "And I would expect you to." He rolled up his sleeves and walked past her to start filling the sink with hot water. He stopped to figure out the child-proof latch on the cupboard so he could open it, then he scowled at the nearly empty dish detergent.

"What are you doing?" Emily asked while she pried Amee away from the box of cereal she intended to carry into the front room.

"I'm going to wash the dishes while you get the laundry started, and then we are going to go over the bills. You got a problem with that?" He looked up and gave a mechanical smile that was gone as quickly as it came.

An hour later they sat together at the kitchen table with a pile of bills, a notebook, and a calculator.

"That's the house payment," Emily announced. "I don't have to pay that anymore, but I do owe my mother-in-law rent. You would think she'd take into consideration that I've paid two payments since Ryan died, and it was supposed to have been in her hands."

"How much is this rent supposed to be?" he asked. She told him and he wrote it down. "And I'm going to get a basic rental contract drawn up, on a monthly basis with no obligation on your part so that you can move out when you choose. We'll send it with a month's rent and tell her we're not sending more until she signs and returns it. I don't want to leave you open for any more trouble with this."

He opened an envelope and adjusted his glasses. "What's this?"

"That's the balance on the car that the insurance didn't cover."

"Insurance?"

Emily bit her lip then clarified. "That's the car he was killed in."

Michael nodded and quickly wrote down the amount.

"And this?" he picked up another one.

"That is the credit card you discussed with that imbecile on the phone yesterday."

"Ah, yes."

Emily continued to inform Michael and watch him write amounts down in two lists: one of monthly living expenses, the other debts that could be paid off and forgotten.

"Now," he said, "have you updated your car insurance since the accident?"

"No."

"If you are technically renting this home now, you need to have that insurance adjusted as well. And do you have medical insurance?"

"Not since Ryan died. It was an employment benefit. We'll be getting a bill for Amee's stitches."

"If it's anything less than ten thousand dollars, they don't appreciate the worth of a pretty face."

He said it seriously, but Emily smiled. He made it all seem so easy, when yesterday it had been a nightmare. Their eyes met and locked. Emily willed herself to turn away but found she couldn't. A smile teased at the corner of Michael's mouth, as if he could read the longing she was trying to hide. Emily cleared her throat and looked down, wondering what she was going to do with these feelings.

"All right," he sighed, "find me your current insurance information and I'll see what I can do."

Michael organized and figured while Emily took care of the babies and rotated laundry. She was getting them ready for naps when he stood and moved to the door. "I'll see you in a while."

"Where you going?"

"Errands," was all he said.

While the babies slept, Emily finished off the casserole Launa had brought and thoroughly enjoyed it. She wished she had thought to feed Michael before he'd left, but she figured he would manage.

Looking over the minimal contents of the kitchen, she decided she would have to escape to the store after the babies woke up so she could fix something presentable for dinner. She was glad Michael had taken the power bill off her hands, which left her that much to get some groceries.

Penny saw Michael leave and came by to catch up while she did some hand mending she'd brought along. Emily sat on the floor to fold laundry.

Michael returned and knocked lightly, but he didn't wait for an answer before he let himself in. "Gossiping?" he quipped, walking between the piles of laundry and mending.

"What else would we do?" Penny replied.

Michael smiled at Emily, who asked, "How did it go?"

"You needn't worry about looking like the wicked witch, as if you could. I paid the power bill and I updated all of your insurance. You are all officially covered for medical as well, but you'll have to fill out these forms and send them in."

"The man's a genius," Penny said to Emily as if he weren't there.

"It doesn't take intelligence to spend money," he retorted, sitting at the table to put on his glasses and review the situation.

A few minutes later Emily passed by with an armload of kitchen linens.

"You must be hungry," she said. "Give me a minute and I'll fix you some lunch."

"I'm fine," he replied without looking up. "I got a hot dog at Seven-Eleven."

Emily put away the last of the laundry and sat across the table from him. "Is it as bad as you thought it would be?" she asked while he contemplated his list.

"No," he stated without looking up, "it's worse." He leaned his chin onto his hands and looked at her. "Exactly what were you intending to do if I hadn't shown up?"

"I didn't have a clue," she admitted. "I guess you could say I was living on faith." She smiled. "It worked, didn't it?"

"Emily, I'm quite serious."

"So am I."

"But you must have had something in mind, some kind of option."

"Besides getting a job, you mean?"

"You wouldn't."

"Not unless I absolutely had to. But if you must know the truth, it had crossed my mind that I might just have to get in touch with an old friend of mine and beg for mercy."

"Would you have done it?" he asked, finding a degree of comfort to think she would have turned to him.

"If I had prayed about it and felt moved to, yes. But it would have been difficult. Let's just say I'm not too proud to admit that you are an answer to my prayers. I need your money."

"It's nice to know I'm good for something," he said blandly.

"I didn't mean it like that."

Michael wanted to believe her, but there was too much evidence that made him feel like *all* she needed was his money. He reminded himself again that she was mourning, that this was difficult for her. And right now, being with her was nothing but difficult for both of them.

"I'll see you tomorrow, Emily." He came to his feet and moved toward the door. "There's not much more I can do with this until then. I'm having money wired in that should arrive in the morning, then I'll get all of this settled. I have a few hundred dollars in traveler's checks, but I think it will take a little more than that to get this out of the way for good."

"Where are you going?" The edge of panic in her voice gave him a little hope.

"I don't know," he said with his hand on the knob. "Maybe I'll go write a book or something."

He closed the door and Emily put her face in her hands.

"If the man had any brains," Penny frowned, "he'd call this Jenny person and tell her he's got other plans for his life."

Emily glared at Penny. "Maybe he loves this Jenny person, and after what I have put him through, I can't expect him to . . ." Her voice cracked. "Well, you know."

"Yes," Penny said as she gathered her mending, "I know. I'll see you later."

Mid-afternoon the next day, Michael returned to the house, his mind made up to back off and give Emily the space she needed. His instincts told him to care for her and to be there. But barriers he didn't understand prevented him from doing any more than he had already done. At this point, he believed the best thing to do was not to do anything.

Emily smiled at him when she answered the door. Despite the struggles she felt within, there was no denying the comfort of his presence, and the emptiness she felt in his absence.

"Come in," she motioned and followed him to the dining room where he silently looked through papers and put them into neat stacks on the desk.

"There," he finally said. "The bills are all up to date, and the debts are paid in full. I even sent a rental contract and the rent to the esteemed Mrs. Hall . . . uh . . . I mean, the other Mrs. Hall."

He smiled, but his expression quickly sobered. Emily couldn't deny the relief his announcement brought, but something inside her ached because of the distance between them.

"Michael, I . . ." she began with an edge of panic, but no words came to her that wouldn't bring out too much emotion.

"What?" he pressed.

"Thank you."

Michael sighed. As difficult as it was, her attitude only deepened his belief that they needed to be separated, if only for the time being.

"I put some money in your account that should be ample to cover your living expenses for a few months."

Emily's heart began to pound. What was he saying?

"You might even be able to afford a new sweater or something." He decided not to tell her how much he'd put in the bank. She'd probably hit him if she knew, and he wasn't in the mood to argue about money. "If you need any more, if anything comes up, just let me know and I'll have some wired." He scribbled something on a note pad, then tossed the pen on the desk beside it. "There's my phone number in Australia. Just ring me up if you need anything." He deepened his gaze into her frightened eyes. "And I mean *anything*."

Michael felt some hope from her unconcealed feelings, but he had to wonder if it was his security she feared being without. Was it possible that she had grown to care for Ryan so completely in those final weeks that she couldn't face up to the part he had played in her life? Or did she just need time? *Time*, he reminded himself. He believed the feelings were still there, and all they needed was time.

"Good-bye, Emily. It was good to see you again."

"Wait." She followed him to the door, panic making her throat dry. She wanted to hold onto him and force him to stay with her. But how could she? How could she intrude upon the life he had found without her? "You're . . . you're really going back to . . . Australia?"

"When I can get a flight," he stated, opening the door. "I left in a hurry. There's business I need to take care of. If you think of anything you need in the meantime, I'll be at the Park."

His words had a finality to them, and Emily told herself she had to accept it. He had answered her prayers. He was helping her financially, and she knew it would be no burden to him. But she had to accept the fact that it ended there.

"Will you write?" she asked coolly.

"Of course," he said as if it was obvious, "but I'll expect you to answer. That *is* generally how it works . . . with pen pals."

Emily nodded, fighting the pain that gathered between her eyes. "Thank you again, Michael. Take care."

"You too," he said, and was gone.

The emptiness Emily felt during the remainder of the day deepened into a tangible ache that filled a sleepless night. Penny found her doing dishes, looking little different than she had the day after the funeral.

"What happened to you?" Penny exclaimed.

Emily looked up, then threw the dishrag scornfully into the sink. "He left."

"And what would you expect, with the way you were treating him?"

Emily looked up in astonishment. "How am I supposed to treat him? The idea that he's found someone else to . . ." She couldn't finish.

"So what if he is engaged?" Penny folded her arms. "Maybe if he knew you still cared, he might change his mind. You'll never know if you don't try. I'd think you could at least talk about it. Maybe he could fast and pray or something."

Enlightenment flooded over Emily. Twice she had been forced to make a decision between two men. At least she could request the same of him. A few days ago, she had thought there could be nothing worse than the financial devastation oppressing her. But now that she was free of that, the thought of living without Michael was far worse. It would take time to deal with Ryan's death, but perhaps if Michael knew that one day . . .

"Penny!" Emily said in panic. "He was going to leave as

soon as he could get a flight. What if he . . . Oh, Penny, I've got to talk to him! If he's on his way to Australia, he won't even get there until . . . Oh, what am I going to do? How could I let him leave this way?"

"It's beyond me."

Emily rushed for the phone book and frantically turned pages. "Maybe he couldn't get a flight. Maybe he hasn't left yet. Oh, please, Father," she shifted her words to prayer as she dialed the number. "Please make him be there."

"This is better than a soap opera." Penny rested her chin in her hand and watched Emily across the bar.

"Oh, hush . . ." she said to Penny, then into the phone, "Yes, has Michael Hamilton checked out yet?"

"Just a minute," the voice replied, and there was too long a wait. "No, he hasn't. Would you like me to ring his room?"

"Please," she said emphatically. It rang and rang until Emily slammed the phone down. "He hasn't checked out, but he doesn't answer. Penny, I've got to find him, to—"

"Get out of here." She pushed her hand through the air, grinning triumphantly. "I'll keep it under control."

"Bless you, Penny. How do I look?"

"Like you haven't slept for a week, and cute. Hurry up."

Emily prayed all the way to the hotel. The complications of her life came down on her like a threatening cloud, but in that moment only one thing mattered. She had to know there was at least a chance for her and Michael to share a future. At least she would then have hope to get her through this transition.

Emily parked the car in the hotel garage, dashed into the lobby, and approached the front desk. "Has Michael Hamilton checked out yet?" she inquired breathlessly.

After a moment it was verified. "No, he hasn't."

"I don't know his room number. How can I—"

"If you want to use the house phone, your call can be directed to his room."

"Thank you," Emily said sincerely and picked up the phone. But Michael still wasn't answering. Not daring to miss him,

Emily resigned herself to loitering near the elevators. He had to show up sooner or later. She just hoped it wasn't too much later.

After twenty minutes and another verification that he wasn't in his room, Emily thought she would die of nerves. She called Penny on a pay phone and gave her a quick update, then waited another twenty minutes before she saw Michael at the front desk. Her heart began to pound as he exchanged conversation and a smile with the girl there. Then he turned toward her, carrying a sack from a local office supply store. Emily turned and discreetly pushed the button to call the elevator, almost hoping he wouldn't notice her. When she turned unobtrusively to see him, he was standing with his arms folded, looking at her smugly.

"What are *you* doing here?" she snapped.

Michael comically turned and looked behind him to see if she was talking to someone else. "This is where I'm staying. What are you doing here?"

The relief Michael felt at seeing her was edged with doubt as she glanced around helplessly.

The elevator door opened and she looked up to say, "I came to find you."

Michael took her arm and urged her into the elevator. The door closed and they felt a sense of motion. "Okay. You found me. Did you run out of money already?"

"That's not funny."

"No, it's not. And I don't find it amusing at all that you can't even tolerate my company—for friendship and support, if nothing else."

Emily felt some of her resolve dissipate into fear. She didn't like the way he used that word *friendship*. She reminded herself that they at least had to talk it through.

"That's what I came to tell you," she said gently. "I'm sorry for the way I've acted, Michael. I don't care who or what is waiting for you in Australia. I need you here, now."

Immense relief washed over Michael, but there was still so much that needed to be said. "We need to talk, Emily."

"Yes," she agreed. She decided it would be better to know the worst, rather than fear it in ignorance. "We must talk."

"I want to help you through this as best I can, but we have to know where we stand."

Emily nodded eagerly. The elevator door opened, but Michael immediately pushed the button to take them back down to the lobby.

Emily searched his eyes for a sign that he might still love her the way he used to. "I hope it won't be a problem to cancel your flight and—"

"I didn't get one."

"Weren't there any available?"

"I don't know. I didn't call." He smiled at her. "I was kind of hoping you'd come and find me."

"You rogue!" Emily laughed and impulsively threw her arms around his neck. Michael laughed too, briefly lifting her feet off the ground with a firm embrace. There was nothing so wonderful as having Emily in his arms. Their eyes met in one of those time-stopping moments, and he didn't want to let her go.

The elevator door came open, but it took them a few seconds to realize it. They turned at the same time to see an elderly couple regarding them oddly. Emily eased away from Michael, who declared proudly, "She wants me to stay."

The couples exchanged places and the elevator moved on. "Come home with me, Michael. We'll talk, and I'll fix you some dinner."

"I don't want you to fix me dinner, Emily. You've got plenty to worry about. We'll order pizza or something."

They drove in separate cars, and Michael arrived just as Penny was leaving. She winked and gave him a thumbs-up signal as she walked across the lawn.

"It's quiet," Michael announced, walking through the open door to find Emily dusting off the top of the T.V.

"Enjoy it," she said. "The babies are asleep, but it won't last."

"Then stop dusting and let's talk." Michael sat on the couch

and stretched his legs. He put his hands behind his head and
Emily set the dust cloth down and turned to face him. She was
relieved beyond words to have him here, but again, facing the
reality seemed unbearable. She didn't want it voiced, as if not
knowing he loved someone else would make it go away.

"So talk," she said, deciding she couldn't begin even if she
wanted to.

"What do you want me to say?"

She didn't answer.

"Sit down, Emily," he said and she did. "You keep telling me
how so much has changed. Why don't you define 'changed?'"

"Why don't you?" she retorted.

"Because I'm not the one who said it. I'm not the one who
stopped writing letters. You know what's going on in my life.
Why don't you tell me what's going on in yours?"

Emily felt a rush of guilt for those unopened letters, but she
only said, "You should have that figured out by now."

"I have figured out that your husband is dead. And I know
that he made some changes before he died, but he still left you
financially destitute. What I want to know is how you have
changed, Emily. What is it that makes you act so delighted to
be in my company?" he finished with a trace of sarcasm.

"Nobody said I'm not delighted to be with you, Michael."

"Emily," he leaned forward, "your marriage has not
enhanced your communication skills. I am not Ryan. Now,
talk!"

"No, you are not," she said as if she resented it.

Michael was tempted to get angry, but he knew that defen-
siveness would not solve the problem or even get to its source.
With purpose he softened his voice. "Did you want me to be?"

"No," she snapped.

"Do you miss him? Is my being here difficult because—"

"Yes," she insisted, "I miss him. My world has fallen apart
since he died. But that doesn't mean I don't want you here.
What I really want is for you to . . . well, if only we could . . .
Oh," she groaned, "I don't know what I want! I don't want to

talk about this. That's what I want."

"Too bad," he stated and she glared at him. "Now, talk."

"Why should I? Why should I open myself up to you, just so you can help me out a little, ease your conscience, then go back to Australia and live happily ever after?"

"What are you talking about?"

"Oh, really, Michael. Ignoring the facts is not going to help the situation any. Don't try to evade it for the sake of my feelings. I'm glad you're here, and I appreciate your help, but I refuse to allow myself to get involved with any feelings for you when . . ." Emily clamped a hand over her mouth as the words came too close to the truth, and the emotion became too much to bear.

"What on earth are you talking about?" he repeated, baffled.

Emily swallowed and moved her hand as she squeezed her eyes shut, hoping to block out the reality. She knew there was no point evading the issue any further. He would make her face it if it took all night.

"I have lived through a lot, Michael. I have tried to be faithful and positive, but honestly, there comes a time when I think it's just too much to bear. The scriptures say we won't be tried any more than we have the strength to handle, but the irony that Ryan would die this way," she sobbed, "just when you . . . when you . . ."

"What?" he nearly shouted in frustration.

"Oh, Michael," she hung her head, "how could God do this to us? Why, after all we have been through, would he take Ryan from me just when you've finally found someone else to—"

"Emily," Michael interrupted, beginning to perceive that the biggest problem here was pure misunderstanding. But surely she should have known that . . . or did she? His mind went back to the issue of unanswered letters. "Is that why you didn't write?"

"What point was there?" she shouted, coming to her feet, fists clenched. "I had no desire to hear all about this new love of yours while I'm sitting here in mourning."

Michael gave a dubious laugh. "Did you even *read* my

letters?"

"Not since the one I got two days after the funeral. You said you'd met someone. That was all I needed to hear. No, I didn't read the others, and I didn't read your wedding announcement either."

"My *what?*" he laughed, narrowing his eyes in an attempt to absorb this. It certainly made her actions explainable, and compassion filled him for the heartache he could see now. He was quick to alleviate it. "Emily, if you had bothered to read my letters, you wouldn't be standing there wanting to throw me out."

"I don't want to throw you out," she whimpered. "I just don't want to think about you finding . . . when I . . . It seems so . . ." She choked back another sob.

"You still love me, don't you, Emily?" Michael said softly, finding immense relief in the evidence.

"Yes," she nearly shouted. "Of course I still love you. I'll always love you. But that doesn't change the fact that—"

"Where are the letters?" he interrupted. "You do have them, don't you?"

"There," she pointed. "Top desk drawer."

Michael quickly went to the desk in the corner of the dining area and opened the drawer. They were easy to find, stuffed together against one side, next to an odd array of office supplies. Michael thumbed through them to find the parchment envelope. He tore it open while he walked back toward Emily, then held the announcement in front of her eyes.

"Read it, Emily. Read it out loud."

Emily cleared her throat and focused on the eloquent printed script. "Byrnehouse-Davies and Hamilton are pleased to announce the centennial celebration of the establishment of the Byrnehouse-Davies Home for Boys and . . ."

Emily looked up sheepishly. There was no need to read further. Finding it difficult to face him, still not knowing for certain, still not over the pain of Ryan's death, Emily turned her back to him and looked out the window.

Michael drew a deep breath. Realizing the reason for the

tension alleviated many fears. "I'm not getting married, Emily," he said behind her ear, "unless you know someone you could line me up with. A pretty young widow, perhaps." He sighed.

"Jenny was a wonderful girl, Emily. She helped me through a difficult transition. But she was a Mormon." He sounded amused. "She fasted and prayed and said she couldn't marry me. She couldn't give me a reason. She just said it wasn't to be, and I knew she was right. If you had read my letters, you would have already known that."

An unbearable mixture of pain and joy rose to Emily's throat. She moaned, and Michael touched her shoulders. "Maybe the Lord didn't want me to marry Jenny, because he knew I was needed elsewhere."

Emily turned to look up at him. "I do need you, Michael," she admitted tearfully.

"I'm here," he whispered. She fell into his arms, emotionally exhausted to the core. While she wept cleansing tears, Michael held her, relishing her closeness. For eleven years he had ached with an emptiness that only now was being filled by Emily's need.

"Oh, look at me." She drew back and wiped at her face. "No woman on earth cries as much as I do."

"Tears are often the result of pain, Emily." He helped wipe the salty moisture from her face. "One day," he promised, "there will be no more crying."

Michael lifted Emily's chin and rubbed a tentative thumb over her lips, as if to test them. She caught her breath and held it when she realized that he intended to kiss her. Their lips met, meekly at first. Michael drew back to check her expression and she exhaled a long, slow breath that caressed his throat.

"Do you have any idea how long I've been wanting to do that?" he whispered. Emily opened her eyes dreamily and shook her head. "Too long," he added just before he kissed her again. The meekness melted into warmth. Michael pressed a hand to her back and Emily took hold of his shoulders as if she might fall otherwise.

A noise from the other room indicated nap time was over. Emily stepped back and cleared her throat as if she'd been caught at mischief. Michael chuckled and kissed her again quickly.

Emily put her hands to her flushed cheeks and tried to remember what they'd been talking about. She hurried to wrap up the conversation.

"I'm sorry, Michael. I should have read the letters. I was just so afraid to—"

"I understand, Emily. Really, I do. If it were the other way around, I would likely have done the same." He smiled and touched her face. "But Emily, I want you to know something. As I told you before, Jenny is a wonderful girl, and I think I could have been happy with her. But . . ." He touched her hair. "She wasn't you. There is no woman on earth as right for me as you."

Emily looked up at Michael, their eyes meeting with wonder. If only she could find words to tell him how much that meant to her.

CHAPTER SIXTEEN

EMILY HUGGED MICHAEL TIGHTLY until Amee's demand came loudly. "I wanna get out, Mommy!"

Michael chuckled and Emily went to get her. After a trip to the potty, Amee came bounding into the front room, only to stop and survey the man seated on the couch. "Who's 'at?" she said to her mother.

"Who is it?" Emily repeated the question.

"Dat's Mikow," she said proudly, then giggled and scampered down the hall.

Michael caught Emily again with his eyes and held her gaze a long moment. She abruptly turned away and pressed her arm around her middle. He wondered if the gesture was an effort to calm a fluttering similar to what he felt. He cleared his throat. "What would it take to bribe Penny to watch the kids again, if she's not busy of course?"

"I don't know, why?"

"I want to take you out to dinner. A nice dinner."

"Really?" she acted surprised and he wondered why. "Do you want me to call and ask her if—"

"No, I'll ask her, but I want to . . ."

Emily grinned. "Doughnuts. But they must be Winchell's."

"I'll see you in a while," he said and hurried out.

Half an hour later, Penny opened her door to Michael Hamilton and two dozen doughnuts. He handed them over, explaining, "I got all different kinds. You know, the ones with the gooey stuff in the middle, and the little sprinkles on, and—"

"All right," she smiled, "what do you want?"

He grinned. "I want to take Emily out to dinner. If you're busy tonight, then maybe tomorrow, or—"

"I don't have any plans except fixing dinner for my family, and I can do that easy enough with a few extra kids."

Michael smiled. "I already took care of that." He set a slip of paper on top of the doughnut box. "I stopped and paid for two large pizzas. You're supposed to call and tell them what you want on them and when to deliver."

"You really know the way to my heart," she chortled.

"Nah, I just know how to bribe. We'll see you at seven."

Michael knocked at Emily's door, then opened it timidly. Allison looked up from where she was sprawled on the floor, watching T.V. "Hi," he said.

"Hi." She turned her attention back to the screen.

"Cartoons," Michael said with glee. "Awesome."

She looked at him dubiously as he settled down to watch with interest. A few minutes later Emily came in from the bedroom with Alexa on her hip. Without a word, she turned off the T.V.

"Hey!" Michael protested. "It was just getting good."

Emily gave him a humorous look of disgust, then said to Allison, "You know the deal, young lady. No television until your reading is caught up, and you pass off those timetables."

"But all the good shows'll be over by then," Allison wailed.

"If you get caught up on your homework, you would be welcome to come home from school and watch the good shows."

"Please, Mom. I'll do it in a while if—"

"I think you heard me," Emily said firmly. "Rewards come after they are earned. In the real world, one does not get paid until the work is completed."

Allison sulked off to her room and Emily drew a deep sigh. Michael applauded quietly.

"Oh hush," she insisted, setting Alexa in front of the block bucket.

"I was not mocking you, Emily. I think you handled that very well."

Emily looked at him deeply and pondered what that meant to her. Ryan would have told her to lighten up and give the kid a break. She went into the kitchen and he followed.

"Did you talk to Penny?"

"Yes, but I think the doughnuts and pizzas talked louder."

Emily chuckled. "She would have done it for nothing."

"I know."

"I shudder to think how indebted I am to her."

"Me, too." He leaned over the bar to watch her dry some dishes. "She has given us much-needed time together, more than once."

"Yes," Emily said, looking slightly melancholy.

"Is something wrong?" he asked.

"No," she smiled. "Just the same old . . . thing."

"Which is?"

Emily didn't know how to explain the gratitude she felt for knowing he was free, or the confusion still hovering around her delicate relationship with Ryan, and the way Michael was now involved, perhaps more than he realized. She chose instead to say, "I think I need to get out. I don't think I was up to appreciating an outing the other night."

Michael chuckled. "I guess reminiscing didn't go over too well if you thought I was getting married."

"No," she agreed self-consciously.

"That reminds me." Michael looked around. "Where's the phone book?"

"Bottom drawer." Emily nodded toward the desk.

Michael found the number and made reservations for eight o'clock, then turned to her and said, "I'd like to stop at the hotel for a minute, if you don't mind. I told Penny we were leaving at seven, and I don't see much point in driving over and back."

"That's fine." Their eyes met, and Emily was surprised at the vivid memory that popped into her head—the memory of how it felt to have him kiss her. She looked down to clear her thoughts. "Make yourself at home. I'm going to fold some laundry, and then I'll get ready." She moved toward the hall.

"Can I help?" he asked, following her.

"No, Michael. I can fold my own laundry. If you're so eager to help, play with the babies."

"Okay," he said brightly.

Penny arrived a few minutes before seven with pizza and doughnuts for the girls. She was on her way to the kitchen when Michael heard from the hallway, "You look pretty, Mom. Are you going out again?"

"Yes, sweetie. Give me a kiss and I'll see you in the morning. Did you get that reading done?"

"Not yet."

"Allison!" Penny called. "I've got food."

Allison hurried to the kitchen just before Emily appeared from the hallway, and Michael stared at her while she fastened a watch around her wrist. He couldn't believe how beautiful she was. At that moment, he recalled one of his mother's adages: Compliments are meant to be spoken.

"You look splendid, Emily," he said with obvious admiration. She rewarded him with a timid smile. "You're every bit as beautiful as you were in college. No," he corrected, "more so."

"Well, I'm glad you think so," she said, walking past him to the kitchen, "since you're the one who has to be seen with me."

"*Gets* to," he insisted. "*Gets* to be seen with you."

She smiled again. "Everything okay?" she asked Penny.

"We're great. Ooooh, where'd you come up with that?" she asked, nodding toward Emily's cream-colored suit and imitation pearls.

"My sister sent it to me. She can't wear it anymore."

"Have a good time," Penny called as Michael followed Emily out the door.

She was quiet as he drove the rented car to the Park Hotel. Emily waited in the lobby while Michael went up to his room to change. She was browsing in the gift shop when he found her. He carried a wrapped package in one hand.

"What does Mickey Mouse say?" he asked quietly, liking the way she wore the watch with her elegant attire.

Emily glanced at her wrist. "He says we have ten minutes to kill."

"Good." Michael took her hand and led her back to the car. He helped her in and tossed the package into the back seat, then drove a short distance where he parked behind the Tabernacle. Together they walked around the corner of the historical edifice, and Michael urged her to sit with him on one of the benches between the building and the lawn.

Emily watched Michael and wondered why he had complimented her appearance so ardently, when he had such a way of wearing those slacks and loafers, and a tasteful white shirt. "You're a handsome man, Mr. Hamilton."

He smiled almost shyly. "Just so you think so." He took her hand. "Your opinion is the only one that counts." Michael squeezed her hand and felt a subtle tension. "Talk to me, Emily. You're still feeling uncomfortable, and that's all right, as long as I know why."

Emily looked around her nostalgically and sighed. "I suppose you could define it as confusion. You did want me to define it, didn't you?" she added more lightly.

He smiled and nodded. "Define 'confusion.'"

"Where did you learn to be so nosy?" she asked, not too seriously.

"My mother did not tolerate unvoiced feelings. If there was one thing taught in our home, it was the need to speak our minds, and to respect what was spoken. Now, define 'confusion.'"

"I don't know," she admitted. "If I knew, maybe I wouldn't be so confused."

"Is it me?"

"Perhaps . . . a little, but . . . it's more than that." She turned thoughtful, and Michael allowed her the silence to contemplate.

She didn't know how all of this would work out, and it

would be foolish to think that there wasn't much ahead that would be difficult. Her life was complicated. To think of a relationship with Michael at this point was difficult simply within the context of dealing with Ryan's recent death. But in another way, imagining a life with Michael was as natural as comprehending the presence of the sun in the sky.

Was this the way the Lord had intended for it to be all along? The idea seemed too overwhelming to even comprehend. But she reminded herself that there was no need to hurry. Mixed with her relief was peace. She knew everything would be all right—now that he was here.

Emily bit her lip in an effort to control emotion and Michael squeezed her hand. She looked up at the expectancy in his eyes and smiled. "There is one thing I am not confused about." She reached over and touched his face, relishing the opportunity to do so without feeling it was wrong. "I'm glad you're here, Michael. And I'm glad you're not going to marry Jenny."

"So am I," he said, pressing his lips into her palm while his eyes never left hers. Emily knew the transition ahead would not be easy, but with the feelings they shared, it would not be impossible.

"Be patient with me, Michael," she said.

"Only on one condition," he said mysteriously.

"And what might that be?"

"That you be patient with me. I'm going to need your guidance and expertise."

"In what?"

"Let's go eat. I'll tell you later."

Little was said as they drove to the quaint little restaurant in downtown Provo. Neither of them had been there since they had last gone together. Much was the same and much had changed, just as it had been with their lives. Michael carried the package in and slipped it under the table where it sat unmentioned through the meal.

In the midst of their steaks with bearnaise sauce, Michael

leaned forward and gently said, "Emily, there is something I need to ask you. But first I must let you know: I do need to go back to Australia." Her eyes widened with panic and he quickly added, "But it won't be for long."

"How long?"

Michael shook his head. "I don't know for certain."

Emily gathered fortitude and nodded firmly. "When do you have to leave?"

"I called from the hotel before we left. A flight has opened up tomorrow."

"Tomorrow?"

Michael couldn't help smiling, if only to know that she wanted him here that badly. "I'll call you every day, darlin'. You can count on it."

"Oh, that's really not necessary," Emily replied casually, attempting to refrain from acting like an utter whimpering fool. "It must be so expensive and—"

"I can afford it, Emily, I assure you."

"Nevertheless, I will be fine," she insisted. Then her lip quivered in defiance of her words. "Just hurry back, that's all I ask."

"I will." His eyes filled with intensity. "And since you're so anxious to have me return, that brings us to what I need to ask you."

"In a minute," she said firmly. "First you must promise me something, Michael."

"Name it."

Emily shook her head slowly. "No, you just promise."

"I don't understand."

"Tell me that you'll keep the promise, and then I'll tell you what it is."

"Is it something within my capability to keep?"

Emily nodded resolutely.

"All right," he smiled quizzically, "I promise. Now, tell me what I've gotten myself into."

Emily lifted a hand to caress his clean-shaven cheek. "Not

until you come back."

Michael's disappointment was enhanced by the severity in her eyes. But he understood. "All right," he agreed. "I'll have something to look forward to."

Their eyes locked, and Emily wondered if he had any idea how much she loved him. She was contemplating the thought of telling him when he returned to his original purpose, quietly repeating his earlier statement with an added sparkle in his eyes. "I'm going to need your guidance and expertise, Emily."

"In what?" she asked calmly, though her insides fluttered violently. She perhaps sensed his motives, but she was uncertain of his point.

"For one thing, in becoming a family man," he stated. Her face lifted toward him expectantly. "Emily, I know it's not been long since you lost him, and I know your feelings for him were mended a great deal in those final weeks. I don't want to replace him, and I don't want to move too quickly, for your sake as well as for the children's. But I have to know where it stands, Emily."

"Are you saying what I think you're saying?" she asked. Her voice trembled.

"I've said it twice before and been told no, but I'm putting my heart on the table again. To look back over the years and all that has happened, I can only believe that you and I are meant to be together. Months ago, when I asked you to leave him, I felt such a peace about being with you; then, when it didn't work out, I thought God had deceived me. I realize now that the peace was justified. It was my own narrow perspective of the timing that threw me off."

Emily put a hand to her heart as his eloquence stirred something deep inside her.

"Emily," he took her hand across the table, "will you marry me? I'll give you all the time you need to feel ready to make the changes. I'll do my best to be a good father to the girls without trying to take away what Ryan left with them. Everything I have is yours." He lowered his voice passionately. "Marry me, Emily."

Emily was surprised to realize she wasn't crying. Her joy was so full that she could hardly contain herself, but perhaps the tears had finally gone dry. She tried in the moments of silence to comprehend all that had brought them to this point. Recalling the reasons she had turned down his proposal eleven years ago, she now saw their relationship from a different perspective. The love and support he offered would bring real and tangible blessings into their lives. And perhaps one day he would join the Church. But either way, her decision was easy now. The path was clearly defined, as all the stipulations in his offer suited her own needs perfectly.

"Why don't you think about it," he said in response to her continued silence. "Fast and pray, then let me know."

"I don't have to." She smiled warmly. "There is nothing in me that has any doubt. You are an answer to my every prayer, Michael Hamilton. I'd be a fool not to marry you."

"I take that as a yes," he grinned.

"Let me clarify it. Yes, Michael, I will marry you."

"It won't be in the temple."

"I know."

"We'll have to live in Australia."

"I know."

"I might not be as wonderful as you think I am once you see the real me."

"That works both directions."

"But I'll make you happy, Emily."

"I know."

"And I'll try to be a good father."

"I know. I said I would marry you, Michael. Now eat your dinner before it gets cold."

"In a minute," he said. "There's one more thing." Without taking his eyes from hers, Emily felt him tug at her wedding rings. She looked down to see them slide easily off her finger. He turned her hand over and pressed them into her palm. "Put these in a safe place, and someday you can give them to Allison. She's the one who will remember her father, and the commitment you shared with Ryan will mean something to her."

Michael closed her fingers around them and added, "It's time to put the past away and start over, Emily."

Emily looked at the rings, then at Michael. She put them into a safe place in her purse and proceeded with her meal. Michael watched in contemplative silence. All at once the reality struck him, and he laughed toward the ceiling.

"What's so funny?" Emily insisted.

"Absolutely nothing," he chortled, reaching across the table to press his mouth over hers. "I'm just so happy I can hardly bear it."

Emily offered a peaceable smile and touched his face. They were barely finished with their chocolate mousse when Michael said, "I have a present for you."

"I hoped it wasn't for the waitress."

Michael brought the box out from under the table. Wrapped prettily with a big silver bow, it was just the right size to hold an item of clothing.

"It isn't a sweater, is it?"

He shook his head with mischief in his eyes.

"Have you been back to K-Mart?"

"I wrapped it in my bedroom in Australia," he said, the mischief in his eyes turning to a glowing sparkle. "I confess, that was part of my motivation for coming."

Only then did Emily recall his saying something about having news to share with her and Ryan, before he had known the circumstances. All the more intrigued, she removed the bow and set it aside.

"I worked hard for this," Michael added, "so you'd best appreciate it."

Emily knew the gift must be of more sentimental than monetary value. Eagerly she peeled the paper away. A smile teased the corners of Michael's mouth as she lifted the lid.

Emily didn't know what she had expected, but it wasn't this. She stared helplessly at the contents of the box until her vision blurred with tears, making her realize that they had not gone dry after all.

She looked up at Michael and he said quietly, "I told you in my last letter that I had a surprise for you, but I wanted to tell you in person. If Jenny did anything for me, she helped me realize that what I loved about you was the very faith and conviction that drove us apart—twice. I had to admit that what kept you and Ryan together was something stronger than I had ever comprehended before in my life.

"When I told my mother what had happened, she said I should stop and think how I might feel if I were the other man in the picture. And when I did that, I couldn't believe the strength behind what you had done. I did a lot of soul-searching, Emily. I went back to church, and for the first time in years I read the Book of Mormon. But I didn't read it as I always had before, searching out its logic. I read it to feel it, and I did feel it. In the same moment that I realized you had been sent into my life with a very defined purpose, I realized that it was true. Not because it was logical, but because the sacrifices and the trials were all very real. And because I was given the privilege of seeing the world through your eyes enough to give me the strength to look at heaven through my own."

Emily wiped at the tears with her napkin and looked again at the framed copy of his baptism certificate, lying among white tissue in the box. She looked up at the sincerity in his eyes, but still she had to say, "I don't believe it."

"I can't blame you for that." Michael turned to the side, a rigid line showing across his jaw.

"No, it's not that. It's just . . . I mean, I knew you had it in you all along, yet there was a part of you so determined to . . ." She faltered, not knowing how to express it without sounding insensitive.

"To be completely self-governing and self-reliant?" he questioned and she glanced down. "Yes, I know." He gave an ironic little laugh and his eyes filled with humility. "I had a . . . strange experience the day I left here last spring, and by the time I got home, I found myself seeing all of this in a different light. When I looked back and heard myself saying to you that my life was good and I didn't see any reason to change it, I could almost imagine God getting a good laugh out of it. You told me last spring that maybe God had something else in mind for me. I think you were right." He leaned forward and his eyes filled with expectancy. "Don't you see, Emily?"

She laughed softly. "No, I'm afraid I don't."

"I was fourteen when I began to have feelings about attending school in the states; feelings that brought me to BYU, and to you. But only last month did it really come to me that I . . . well, I think God wanted this for me, even then. I don't know why, but I'm forever grateful for His patience with me. And for you, Emily, for having the strength to be obedient to His will and allow me the opportunity to grow and become humble."

Michael leaned back and chuckled. "Do you know what's really funny?" She shook her head. "Actually, I suppose it's not funny, but . . ." His brow furrowed reflectively. "After you left me eleven years ago, I was so miserable that I told God I would join the Church if I could have you back. When you didn't come back, I began to believe I had offered myself in vain, and I became all the more bitter.

"After you told me good-bye a few months ago, I told God again that if I could just have you back, I would join the Church. Then I stopped to ask myself, as if He were asking me: *Then why didn't you do it years ago?* It came to me one day when I was out riding. God doesn't work that way. So I turned it around and decided that if I wanted to be happy, I had to join the Church first. But honestly, at that point, I never dreamed I would ever be here . . . like this. Once I was baptized, I knew I could find happiness with whatever life gave me, and yet . . . here we are, and I have to wonder why I am so blessed."

Emily saw moisture glisten in his eyes to match her own. There were no words to express what this meant to her, but he seemed to understand by the way he summed it up neatly.

"I'm a Mormon now, Emily. I can't marry you in the temple, but I can take you there next year, and I can give your home the benefits of the priesthood, because I am going to live worthy of it . . . live worthy of you."

Emily was speechless. She squeezed his hand across the table, but it didn't begin to express the joy inside her. Their eyes met and locked in a way that was becoming familiar, and Emily could almost believe they had shared these feelings in another time, another place.

Feeling as though she might burst, Emily impulsively stood and urged Michael to do the same. Again their eyes met as she pressed a hand to the back of his neck to brace herself. She felt him suck in a sharp breath as they made contact, then he held it as their lips did the same. A moment later, Michael drew a deep breath and wrapped her in his arms. He returned her kiss eagerly, leaving her certain that he loved her, he needed her, he would come back to her. But above and beyond all of that, of his own will and choice, Michael had wholeheartedly embraced what mattered most to her in this life. They would truly be one in all things.

Emily felt a laugh erupt as their lips parted. Michael's eyes silently questioned the reason.

"I'm just so . . . happy," she declared, thinking it sounded trite.

"As you should be." Michael smiled exultantly as he quoted scripture: ". . . and bring save it be one soul unto me, how great shall be your joy."

About the Author

Anita Stansfield is a prolific writer who always has several works in progress. *First Love and Forever* is her first novel published in book form; another romantic novel, *Candle in the Rain*, was serialized in the *Utah County Journal*.

Anita has been writing since she was in high school. Her work has appeared in *Cosmopolitan* and other publications. She is an active member of the Romance Writers of America and the League of Utah Writers.

Anita and her husband, Vince, and their four children enjoy outdoor activities such as camping, hiking, and Mountain Man rendezvous. They live in Orem, Utah, where Anita is Young Women's president in her ward. Her other interests include dance, choreography, aerobics, and drama.

The author enjoys hearing from her readers. You can write to her at:

P.O. Box 50795
Provo, UT 84605-0795